Playing Games
The Reboot

A lesbian love triangle

Kendra Spencer

Cover Design: Marion Designs

Editor: Crystallized Editing

This book is dedicated to my harshest critic that made me level up, Christiana Harrell.

#PlayingGamesTheReboot is also my dedicated literary fuck you to my anxiety.

Acknowledgements

None of my writing ability is soley mines alone. The Lord blessed me with this flair and I thank him every day for my gift. Thank you Lord, thank you Jesus. All praises due to you.

Ms. Crystal Collier, of Crystallized Editing LLC, thank you for your work and prompt service. I look forward to working with you on future endeavors. Authors, if you reading this, she is the lady you need to work with!

Playing Games the 2012 edition was fabulous. However, when I received my proof copy I had a rash fear, anxiety made me doubt my skills so I "fixed" it. It took on a Ronnie/Kenni sort of pattern and trust me I knew better. As a child I made notes from about book writing and that was a big NO NO. It took for Christiana Harrell to point it out among other things. She incited me! I remember being at work like who the fuck wrote this review?! I felt personally attacked honestly I thought it was a family member. Once I calmed down and flipped through the book I came to realize she was right about some of what she said. Immediately I set out to fix it. When I did attempt though it didn't feel right, it felt like I was taking away from the tone of the novel. At that time also Playing Games II, Players Ball was already finished. Then, my laptop with my, Playing Games 2012, files were stolen. So, I set out to show my maturity and elevated literary skills with Players Ball.

Eventually it began to bother me again especially with my goals of audio books and movies. It was time. It felt right and here we are.

It was a joy to dive deeper into the characters. Enjoy and don't forget to leave a review!

Prince #33

Quick Reference Notes

Stud: a masculine lesbian labeled due to the manner of her attire

Stem: A versatile woman, her style of dressing is androgynous. She can do both masculine/feminine wear

Fem/Femme: The feminine woman. You may not know she's gay because she doesn't dress any different than a straight woman.

No label: Simply put a lesbian but she doesn't identify as any of the above stereotypes.

Prologue

"How y'all doing? Welcome to Flyy Footwear," Ronnie called out a greeting to a pair of men who had walked into her store. "Let me know if y'all need some help," she offered them from her position behind the register.

"We do," one of the men boomed immediately. "We need them new Jays."

"I got it, Ronnie," a male employee told her and started to move from his position, towards the gentleman to inquire about the sizes they needed.

Ronnie shrugged and stayed where she was. The drawer was in her name, so at least she didn't have to worry about anyone messing up her money. A mother and her child stepped up to check out. She took care of them, joking amiably while attempting to upsell other products.

"Nah, bra. I'm sick of this gay shit. Everybody wanna be gay now. Boys and girls. Like, why the fuck a man want to kiss another man? That's that sweet shit. And these fuckin dykes runnin' around, thinkin' they men and shit," a male's voice stated loudly, prompting Ronnie to look up and notice that they were behind the woman she was cashing out.

Her jaw flexed with the tension of holding back her temper, and she took a deep breath. "Y'all have a good day," she stated to the older woman stiffly, who gave her an apologetic smile.

The man spouting homophobic rhetoric stepped up to her register, setting his shoe boxes on the counter and grabbing a few cleaning agents that were next to him. "I don't need nothing else, so don't ask. That's it."

"That shit don't bother me. Shit, as long as a nigga don't come at me with that sweet shit, I'm cool," his friend standing behind him in line with a box of shoes added.

"Man, you crazy." He watched Ronnie ring up his items. "These lil faggot-ass lil boys and dykes everywhere. That shit irritating."

Unable to remain quiet any longer, Ronnie looked up at him, staring into his eyes. "You know it's kids in this store, man. Could y'all keep that in mind and, you know, be respectful to others?"

The light-skinned man who was bothered by homosexuals scoffed. "So? They need to hear that shit," he sneered with a smile peering at her closely. "What? I hurt yo dyke-ass feelings?"

A pink tongue slid out, wetting her darkened lips. "Look, man. I ain't gotta ring you out, homie. You can leave. You being mad disrespectful."

"Fuck you and yo dyke-ass feelings. Take my money and give me my change." He threw the total amount shown onto the counter and waited for her to take it.

"My nigga, you can leave," Ronnie dismissed him, sliding his money to the side and putting the bag with his shoes in it on the counter behind her. "Hey, can I help you?" She looked around him to the next customer.

"Bitch," the man uttered, glaring at her and nudging his laughing friend, who was next in line, out of the way.

A hand dropped onto her shoulder, gripping tightly. "I'll handle this," her supervisor stated. "Take your break."

"Nah, I'm good," Ronnie told him, but before she could say anything to the man who still stood at the register, another employee sidled up next to her and physically steered her to the backroom.

"Fuck this job, bra!" she spat vehemently, ripping off her shirt and tossing it to the ground. She kicked a stack of shoe boxes over and started to head back out towards the main area of the store.

"Ron, just go on break, yo," the male employee told her, blocking the door that led to the store. "Smoke a blunt. Calm the fuck down. You told me you wanted this job, remember?"

"Fuck you! You calm down! Fuck this job! I made more money in the streets anyway!"

"So, you wanna go back to that?" he asked, incredulously. "Why you ain't just stay on at the club?"

"Because I don't need no fuckin' handouts! I can get it on my own. And I told you, I'm done with the streets."

"Prove it. Go smoke and calm down. Don't let nobody stop yo money, man, you tripping."

"Fine," Ronnie bit out, storming out the back entrance.

Swiftly weaving through the mall, Ronnie made it to her pimped-out ride: a truck she'd splurged on when she was getting dirty money. She sparked her blunt and began taking deep breaths to ebb away the remnants of her temper that still simmered. Ronnie locked eyes with her reflection in the mirror while smoking, silently reminding herself that she was paving her own way and that situations like this came with the territory, just like in the streets. Once she was finally marginally calm, Ronnie sprayed on some cologne and exited the truck.

"Man, fuck that dyke, bra. How the fuck you ban me from the mall over a fuckin' dyke?" a male voice questioned angrily from somewhere in the parking lot.

Her eyes narrowed and her fists balled up. She reached back in her truck, up under her driver's seat, and retrieved her nine, sticking it into her waistband. Catching sight of the two men who had been in her store moments ago, Ronnie leaned against the edge of her truck in anticipation of the approaching men. They stopped a few feet shy of her upon seeing her.

"I told you to watch yo mouth," Ronnie told him.

"Fuck you, bitch."

"Yeah, whatever, nigga. You was real muthafuckin' disrespectful in there. What's up now, nigga? Punk ass."

"Bitch, you wanna be a nigga so bad. I'll knock yo ass out like one!" he spouted.

Ronnie lifted off her truck, and her white tee raised a bit, exposing the gun tucked into her waistband. "Shit can get real ugly in this fuckin parking lot, homie. What's up?"

He went to take his shirt off, ready to fight, but the other man, who had stood silently at his side the whole time, saw the flash of the gun. He pushed his friend away.

"Jeremy, shut the fuck up and come on, man. She strapped." He pushed him further away from Ronnie.

The loud-mouthed one glowered at her but didn't say anything else. He walked stiffly away with his friend.

*   *   *

"Kenni!" Jeremy bellowed for his sister, storming into his mother's house. He heard music and barged into her room to see Kenni and her friend, Sayvonne, staring at him blankly.

"What, Jeremy?" Kenni snapped. She looked at his empty hands, then down at his feet. "Where my shoes?"

"I ain't get them." He plopped down on her bed. "What's up, Von?" he greeted the darker toned girl.

"Hey," Sayvonne muttered.

"Excuse me? So, why didn't you get my shoes? You told me you would buy me the new Jays," Kenni demanded to know.

"This stupid bitch at the store got me fuckin' banned from the fuckin' mall."

"Let me guess, for cussing and carrying on ignorantly?" Sayvonne muttered.

"If you wasn't my sister's friend, I'd slap the shit out of you," Jeremy threatened.

"And then you would be left wondering how a girl kicked yo ass so fast," Sayvonne retorted quickly.

"Jeremy, shut up! I'll be damned if you hit my friend. And I want my shoes! You told me you was gonna get them." She threw a remote at him. "Just give me the money. Me and Von will go get them. Damn!"

"Well, go to a different store first. Don't go to Flyy Footwear. If you do, let me know if that dyke-ass bitch say something stupid to you," Jeremy ceded, pulling money out of his pocket for her.

"Whatever. C'mon, Von," she dictated to her friend, who twirled her keys on one finger.

*   *   *

"So, you just gonna say fuck the shoes and blow the money he gave you?" Sayvonne questioned her friend Kenni, who had already spent two hours, browsing everything but a shoe store.

"He still gonna buy them for me. Or my mama will," Kenni stated simply, with confidence. "You know they will." She blew a kiss to a stud who had her girlfriend with her.

"How you just gonna be blowing kisses to other girls' girlfriends?" questioned Sayvonne with slight amusement.

"Cause I can do that," responded Kenni with a neck roll while flipping her flowing, light brown hair over her shoulder.

"Umm-hmm," said Sayvonne, following her through the maze of tables in the mall's food court to Coney's Galore. "You gonna get yo ass beat one day doing that shit."

"What you say?" inquired Kenni.

"You gonna get yo ass beat one day doing that shit," repeated Sayvonne.

"Shit, I bet I don't."

As they stood in line, waiting for their order to be taken, three boys got in line behind them. Sayvonne heard them telling one another to 'go holla at her' and saw them nudging each other from her peripheral. They finally ordered, and as they headed towards their table with their food, one of the average-looking boys blocked Kenni's way.

"Yo, ma, can I holla at you?" he asked, holding his cell phone out so he would be ready to enter her number if she gave it to him.

"Nah, I'm gay," answered Kenni.

Sayvonne's plump lips curled into a smile as the boy made a face.

"Damn, girl, it ain't that serious. You ain't gotta lie to me if you ain't feeling me," he spat at her angrily, holding onto his name belt that read TayB.

Kenni cut her eyes at him, placed the food on the nearest table, then spun around angrily to face him. "Muthafucka, I ain't lying! And if I was, I wouldn't wanna mess with yo dusty, ugly ass anyway with them old-ass Jordan's on that came out fucking last year," she retorted, her head whipping every which way with every word.

"Fuck you, bitch," he spat back at her, walking away towards his friends.

She raised her hand, aimed to push him in the back of his head, but Sayvonne intercepted and gave her a look that said to calm down.

"He lucky my brother ain't here. Jeremy would've beat his ass," fumed Kenni.

"Whatever. Quit acting ghetto in the mall before we get put out," reprimanded Sayvonne.

"Whatever."

*   *   *

Sitting at the food court by herself, Ronnie finished off her meal and gathered up the bags she had accumulated from her after-work shopping venture. She smiled as a butter pecan-toned female stopped in front of her. She'd seen the cutie already from afar with another female, but hadn't approached.

"Hey," Kenni greeted her.

"What's good, ma?" Ronnie greeted in return, looking the slim girl up and down and licking her lips.

"Where yo girlfriend at? You sexy as fuck," she commented, praising the brown-skinned, tattooed stud.

"I ain't got one of those. Where yours at? She know you talking to me?" Ronnie bantered.

"I wouldn't be over here if I had a girlfriend."

Smiling widely, Ronnie asked, "What's yo name?"

"Kenni with an I," she punctuated with a smile and a pop of her lips.

"I'm Ronnie."

"Where yo phone, Ronnie?"

"In my pocket," Ronnie responded, about to drop her bags and retrieve it.

Ronnie was shocked into stillness when Kenni stepped into her personal space and slid her hands into both of her front pockets. Kenni pulled her phone out, saved her number, and put the phone back. She pecked her on the cheek and stepped back, grinning.

"You got my number, now put it to use," Kenni stated, walking away towards her friend.

Chapter 1

"Who got you over there geeking?" Kenni's other best friend, Layla, questioned when she peered over at Kenni, who was stretched across her bed with her phone glued to her hands. "You over there smiling and laughing and shit," she remarked, twisting the cap back on the nail polish she was using on her nails.

Another giggle slipped out, and Kenni looked up at her, grinning like the Joker. "I met somebody at the mall." Her attention went right back to her phone as a new text message came in.

"And you just now telling me?" Layla threw the nail polish bottle at her. "I'm listening."

"She a stud," Kenni said, flipping onto her back with her phone in the air. "She like my height, but a lil bit taller than you and a lil lighter than Von."

"Fuck all that," Layla dismissed. "She got money?"

Gray eyes rolled in Kenni's eye sockets. She sat up, typing a response. "I guess so. She had some bags with her."

"Big or little? From where?"

"Oh my God!" she exaggerated. "Lay, everything is not about money. She funny as fuck.

She make me laugh. Since I gave her my number, all we been doing is talkin' nonstop. Like, she even send me paragraphs in the morning."

Her friend gave her a mock look of disgust. "Have y'all fucked yet? You acting sprung already."

Again, Kenni rolled her smoky gray eyes. "No!"

"Man, if you don't quit holding onto that lil virginity and catch a nut. You gonna fall in love the first time you get hit," Layla teased.

"Whatever! I got head before."

"Girl, so? I got head back in like seventh grade. Wait till you get that thing stroked right. You gonna be in love for real."

"Oh my God, whatever. Anyways, I like her."

"Aww, shit. You sprung already." A teddy bear flew at Layla's head, bouncing off the hat she had covering her hair. "Hey! I'm just saying. It's cute, though," she smiled at Kenni. "She better not hurt you, though. Cut me in on one of her friends if they got some money."

Laughing, Kenni muttered, "I got you."

*   *   *

"So, you only have one real sister, but three stud brothers and a fem play sister?" Kenni questioned into the phone about Ronnie's family while she stretched across her bed after dinner.

"Yeah. My real sister, Arianna, older than me, though. Hell, I'm even one of the youngest in my squad, too. Me and Lil Buddy the youngest."

"Oh, okay. I have an older brother named Jeremy." Her words were cut off as Jeremy stepped into her room.

"Who the fuck you telling my government to?" he demanded to know immediately.

"Speak of the devil," she muttered to Ronnie and looked up at her brother. "Jeremy, get out my room!" Instead of complying with her demand, he took a seat on her bed and reached for her phone. Kenni smacked his hand down and rolled away from him. "Oh my God, Jeremy, leave! Ma!"

"Look at you sounding like a spoiled lil baby," chuckled Ronnie.

"I am," Kenni admitted, jumping up and running to her mother's room. She barged in and collapsed onto her mother's bed where she lay, watching TV. "Ma, tell Jeremy to leave me alone. I'm on the phone," she pouted.

"Aww, you went and told?"

With eyes that matched her daughter's, Beaunna looked at her son, standing in the doorway, then turned back to Kenni and asked, "Well, who you on the phone with, baby?"

Jeremy let out a whoop of triumphant laughter and dove across the bed, towards where his sister had scrambled to. Her mother and brother attacked her on both sides, tickling and reaching for her phone. Beaunna succeeded in the phone grab.

"Hello?" she spoke into the phone. "Who is on my daughter's phone?"

"Y'all jumped her?" Ronnie concluded from the background noise that had hit her ears. "That's terrible, Miss Mama. My name Ronnie, though."

"Nice to meet you. My daughter is a spoiled brat, you sure you wanna deal with that?" Beaunna moved away from Kenni, who attempted to get the phone back from her. She stood behind Jeremy and poked her tongue out at Kenni.

"She gonna be worse with me because I got plans on spoiling her, too."

"Yeah, okay. I hear you. How long have y'all been talking? She been walking around for the past few weeks, smiling all at the phone. Her yellow ass blushing right now."

"Ma!" Kenni laughed.

"That's about right. I met her a few weeks ago at the mall, and we been talking ever since."

"Okay, well take care of my baby."

"Yes, ma'am."

"Because if you don't, I'ma be the one you deal with!" Jeremy made his presence known as the phone was handed back to Kenni.

Kenni ducked under her brother's arm with her phone back in her hand. She muttered to Ronnie, "Ignore them. So, is yo peoples like mine?"

     *   *   *

"Who the fuck?" Ronnie muttered to herself, hearing someone knock on her front door. "Who is it?" she hollered. "Who is it?" she yelled again when she didn't hear a reply. Ronnie grabbed her pistol off the counter. "Who is it?"

"Lil Buddy!" a voice finally yelled back from the other side of the door.

A grin split across Ronnie's face, and she tucked the gun in her waistband. "My nigga. What's good?" she greeted the stud on the other side of the door with a handshake.

"Shit, what's good, nigga?" Chantel, affectionately called Lil Buddy by their group of friends, strolled into her apartment.

"Where you coming from?" Ronnie questioned, pulling out two beers from the fridge.

"I went to go see my pops."

"Oh, word? How he holding up?"

"Shit, he good. You know that. He in the pen, still moving like he free type shit."

"I can dig it."

"What's good with you, though? I ain't seen you in a few weeks. You ain't even been at the club," Chantel stated, cracking open her beer.

Out of their crew of friends, Chantel and Ronnie had always been the closest. Being the youngest and the ones who had run the streets the most had a way of solidifying their bond. Ronnie should have known if anybody was going to pull up and call her out on her shit for distancing herself from the family, it would be Chantel. She smiled apologetically at her. "Man, I just been working, yo."

"Nigga, why?" Chantel laughed. "We own a whole-ass club and you slaving at some mediocre bullshit for what? Man, roll up, fool. I'ma match you."

"Man, T own that bitch for real," Ronnie declared, expressing her true feelings about the five-way joint ownership of the nightclub. "We ain't put up no money. Nigga, me and you wasn't even old enough for the liquor license and shit."

"Nigga, T ain't put up no money," Chantel laughed in disbelief. "Yeah, we wasn't old enough for that part, but damn, nigga, was you high when we filled out paperwork? All our names on that shit, na mean? T name on more because she older, but we all got equal parts. We all eating."

"I don't know, man. I just started feeling like I needed to go get it on my own, you feel me? Shit, I always did in the streets." She sparked the blunt she had rolled up. "I gave my word I wouldn't trap, so I'm just proving to myself I can get it with no help."

Old habits die hard. Both studs had to carve out their own path to take care of themselves due to a lack of familial support. The streets had lured them in early. To leave the streets and stay completely legit was still a process Chantel could understand.

"I feel it, just don't forget about yo family, man," she spoke. Their group of friends had blossomed into something that wouldn't make them closer even if they were blood-related.

"I won't," Ronnie promised. "But, yo! I met a bad lil redbone at the mall the other week."

Looking up from the blunt she was rolling, Chantel grinned at her. "Oh, word? What she looking like?"

"Redbone, slim with some long hair, like that mixed or foreign shit," bragged Ronnie.

Chantel smirked. "You ain't get her number, though."

"Nigga, you tripping. She damn near threw herself at me for me to have the number." She passed the blunt back to the other stud, who had just lit her blunt as well. "Real talk, I been talking to baby for like two or three weeks now."

"You hit yet?"

"Nah."

"Fuck is you waiting on?"

"Man, I been working and she been in school. We ain't even been out and about yet."

"School?" She looked at her stud brother curiously. "Nigga, college school or like high school?"

"High school," Ronnie admitted with not a hint of embarrassment. "She sixteen. Her birthday coming up soon, though."

"Hey, no judgment, nigga. You still a fresh nineteen and it's within four years," Chantel remarked. "Now, if you twenty-two, twenty-three with a sixteen-year-old, I might have to call you something," she told her seriously, then flashed a grin. "Shit, I might still call you something."

A smoke ring and a middle finger was aimed her way. "Fuck you, nigga."

"So, where you taking yo daughter out to?"

"Oh, you got jokes, huh?" Ronnie chuckled. "I'm taking her to the movies and Casanova's."

"Oh, you trying to get some pussy in the theater, huh?"

"You know I'ma get it."

With a glance at the time, Chantel set her blunt cottie in the ashtray and stood up. "I'm about to get up outta here. I gotta get Dreamz from Mya, so she can get to work."

"Yo ass, man." Ronnie stood as well. "Happy wife is a happy life looking ass."

"Yeah, aight. It's really happy spouse, happy house, lil nigga," she clarified. "Make sure you take yo new lil boo to something age appropriate. Ain't no R-rated nothing, nigga. And you better get her the crazy straw with her kid's meal from Casanova's."

The two friends cracked up laughing. No harm, no foul, despite the shit talking they slung at each other. They shook hands and made their way to the front door together.

"Aight, bro. Be safe, nigga."

"I got you, you too. Call me and let me know how the play date went, though, bra."

"Fuck you, Lil Buddy."

"Mya do it better!" Chantel yelled back from the hallway with laughter infecting her voice.

*   *   *

It was finally date night. After several weeks of talking, getting to know one another, sending pictures, and a whole lot of easy banter, Ronnie's eyes perused Kenni in the physical from head to toe. She loved what she saw on the outward appearance of the young woman. The bits of exposed flesh caused her to lick her lips in anticipation. Her hand drifted to the controls on her door, pressing lock when she went to grab the door. Ronnie snickered to herself, watching Kenni smack her lips and roll her eyes.

"Open the door," she demanded, though unable to clear the grin from her face.

The window on the passenger side slid halfway down. "I'm sorry, ma'am. What'd you say?"

"Ronnie," Kenni whined, stomping her feet. "Please."

She pressed the unlock button and quickly pressed it again when Kenni tugged on the door handle. Those pink lips popped against each other again, and this time, she unlocked the doors, allowing the woman entry into her truck.

"Punk." Kenni pushed her shoulders.

"Nah. Never been that." Ronnie started to drive away from her home. One of her caramel hands drifted to a standstill on her blue jean-clad thigh. "So, what you tryin' to go see?"

Pretending to think, a finger went to her face, and her lips pursed into a duck shape. "That new movie with Tiffany Johnson."

"That shit look stupid as hell," the young stud protested with her grill flashing from the catch of the lights.

"So, that's what I wanna see!"

The hand on Kenni's thigh drifted closer to her crotch. "You like scary movies?"

A raised eyebrow and a conspicuous hand grazed over Ronnie's, removing it from her groin area. "I don't like scary movies."

"Aww, so who the punk now, punk?"

"So, we going to see my movie or I'm not going in."

Twenty minutes later, Ronnie was sitting in the theater with her arm draped across Kenni's shoulders, waiting with the rest of the crowded theatre for the previews to come to a close, the lights to dim, and that dumb ass movie she didn't want to see to begin. The large, overpriced drink was in a cup holder on the other side of her arm. She took a drink and offered it to her date, who declined. In her lap, was the extra-large bag of popcorn, and when that was denied as well, she set it down on the seat next to her.

Since nothing was in the way now, Ronnie turned Kenni's face to her and captured her supple lips into a kiss. Her hands cradled her face, sipping at her lips until her tongue came alive to play. One of her hands drifted away, moving down to pinch her nipples, breaking a moan free from her.

Abruptly leaning away from her, Kenni took a calming breath, eyes fleeing to the movie screen. When she leaned back in to meld her lips against hers once again, the young lady placed a hand on the flat-chested woman. Music boomed from the surround sound, ending the previews, and signaling the start of the movie.

"Baby, the movie about to start."

"So?" Ronnie said, moving her hand out the way so she could kiss her again.

"So, I wanna watch it," Kenni snapped at her, her neck rolling.

Grumbling in protest, she sat all the way back and brought the popcorn back to her lap. "Aight."

*   *   *

Movie over, cruising into the parking lot of a classic, old-school-style diner that was popular after a movie date, Ronnie glanced over at Kenni.

She had been quiet since the movie ended. They hadn't even discussed what had happened in the movie. Not that Ronnie knew anyway because she had gone to sleep shortly after the movie begun, after it was clear she wasn't getting any in the theatre.

"I know you been to Casanova's before, right?" She attempted to break up the silent solitude. A shake of her head indicated that Kenni hadn't been to the establishment before. Ronnie hopped out the metallic blue Cadillac Escalade and went to open the passenger door.

"Thank you."

"You welcome."

The two got settled inside and even placed their orders, but still drifted into quietude. Ronnie peered at the young woman across from her, wondering what the hell had stolen her attention from her. She definitely wasn't getting any pussy if she couldn't keep her attention.

"Look, I ain't one of yo lil hoes you usually deal with," Kenni spat out like she'd heard that last thought.

Amusement slowly etched across Ronnie's facial features. So, this was what had her bothered. She let out a chuckle. "Aight, now what you tellin me that for?"

"Because you tried me like a hoe in the movies. I don't do that. I don't go out in public just to have sex."

"You know you dealing with a freak, right?"

"I don't care," Kenni fumed. "We ain't gonna *freak* on our first date." Her wet lips drew the words out. "I ain't like that. When I want it, I'll let you know."

"Yeah, aight."

*   *   *

"Look, I ain't one of yo lil hoes you usually deal with." The statement Kenni had proclaimed to break up the tense silence over a late dinner was stuck in Ronnie's head. She laughed to herself. The women she'd dated and had engaged with sexually were definitely not as prude as her. Driving back towards her house, she replayed their date and conversations leading up to it. Remembering her stud brother wanted details, Ronnie picked up her phone and dialed her number.

"Yo, what's good?" Chantel greeted on the first ring.

"Shit. Shit, what's good? Aye, I took lil baby out," she immediately divulged.

"Finally," Chantel joked. "How it go?"

"Man, nigga, we went to see that bullshit-ass movie, *Torn*."

"You say it like y'all was actually there to watch the movie."

"Man, nigga, we did!" she finally blurted, laughing. "Shorty was never going for that theater action. I ended up going to sleep on her shit. She real live watched the whole damn movie, man."

On the other end, Chantel guffawed and passed the message on to her girlfriend, Mya. "Aah, salty balls."

"Man, you hear me? Like, the fuck. I ain't not had no action in the movies since I was a kid and still wet behind the ears," she boasted, thinking about it. "Baby gonna have to get with it or I'ma leave that ass behind."

"What about after Casanova's, though? You still ain't hit after that?"

"Nigga, why she tell me at Casanova's—mind you, she was quiet as fuck after the movie, on the way there, and when we get there. She finally bust out with, I ain't one of them lil hoes you usually fuck with."

"So, I take it you ain't get no pussy at all then, huh?" laughed Chantel.

"Man, nah! Shorty like we ain't gonna fuck on the first date, then turned around and said something like, she'll let me know when she want it." Reminiscing back on her past, Ronnie couldn't recall a female ever being bold enough to tell her no. It was kind of a turn on. Now that she thought about Kenni and the slim shape of her body, coupled with the backbone to tell her no, her creamy, high yellow skin made the desire to slice the butter between her legs and put it in her mouth increase. "Fuck you, nigga!" she jested, cutting off Chantel's chuckles.

"Aye, don't be mad at me because you ain't get that pussy. You better call up some act."

"Nah, I can't now. This shit personal. I'ma keep rockin' with shorty."

"Why?"

"Nigga, I ain't never been turned down! I gotta hit now!" She got out the car, heading into the house, and threw her chin up in greeting to her neighbor, who was walking out the house with the police officer she was dating.

"Yeah, aight! Shorty got yo nose open."

"Nah, nigga. It's the principalities," retorted Ronnie, her attention stuck on her female neighbor's backside. "Damn, that muthafucka lucky," she commented about her neighbor. She loved when shorty came to buy weed from her because she always stayed to kick it, and the eye candy was fucking sinful with all her curves and all that ass. "She wanna wait, cool, but I'ma drive her ass crazy till she beg me for it," said Ronnie, getting back to the original conversation about Kenni. Her phone beeped, alerting her to a new call. "Yo, I'ma hit you back in a lil bit, nigga."

"Yo girl calling?"

"Nah, never that. This my sister hitting me up."

"Yeah, aight."

"Aight, bro."

*   *   *

"You wanna be a foreign language translator?" repeated Ronnie, putting her game controller down like that was interfering with her ability to hear the voice on the other end of the phone. "For real? Do you even gotta go to school for that?"

"Yes, for real, and yes, you have to go to school," Kenni told her. "I wanna interpret foreign language and get a job with the government."

"Why you like foreign language?"

"Why not? Black people have a lost culture after slavery, and it's hella different languages and cultures in Africa. That was my main reason, at first. After studying new shit in school, though, I love learning new cultures and languages."

"True. True."

"What about you? What you wanna do?"

Fuck, was the instant asshole answer that popped into her mental. Out loud, Ronnie responded, "Shit, I just wanna get money, look good, and be able to take you around to different countries. You gotta be my translator, though."

"You know I got you, boo."

"I wanna take you somewhere," she revealed suddenly.

"You already planning another date and you just seen me Saturday? Ooh, you like me," Kenni teased.

"Damn right I do."

"I'm surprised. I ain't think I was gonna hear back from you since you ain't get none. I'm sure you got lil hoes who would drop them panties for you before you could say so."

"Nah, I ain't got none of those, and even if I did, I want you, and they not you. I ain't tripping because I like you," she answered. "So, what you got going during the week?"

"Nothing that I can't work around, so I'll have time for you."

"Aight, bet. I can't wait to see you again."

A huge yawn ripped from Kenni, and she uttered, "Excuse me," while snuggling deeper into her bed. "I can't wait to see you again, either."

"Aww, you sleepy, lil baby." She picked up her game controller and rested the phone between her ear and shoulder. "Shit, go ahead, ma. I'll talk to you tomorrow."

"Or you can get in the bed like me, and we can stay on the phone."

"Shit, can I get in yo bed with you?"

"Another night, maybe, but tonight, my brother here and he a cockblock."

"Oh, word? I can't wait till that night then."

"Me either, but for now, you should go get in the bed like I'm already in yo room waiting for you."

Placing the game controller back down, Ronnie chuckled and headed for her room. She put the phone on speaker and stripped down to her basketball shorts and sports bra. "Aight, I'm in the bed," she proclaimed after putting her phone on the charger, climbing into her bed, and settling under the covers.

"Good. Now pretend like you holding me and go to sleep. Goodnight, Ronnie."

"Goodnight, ma."

*   *   *

"Mama!" Kenni zoomed down the staircase, screaming for her mother. She found her in the kitchen, sipping from a coffee mug nonchalantly. "Ma!"

"Yes, however unfortunate it is at times, I am your mother, child."

Her eyes rolled at her mother's attempt to make a joke. "Von needs me to come stay with her tonight and help take care of the kids."

Beaunna took a drink of her herbal tea, looking at her daughter, waiting to see if she had more to say. "Okay, are you asking or telling?" she asked when Kenni looked at her just as expectantly.

"A little bit of both."

"Okay. Tell Von to let me know if she needs anything."

"Okay!" She made a dash back out of the kitchen but walked back slowly when she heard her mother call her name. "Yes, mama?"

"Your middle of the week date, girl." Beaunna balled up a paper towel and threw it at Kenni's head. "How did it go?"

She pulled out a chair from the dining room table, plopping down into it. A huge grin split her face. "Mama, she—he is soo sweet." She corrected herself quickly since she hadn't come out of the closet to her mother yet.

"Ooh, you sound like you got it bad. Where did y'all go?"

"Okay, so look, after our first date, we was talking, and I had said what I wanted to do in life, you know, working for the government as a foreign language translator and interpreter, and how I like learning new languages and culture." Kenni paused for dramatic relief. "Ma, we went to the park—"

"The park? Hold on, this is not where I thought this was going."

"Ma, just listen." Kenni snagged her arm. "We went to the park, and Ronnie rented one of those little boat things, a canoe. He brought a speaker and a bookbag with him. We was on the river for a lil while, kicking it, listening to music and talking. But Ronnie found this lil spot, and we got out the boat." Her grin stretched wider. "Ronnie had a whole blanket and food in the bookbag. He even found this French hip hop mix on YouTube. It was so sweet."

"Oh, he then tugged my baby's heartstrings," Beaunna grinned at her daughter. "It do sound sweet and romantic, baby."

"It was! Oh my God, mama, it was everything!"

Kenni's phone started ringing, and she let out a squeal of delight. "This her! I'ma go get ready!" She kissed her mother's puzzled face, running out of the kitchen.

*   *   *

"So, how you pull this off? Yo moms was cool with you spending the night with me? I thought you was her lil spoiled baby?" jested Ronnie, driving back towards her apartment so Kenni could spend the night with her.

"Spoiled, I am," she grinned. "And I always get what I want." She stuck her tongue out at her.

"Oh, you do now?"

"Yeah, I do. I got you, didn't I? I saw you at the mall and pushed down on you, lil daddy."

Ronnie laughed. "I saw you first, though."

"No, you didn't." She playfully pushed her.

"Yeah, I did."

Kenni rolled her eyes. Mischief sparkled in her eyes, and a smile flashed on her face as she reached between Ronnie's legs, feeling the crotch of her pants. "Where yo nuts was at then? Oh, I forgot, you got a pussy." She kissed Ronnie on the cheek, snickering to herself.

"Girl, I gotta dick! You can find out when you ready! But I knew you was going to come to me," Ronnie confidently told her.

"Aww, here we go! Whatever!" She went to get out of the parked car, but Ronnie stopped her.

"Check dig. I should've told you this before, but my house ain't clean, I ain't got no food, and I got roaches."

"Roaches better than bed bugs. We can order some food and clean up while we wait." Undeterred, Kenni kissed her on the lips. She pulled Ronnie's bottom lip into her mouth, sucking on it.

"Damn," Ronnie grunted with approval once they separated. She jumped down out the truck, leaving the young stud to scramble after her towards the open trunk. "I was just playing. I got some food." She pulled bags out her trunk. "I know you probably can't cook as good as the kid, so I just kept it simple."

"Can't cook? Girl, who? I'll make you fall in love with my cooking."

"Yeah, aight. Listen, I got some burgers, fries, and salad. You cook for me, I'll cook for you, and I bet you I'll have you in love by ya first bite."

"Yeah, aight. We'll see."

*   *   *

"Okay, I give! I give!" shouted Kenni, laughing. "You cheated," she wheezed with a smile on her face after Ronnie had rolled off of her as the wrestling winner of the triathlon activities.

"Nah, I ain't cheat," Ronnie jested back, extending her hand to Kenni, who was still laying flat on her back on the floor of the living room.

"You just lost." She snatched her hand back from her before she could grab it. "Ahh, thought you had a friend."

Quickly rising to her feet, Kenni stomped her foot, fuming with petulance. "That's why I beat you at *Mortal Kombat*," she told her, arms crossed over her chest.

"You cheated!" cried Ronnie in astonishment. "You smacked my controller down."

"Oh, now I cheated, but you didn't?" she joked.

"It's cool. I told you I would win the cooking contest, and I won the wrestling match," Ronnie gloated. She thought back on their wrestling match and murmured a second later, "Shit, I need to teach yo ass how to fight."

"I can fight," Kenni stated with her chin raised in the air.

"Man, whatever."

"Besides, I got you to protect me anyway. I ain't got no reason to fight."

Ronnie rolled her almond-colored eyes. "Yeah, I got you, ma, but shorty, I gotta teach you some moves. C'mon."

She led Kenni back to her bedroom, flipping her light on. Her room was a little messy with clothes everywhere. The bed was pushed against the wall, unmade. On top of her dresser was a mirror that was spotless; however, on the actual dresser, there was a clutter of cologne, cigarillo packages, and a few cups she must've drunk out of but had failed to throw away. Next to her bed was a nightstand with more cigarillo packages, an ashtray that was overflowing with ashes and tobacco guts, and a jar of blunt cotties. In the back corner of the room, the off-track closet doors bulged from the surplus of its contents.

The real reason for coming to her room was on the other side of the room, which was where Ronnie had moved to, stripping out of her shirt. A punching bag stood next to her. She beckoned her over.

In only a sports bra and her pants, all of her tattoos on display, Kenni was rooted to the spot, salivating. Her tongue slipped out over her lips. When she caught sight of Ronnie's smirk, she rolled her eyes, stepping towards her.

"Hold up," Kenni muttered before Ronnie could begin speaking. She took a step back and took off her shirt, following Ronnie's earlier actions by throwing it onto the bed.

The same way she had devoured her exposed flesh, she watched her eyes roam over her as well. Under her heavy scrutiny, Kenni felt naked, despite the bra and pants she wore.

"Ready now?" Ronnie asked, smirking.

"Yeah. You know I just had to get like my daddy first," she grinned at Ronnie. "I'm ready."

"Aight, look. Watch how I'm standing and throw this punch." She jabbed the bag. "Yo turn."

Biting down on her lip, Kenni stood squarely in front of the bag with her feet close together. She threw a straight punch at the bag.

"Nah," Ronnie chuckled and moved so she was standing behind her. She nudged the back of her knees, making her bend a little. One of her feet slid between Kenni's, and she motioned for her to spread her stance. "Yo legs is yo base." She touched her thighs. "This where yo strength come from." Slowly, she brought her hands up to her hips. Ronnie pressed a kiss to her shoulder, then maneuvered her body into a fighting stance and stepped back.

Standing stock, still in the position, Kenni looked back at Ronnie. "Now what?"

A chuckle slipped out, and Ronnie stepped back into her space until they were pelvis to ass. She took Kenni's arm and slowly went through a left jab motion, then a right jab. "Left," Ronnie said and snapped their bodies, quickly connecting with the bag. "Right." She jabbed with Kenni's right hand. "Left, right." She moved their bodies quickly for the one-two combo. "Left, right, dip." Their bodies ducked. Ronnie stepped away from her, letting her hands drift away from her body. "Now, you do it."

"Okay, I got it now, baby."

"Left," Ronnie commanded. "Right, left, right, left, right, dip." She nodded with pride at Kenni executing it just like she had shown her.

Kenni spun around to face her, grinning with triumph. "See, I told you. Left, right." She threw soft punches at Ronnie. "Left, right, dip."

Deftly weaving, Ronnie tackled her onto the bed. "So, you gonna use what I just taught you on me? For real?"

"Yeah, you know I had to check yo skills out," laughed Kenni.

"Oh, word?" Her eyes dipped down to her lips. "Check my skills out, huh?" Ronnie grazed her lips across hers.

An answering pair of wanton lips charged Ronnie's, refusing to end the kiss. Ronnie's hands moved from her waist, down to her hip, grasping firmly. Kenni's tongue came out to join the fray, and she caught it, sucking on it and flipping her tongue against hers. A small moan came from Kenni when a hand between her legs, massaged her sweet spot. She whimpered in pleasure again, biting her lip with Ronnie kissing along her neck.

Kenni bit Ronnie's ear and sucked her earlobe into her mouth. "You ain't slick."

"What you talking about?" she questioned, staring down at her.

"You trying to get my goodies," accused Kenni with a smile.

"Girl, I don't want yo goodies," Ronnie feigned offense. Kenni pushed her away, but Ronnie pulled her back to her. "I think you want me to have yo goodies, though." She nuzzled her neck.

"Whatever," Kenni laughed and shoved her. "Why you ain't got no books?"

"Books? What, you wanna watch a movie?"

"I said books," Kenni laughed.

"The fuck I'ma do with a book? You wanna watch a movie?"

Her stone-colored eyes rolled in their sockets. "No. I want you to read me a book."

"Well, shorty, I ain't got no books, no magazines, none of that shit. I can read yo ass a text message."

Kenni flipped her the bird. "Lucky for you, I brought a book with me." She stuck her tongue out at her.

"You brought a book with you?" Ronnie questioned dubiously.

"Yes!" She rolled her eyes and leaped up to retrieve her bag from the living room. "See," she stated, handing Ronnie the book.

"*The Coldest Winter Ever*? The fuck boring-ass shit this about?"

"It's not boring!" Kenni snapped, snatching the book back.

"Yeah, aight," Ronnie replied, closing her eyes.

"Roll a blunt. I'ma sit on yo lap and read to you until the blunt gone, and if you can listen the whole time, I might just let you kiss me again."

Ronnie's eyes sparkled with challenge.

"Well, come on with it then."

*   *   *

"Go in the house," ordered Ronnie from her driver's seat where she sat, watching Kenni, waiting for her to go into the house so she could pull off.

"Drive off," Kenni demanded back.

"I will when you go in the house."

"I'm at my front door. Drive off. Bye."

"Girl, get yo ass in the house!" Ronnie shouted at her.

With a giggle and a wave of her fingers, Kenni succumbed to her dictation. She breezed into the house, all smiles. "Hey, mama," she beamed at her mother, who was sitting in the living room.

"Look at you, all smiles," Beaunna commented. When her daughter continued to grin, she asked, "So, you wanna tell me where you been?"

"Ma," Kenni began, ready to spew her fabrications.

"And don't fix yo mouth to lie to me because I know you wasn't at Von's, helping out with the kids."

The smile dropped off her face. Busted.

"Yeah," her mother commented with a raised eyebrow. "So, where the hell was you at?"

"Ma, I promise I wasn't out there doing nothing bad or crazy."

"Girl, where the hell was you at? And don't you lie to me!"

"I spent the night with my friend, Ronnie," she admitted with downcast eyes. Before the fire could spew from her mother's mouth, Kenni rushed to say, "I didn't have sex. Ma, we didn't have sex."

A look of doubt flashed back at Kenni. "And how old is this Ronnie?"

"Nineteen."

She pursed her lips together and ran her eyes over Kenni's face and neck, looking for sexual bruises. "So, what was y'all doing if y'all didn't have sex?"

Pure happiness washed over Kenni's face as it glazed over, recalling her time away. With a smile, she told her mama, "We talked, watched movies, had a cooking contest, and played the game." She chuckled to herself and said, "She gave me boxing lessons and let me read to her." She grabbed her mother's arm, not realizing she had slipped up yet again by saying she instead of he. "Ma, it was soo much fun, and I'm still undefeated in *Mortal Kombat*."

Beaunna waited for a beat, then suggestively asked, "Anything else you wanna tell me about Ronnie?"

Kenni's face blanched in confusion. "Nooo… we didn't have sex. Oh!" She reached into her purse and pulled out a gift card. "Ronnie paying for us to have a spa date. Massage and a mani and a pedi."

"Girl, shut up," Beaunna stated, impressed. "Okay, I think I'ma need to meet this, uhh, Ronnie." Beaunna stood, dropping a kiss on Kenni's forehead. "My baby falling in love."

"Ma!" Kenni grinned.

"Now, where we doing this spa date at?"
*   *   *

On their next date, Ronnie sat across from Kenni at a park with a box of pizza on the table between them. She grinned, watching Kenni eat. When Kenni reached for another slice, she asked, "Yeah, it's good, ain't it?"

With a mouthful of pizza, all Kenni managed was a grin and a nod as a response.

"Told you I knew where the best pizza in the city is."

Kenni swallowed what was in her mouth and washed it down with the juice they'd bought from a corner store, "Aight. Ain't nobody say all that now."

"Name a better pizza place," Ronnie dared her.

She took another bite of her pizza, gesturing to the motion of her eating. "I can't right now while I'm eating," she mumbled around her food.

"I won," Ronnie declared with laughter.

"Eat yo food," demanded Kenni with a roll of her eyes.

The two finished eating, threw their trash away, and started to walk up the busy strip of the college area. Kenni wandered in and out of several boutiques, casually looking around while Ronnie smoked a blunt discreetly. Exiting one store, she found her girlfriend standing outside, rolling up again.

"What's wrong with you?"

"Huh?" Ronnie looked up at her. "Nothing." She brought the lighter to the end of the blunt in her mouth.

"Ronnie, what's wrong?" Kenni questioned, stepping into her chest and pushing the blunt away.

A quick mental spurt of confidence whispered to Ronnie. She tucked the blunt behind her ear and looked up at Kenni after taking a deep breath. "You wanna be my girlfriend?"

Laughing, she replied, "Baby, I been yours, and if you got any hoes hanging around, you better tell them to gone."

Ronnie chuckled. "Nah, I'm all yours, shorty. You all I got eyes for, and you all I want."

The grins on both their faces beamed brightly at one another. Their lips met each other halfway. Eyes closed, both women quickly forgot about the people maneuvering around them on the sidewalk, the cars beeping as they cruised down the streets, and even the color of the sky. There was only the frequent urgency of their lips to continue to mash against one another.

"Get a room!" somebody hollered from a passing car.

Their lips disconnected as they both turned towards the source speeding away and hollered, "Fuck you!"

*   *   *

Later that evening, Kenni sat in her room with a history book open, smiling like a clown at her phone as she texted back and forth with Ronnie. Her room door burst open, jarring her into dropping her phone. The uninvited ass, Jeremy, scooped it up. He immediately started to read her messages.

"Jeremy, what the fuck? Give me my phone!" she screamed at him, reaching for it, though he held it out of her reach.

"Hell nah! Mama told me you had a lil boo. I bet you ain't tell Mama it's a dyke."

"Give me my fuckin' phone! What the fuck is wrong with you?"

"Yo dumb ass! Out here on that dyke-ass shit. That's that dyke bitch from the mall. I should break this shit since you wanna be gay now!" He cocked back with the phone in his hand.

"Why the fuck is you even mad if I was?" Kenni screamed at him, eyes on her phone, which beeped, indicating she had a message. "Dummy, I can't get pregnant."

"So, you gonna lie to my face now? Me and my boys ain't see yo dumb ass kissing that fuckin' dyke on the strip?"

She took a deep breath. "Jeremy, I don't know what the fuck you got against dykes, but you gonna have to get over it. I like females! I'ma fuckin dyke! You happy?"

"Fuck no, I ain't happy! That shit ain't natural. That shit ain't in the Bible—"

"Muthafucka, you don't even go to church!"

"Mama want grandkids from both of us, how the fuck that's gonna happen? Leave that dyke-ass bitch alone! And I ain't gonna tell yo dumb ass again!" He threw her phone on the bed and turned to leave.

"Or fuckin' what?" Kenni laughed spitefully. "Yo punk ass gonna tell Mama on me like you always do? Snitch," she hissed.

Jeremy rounded on her with spittle flying from his mouth. "I ain't no fuckin' snitch, but you gonna leave that dyke-ass hoe alone!"

"Negative! No the fuck I'm not gonna leave my fuckin' girlfriend alone for you!" She cocked her head remembering suddenly, "And I know why yo dumb ass in yo feelings. You still mad 'cause Nikki left yo ass for a bitch!"

"Fuck that bitch and fuck you, too! Don't call me when that dyke start beating yo ass for that slick-ass mouth." He swept everything off of her desk as he headed out her room.

"Nigga, you can't even fight! And you throwing shit like a bitch! Fuckin' pussy," she bit out, glaring at the shut door.

Chapter 2

"Baby, you betta ask about me," bragged Ronnie as the two walked away grand prize winners from a basketball game. "Ya boy got skills." She held the big, stuffed tiger up proudly, waiting for Kenni to give her her props.

"Oh, ask about you, huh?" Kenni smiled teasingly. "So, everybody at this fair know who you is?"

In mock disbelief, Ronnie stared at her, uttering, "You damn right."

Gray eyes rolled before locking onto a giant slide. She grabbed her arm in excitement. "Ooh! Come on, I wanna get on that."

"You wanna go down that big-ass slide for real?"

"Yeah," Kenni answered honestly, her lips smacking together. "Why?"

"Punk ass." Ronnie rolled her brown eyes back at her. "You just trying to get out of riding Somersault."

Kenni looked to the right at the ride they were passing. It flipped you over forward and backward. People were screaming in fun, some in terror, however, as she saw that all of the passengers weren't fully in their seat as the ride tossed them every which way. Her attention zeroed back in on the line for the slide. "Ain't nobody scared of that ride."

"Yeah, aight, we going on that next then."

The answering look Kenni sent her made Ronnie crack up. She'd clearly said without saying, *no the fuck we ain't.*

"Eww, baby, look at her," Kenni murmured. "She got her muffin top all out like it's sexy," she commented on a woman further up in the line.

Checking to see who she was talking about made Ronnie fall apart in laughter again once she caught sight of the woman. "That's yo boo right there, quit playing," she jested. "She wore that just for you."

"She wore it just for me to talk about her."

They shared another bout of laughter at the woman's expense. Ronnie's eyes bounced around the line, checking people out, trying to decide on their next unknowing victim to help them kill time as they waited in line. Her eyes connected with a short, Hispanic woman, who flashed her a smile. Ronnie smiled back at the woman politely, and Kenni smacked her in the chest.

"I know you ain't forgot I'm still standing here!" Kenni snapped out, drawing looks from people in line. "Don't be looking at no other bitches while you with me."

With concentrated breaths, Ronnie calmly switched the bill of her snapback hat to the back. Her jaw twitched as she stepped closer to Kenni. "Girl, you betta keep yo muthafuckin hands to yo-got-damn-self," she warned.

Kenni's lips pursed and her arms folded across her chest. She looked Ronnie up and down, then spat, "What you gonna do about it?" she smirked, glancing around at the people who were watching them.

Ronnie's eyes followed the path Kenni's had taken, taking note of the observant audience they had acquired. She cut her brown eyes at her, smiling. "You don't wanna find out."

"Whatever." She dismissed the blatant threat. "I know you betta not be looking at no other bitches while you with me, though." She spun on her heels, facing away from Ronnie, her arms folded across her chest.

Ronnie opened her mouth to say something, but her eyes snatched her voice away as they roamed over Kenni's backside. Even from the back, she was sexy. Not thick like a Snicker, but her buttery pecan skin, the way her jeans fit around her waist and hugged her hips transformed her irritation to sexual frustration which she couldn't wait to unleash. She licked her lips, imagining hitting her from the back, visualizing kissing, biting, licking and sucking all over her smooth skin. She stepped closer to her and enveloped her from the back, making sure to press herself against her ass. Ronnie began to play with her neck, kissing and licking, sucking and biting to Kenni's delight.

The anger melted away with Kenni licking her lips in desire. She turned around to face the stud and wrapped her arms around Ronnie's neck. Their lips bounced off each other and met up again, conveying the budding desires that were building within them.

"Yo! It's y'all turn," a voice complained behind them.

"Thank you," Kenni stated once she had broken away from Ronnie and looked over her Polo shirt.

The two sat on the same rug with Ronnie in the back. The ride manager raised his arm, then proclaimed, "Go!" to all the people across the six lanes. Ronnie pushed off, and they sped down the slide, up and over its hills. Kenni laughed, enjoying the breeze on her face. As the slide came to a straight away, slowing to a stop, Kenni looked towards the sky.

"Baby, come on, it's 'bout to rain." Kenni jumped up, pulling her.

"Nah, it ain't," she said without looking up. "You trying to get out of riding Somersault," she accused her.

"No. I felt a raindrop while we was going down the slide."

"Nah, you didn't," Ronnie smirked. "You punking out." At her last word, a raindrop tumbled onto her lip.

"See, I told you," laughed Kenni.

"Whatever, a lil rain don't stop no show. Bring yo scary ass on." Ronnie gently pulled her towards the line for the roller coaster.

"Baby," Kenni pouted. "The rain gonna mess up my hair."

"It ain't even raining for real. It's sprinkling."

"Whatever." She folded her arms across her chest, turning away from her. "I'm hungry," Kenni announced a second later, turning back towards a silent Ronnie, who smirked at her.

"Nah, you scared is what you is. It's okay that you scared, just gone 'head and say it."

"Whatever." She whipped her neck around and stalked out of the line she had been dragged into. "I'm going to get something to eat. I don't know what you about to do."

Smiling and laughing to herself, Ronnie shook her head. She jogged up to Kenni and grabbed her from the back. Ronnie kissed her. "Aight, I'ma let you slide," she smirked, glancing at the world's largest slide.

"Whatever," she punctuated with a smack of her pink lips.

Ronnie kissed Kenni's neck and up to her ear as the two stood in line to get food. "Umm-hmm. It's cool, baby. I ain't gonna tell nobody after I tell everybody."

Kenni, who had been smiling, enjoying the feeling of Ronnie's dark lips on her skin, stopped abruptly and shoved Ronnie. "Fuck you."

"Fuck me then." Ronnie stuck her tongue out, wagging it at her, then flicking it.

The laughter Kenni expelled died off quickly as the rain began to spiral out of the sky. She instantly pivoted, seeking refuge under the side of a building.

"Baby, what's wrong?" Ronnie inquired, laughing. "You scared of a little bit of rain?" She tried to pull Kenni into the rain.

She squealed, "Ronnie, no, stop!" while resisting the tugging on her arm. She tugged Ronnie back under the ledge with her.

Face to face, with only a mere inch of separation, Ronnie licked her lips and flattened her palms against the side of the building. Her honey-brown eyes searched Kenni's crystal-gray eyes. When Kenni opened her mouth to quiz her on what she was looking for, she pressed a kiss to her lips.

They tasted one another's lips as if it were their first time. A heady sense of desire threatened to overwhelm the pair, but they basked in the moment, lips dancing slowly against one another. Tongues intervened. Kenni's slid across Ronnie's bottom lip before she pulled it into her mouth. Ronnie repeated the move, flicking her tongue against the flesh she held captive in her mouth.

Soft moans from their kissing pushed Ronnie to be more brazen. She twisted Kenni's nipples, pinching harder as she kissed harder. Her lips moved to her neck. She switched the tempo up, lips grazing across her skin in haste as Kenni moaned every time her lips touched her skin.

The hands toying with her nipples wandered further south. Ronnie covered her mouth with hers, drowning any ideas of protest. She unbuttoned and unzipped her jeans. Kenni's hand flying down to grab hers brought Ronnie's hand to a pause. Her other hand yanked her head back so the rain could fall down on her face. She diverted the attention of her hand below, resting on Kenni's exposed panties with a kiss then a lick down her neck, which she clamped on lightly and sucked. Ronnie made her way back to Kenni's lips, and Kenni's arms went around her neck.

Seizing the opportunity, Ronnie snuck her hand under her pants and panties. A low, sensual moan burst out of Kenni when her finger slid over her clit. Grinning, Ronnie flicked her finger across her clit swiftly, emulating a come here motion.

"Ooh, shit, Ronnie." Kenni's hand clenched the black shirt she wore, screwing up the artwork on it.

In response was a smile, and the reward for Ronnie continuing to stroke her now drenched cat. Ronnie's finger slid down her clit and dipped inside of her opening, swirling around and smearing the juices back on her clit.

"Damn… Shit, baby. Don't stop. Don't stop, baby. Ooh, shit," Kenni groaned, her hips gyrating on Ronnie's fingers. "Fuck, baby. I'm about to cum," she whispered in her ear, pulling her earlobe into her mouth.

Ronnie smiled, watching Kenni's face contort with pain and pleasure. Kenni's mouth opened, uttering a slight scream as her thigh muscles tightened.

"EXCUSE ME, LIGHTNING WAS SPOTTED! THEY CLOSING EARLY!" someone yelled to the couple as they ran past them.

Kenni fanned them away as her juices charged out of her. Ronnie zoomed in on her lips, kissing her passionately. Abruptly, she broke away and snatched her hand from her lady parts. Kenni watched her in confusion, then a blush and a smile crept over her face when Ronnie began licking her fingers.

"You so fucking nasty," she finally commented.

"Don't I know it, though." Ronnie took off her jacket and placed it over Kenni's head. "C'mon, they then closed this shit."

Hand in hand, the two took off towards Ronnie's truck. Once settled in the truck with the heat and defroster on, Kenni curled up in the front seat. "So, why don't you hustle no more?"

"I still do a lil bit, not as much or as hard as I used to, though. Na mean? I might flip a lil pack every now and then, but that's it."

"Yeah, I got that from the phone conversations, but you never told me *why*, though," she replied with an added eye roll.

"Man, I don't know, shit. We started going hard like freshman or sophomore year. Niggas was eating. We was in fucked-up situations, ya dig, so we had to. Then, one a my stud brothers, her older brother got killed in Iraq. That was our nigga. He fucked with us heavy but hated we was in the streets. He saw potential in us that we ain't see." Ronnie shook her head sadly. "I thought he was bullshitting about taking care of us if we left the streets alone. Like, nigga, how you gonna help us if you all the way in Iraq? Then, that nigga got killed over there, but all the cash he had racked up, he left to us and shit. Told us to put some use to it. Open a gay club or something. So, we did."

The young woman's eyes ballooned, and she could practically hear one of her best friend's screeching in her ear. "You own a club?"

"Partially own," Ronnie corrected her. "But yeah, though."

Kenni grinned, flashing a set of perfect, white teeth. "So, why you fucking with me then? You own a club. You can have any bitch you want, for real, so why me?"

Ronnie licked her lips and smiled. "You could be right, but I ain't that type a nigga. If I'm single, I do me, but I ain't never been a cheater. I do me until I find something worthy enough for me to stop. But you, though, you attracted me when you first walked into the food court. I peeped you, but you ain't know it, though. Then you made yo move." She laughed and rubbed her chin, looking at Kenni with a smile. "You knew what you wanted and went for it. I respect that shit."

The two shared a laugh.

"You know, you say all this like I'm yo age, though. My age don't bother you?"

"Why should it? Shit, I just turned nineteen. And it's bitches that's nineteen that act like they twelve and shit—"

"Hold on." Kenni cut her off with a laugh. "I ain't twelve now, though."

"You know what I mean, though. Young minded-ass hoes. You sexy as fuck and you smart. You actually got goals, and you ask me about mine. You make me think and want more for myself, you feel me? You silly as hell and we can be goofy together. I don't know, you just got me, shorty. You

got a lil punk-ass temper, but I like it, though."
They laughed together. "You got a mean-ass lil
jealousy streak, but it's cool. I like that fire in you.
Shit, I gotta temper, too. But, with all that, why
should I let two years stop me from dating you,
getting to know you and shit?"

Kenni beamed, biting her lip. She turned
Ronnie's face towards her so she could kiss her lips.
  *   *   * "The
fuck is you looking at?" Kenni spat over her
shoulder, staring at a woman who had caught her
eye as she followed Ronnie into her apartment.
"Did you fuck her?" she questioned when Ronnie
nodded a chin in greeting at the woman and closed
the door.

"Nah," Ronnie chuckled. "Why?"

"Because she staring at me like she had a
fuckin' problem or something."

"She probably just wondering who you is. I
don't bring people besides the fam to my house.
That's the homie, though. She cop bud from me
from time to time, and we kick it and shoot the shit.
Her dude the police, so she don't be trying to smoke
in her house."

Kenni made a hmmph noise. "Well, you
need to be careful. She might try to set you up or
something."

"Look at you, all worried about me," Ronnie
smiled.

"Yeah, whatever, I'm just saying," smiled
Kenni.

 "So, you only cuss when you mad?"
"No."

"Umm-hmm. So, you gotta be mad, talking shit or on some nasty shit, but mainly when you mad, you sound like a drunk sailor?"

She laughed. "What?"

"You thirsty?"

"I don't drink, but I'm cool. Thank you, though."

"You hungry?"

"Nah," she smiled, peering at her curiously, wondering why she was being asked all of these questions.

"Well, damn. Shit, do you smoke?" Ronnie picked her blunt up off the living room table.

Again, Kenni shook her head no.

"Damn. Oh for three. Shit, I was just trying to, you know, take care of you, but shit, I'm 'bout to blow this then. C'mon, sit down with me. I ain't gonna bite you unless you want me to."

"Maybe." She flashed a smile and began to walk towards Ronnie, who was seated on the couch.

When Kenni was close up, she pulled her down on her lap. Kenni giggled and looked down at Ronnie, biting her lip. She watched her smoke the blunt, almost transfixed by the sight.

"What you looking at? Yo scary ass trying to hit the blunt now?"

"I ain't scared," she responded with a neck roll. "Let me see it."

An impish grin peeked at her. "Nah," Ronnie declined, moving the rolled-up, funny-smelling cigarette away from her. "You don't know nothing about this cush right here. It's not for kids."

"Fuck you," Kenni snapped.

"Right now?"

"Whatever."

"Turn back around so I can blow you a shotgun," Ronnie told her, chuckling.

Her eyebrow raised in curiosity. "A what?"

"C'mere," she commanded as she hit the blunt. Her chest filled with smoke and she gave out her next instructions. "Wrap yo lips around it and inhale. Hold it in for as long as you can, then swallow it." Ronnie hit the blunt again and flipped it around so the lit end was in her mouth.

Heeding Ronnie's prompts, Kenni wrapped her lips around the blunt. Slowly, the smoke began to expand across her chest. Their eyes locked onto one another, declaring a silent war of who would back away first. Determined to win, Kenni swallowed the smoke that had already filled her, and it came out through her nose, freeing up more room for her to continue to take what Ronnie dished out. Ronnie's eyes twinkled with something akin to pride before her competitive spirit took over, and she pushed the smoke out harder, filling her lungs more quickly now.

Casually, with a slight coughing fit, Kenni leaned away from the blunt, exhaling. In triumph, the stud hit the blunt the correct way, watching her catch her breath. She looked at her curiously when Kenni motioned for them to do it again.

"Oh, so you about this life now? You think you can smoke now?" teased Ronnie.

"I told you I ain't no punk, and I ain't never scared," she smiled with low eyelids.

"Yeah, aight." The blunt was offered to her. "Go 'head and puff away then, baby badass. You got it."

Kenni took the blunt from her gingerly. She imitated the manner of how she had seen Ronnie hitting the blunt and exhaling. The effect was almost instantaneous as her shoulders drooped, relaxed, urging her to continue.

For a while, Ronnie only watched, enjoying the sight. When the young woman continued to smoke with no sign of passing, she tightened her grip around her. A sigh of contentment slipped out, and she kissed her on the side of the neck. The repeated touch of her lips began to warm the surface of her skin, the moans emitting from Kenni swirling around them like an intimate, sensual seduction. She pulled her face to hers, smashing their lips together and sucking on them. Slowly, Ronnie pulled out of the kiss and took the blunt from Kenni's hand.

Hands free and body ablaze with a turmoil of need, Kenni turned around and straddled her. Not one to be outdone, she started with Ronnie's neck as well, making her way behind her ear and licking. She kissed along the stud's jawline, dipping down sporadically to suck on her neck. Eventually, she found her way back to the lips on her face, and both of their tongues came out to frolic with one another.

The burning blunt was moved to the ashtray. Ronnie stood up with Kenni locking her legs around her waist. When she noticed Kenni reaching back for the blunt, Ronnie picked it up, putting it in her mouth. Kenni stole it from her, so she leaned forward and initiated a shotgun, blowing the smoke into her while she navigated the two to her bedroom. She took the blunt from her and threw her onto the bed.

Standing at the foot of her bed, Ronnie watched her girlfriend rubbing her legs back and forth, staring back at her seductively. She started to undress, and Ronnie held in a breath in anticipation.

"What you waiting on?" Kenni asked. "I'm ready, baby," she declared.

"I got you." Ronnie handed her the blunt and disappeared into her walk-in closet. She reemerged in her boxers and strap-on.

Kenni giggled as she helped take off her panties and pants. When Ronnie loomed over her, coming in for more kisses, the giggles turned into full-blown laughter.

"What the fuck is you laughing for?"

"What is that?" Kenni giggled, touching the strap-on penis that was touching her leg. "Take that off."

"What?" Ronnie damn near retreated off of her. "This my dick, what you mean?"

"I don't like straps," she told her simply, then kissed her. "But I would like for you to use yo fingers and yo tongue." Kenni continued to kiss her while loosening the harness.

No more protests, she allowed Kenni to remove her toy. From her position between her legs, Ronnie dipped her face down to kiss her. The thumbs of her hands stroked against her pearl until her juices seeped over her fingers. She paused from teasing along her neck with alternating kisses and licks to suck the juices off her finger.

Her hips rose in anxiety, searching for Ronnie's fingers. Ronnie chuckled and pressed herself against her, rolling her hips. Moans ripped from Kenni at the direct clit to clit stimulation. One of Ronnie's hands went to her nipples. She twisted the little buds between her fingers, tugging on them gently as their hips rose and fell against one another.

Fingers dug in and raked across Ronnie's back, the shooting sparks of an emotion Kenni couldn't quite yet fathom, forcing her eyes to flutter. She gasped audibly when Ronnie suddenly slid down and covered her pussy with her mouth.

"Oh my God," she groaned, feeling Ronnie's tongue slide languidly down her inner parts. "Fuck… fuck… fuck," Kenni panted, clutching Ronnie's head.

From down below, Ronnie grinned, loving the sounds she heard. Her hands wrapped around Kenni's thighs, pulling her down closer when she tried to retreat from the feeling. She devoured her clit, pulling the nub into her mouth, her head moving side to side, and her tongue flicking against it.

"Oh my God, baby… Please, don't stop… Shit, baby," Kenni whimpered. "Ooh, fuck." Her toes curled up as her first orgasm ripped through her body.

Ronnie groaned in pleasure, sucking and swallowing the juices she produced. She released her thighs and pushed her legs back towards her ears. Softly, she blew down on the glistening pink spread out before her. That juicy jumped and quivered in response. Just like it had been invited, Ronnie's tongue skated out to dance alone on her clit. First, at the top, then skirting down to the underbelly of the base and around the orb, only to make its way back up again.

"Fuck," she cried out, sitting straight up with her body shaking. "Ronnie... oh my fucking God... Shit!" Kenni panted. "F-f-f-fuck," she stammered at the feeling of two fingers slipping inside of her. Her body collapsed back onto the bed. "I'm about to cum. I'm about to cum."

Deftly, her fingers moved in and out with a come here motion. Tickling her clit, Ronnie's tongue scurried across the top of her clit. The hold Kenni gripped her head in intensified as her body contorted in on itself, orgasmic fireworks shooting off in her body. She pushed at Ronnie's head, trying to free herself from the mouth that was slurping up the essence that had been exiled from her.

"Fuck," Kenni stammered, her body still trembling, legs tightly closed.

"Open yo legs so I can finish what I was doing."

Without even looking at her, Kenni shook her head no. "Hold on, baby."

Grinning like the Grinch that stole Christmas, Ronnie suggested, "Clean my face off then."

Kenni immediately lifted her tongue to oblige. She kissed Ronnie on the cheek when she was done. "Wake me up in a lil bit. I gotta get home soon. My mama be tripping sometimes about curfew," she whispered in her ear and fell back, lightly snoring before she hit the bed.

"I got you, ma." Ronnie, filled with pleasure and an immense amount of proudness, kissed her forehead.

*   *   *

The next day, the couple was on the phone, talking. Ronnie meandered around her home, straightening up. A bag of weed and her scale sat on her counter.

"What's wrong? Why you get so quiet?" Ronnie questioned Kenni.

Kenni let go of the drapes in the living room and headed back towards her room. "My brother bitch ass just pulled up."

"Damn, what he do? Fart on you?" she chuckled. "Why he gotta be all that? I thought y'all was cool?"

"We is, but he been on some bitch shit lately. Like, he saw us the other week when we had pizza, so he had this big-ass fit about me being out in public with a stud and for being gay."

"Oh, he one of them muthafuckas. What, a dyke then cuffed his bitch?" Her girlfriend giggled but didn't respond, so Ronnie fired off another question. "So, what you think about what he was hollering about?"

"Fuck what he talking about. The fuck I look like, breaking up with you for him? I like girls, and I'm not ashamed of that."

"Hold on, but I'ma grown-ass man, though," laughed Ronnie.

"Whatever. I like women, Ronnie, and you got ass and titties just like me."

"Girl, I got muscles, a lil baby booty, and a big-ass dick you ain't ready for."

"Whatever," Kenni giggled. "Anyways, back to my brother—"

"Yo bitch-ass brother, you mean."

"All right, don't come for my brother now. I'll have to kick yo ass."

"Yeah, aight. You better keep yo hands to yoself. You called him a bitch-ass brother first. I thought that was his name anyways."

She chuckled. "Whatever. Anyways."

"Yeah, anyways. I'm glad you not scared to rock with me even though yo brother don't like that shit."

"Fuck him. He'll get over it."

"Shit, I already know. He ain't got no choice because I don't plan on leaving yo lil pretty ass no time soon."

"Good, 'cause I ain't going nowhere, either."

"I ran into that type of nigga before at my job. I ended up having to flash my gun at his bitch ass."

"Damn, what he do?"

"Dude came into the store, talking all loud, cussing and shit, screaming about dykes and shit. I told him to chill, you know, because it was kids in there. Dude got beside himself, so I told that bitch-ass nigga to kick rocks."

"Where was this?" Kenni questioned.

"The day I met you, I think." She paused. "Yeah, 'cause I had just got off work when you stepped to me."

Kenni shook her head sadly. "You remember what he look like?"

"Shit, I don't know. Light-skinned, waves, a bitch-ass nigga."

"I think that may have been my brother," she admitted softly.

"Why you say that?"

"Because he was supposed to buy me some shoes, but came back home without them, talking about he got kicked out the store by this dyke."

"He say what store? I work at Flyy Footwear."

"Oh my God! Fuckin bitch!" Kenni shook her head. "That was his ass!"

"Aww, man. Dude almost got beat the fuck up."

"Just ignore him."

"Man—"

"I will beat you up over my brother," she interjected. "Don't make me fuck you up, Ronnie."

"Whatever, shorty," Ronnie smiled. "You couldn't bust a grape. That lil pussy can bust all in my mouth, though."

"You silly," Kenni smiled, recalling how orally talented she was.

"Shit, for real. I want that pussy in my mouth right now."

"If you wait till later, I got you, baby."

"Oh, word? Shit, bet. Why not now, though? I ain't doing shit, you ain't doing shit."

"Because you being thirsty," Kenni laughed. "Nah, I'm playing. I'm about to go cook for my mama. She about to pull up."

"Aight. I got you, baby. Call me when you ready."

"I will, baby."

"Aight."

"Bye," Kenni murmured into the phone, hanging up and putting it on the charger.

*   *   *

"Soo, dinner is good." Beaunna praised her daughter's cooking while looking back and forth between her two children, who were eerily silent.

"Thanks, mama," Kenni said.

Beaunna looked at her oldest child, her son, but he didn't respond, only continued to eat. "Jeremy?"

"What's up, mama?"

"Is the food good?"

Jeremy shrugged one of his shoulders. "It's aight, Ma. Could be better." He jabbed at his food.

Her eyes narrowed at her brother. "Well, I'm glad you like it, mama, because it was really only for you."

"What's going on with y'all?" Beaunna questioned, looking between the two glowering at each other.

"Nothing," Kenni bit out, dropping her eyes down to her plate.

"Oh, now it's nothing?" Jeremy raised an eyebrow at his sister.

Their mother sat between them, eating silently, following the conversation back and forth.

Sometimes, the best way to glean information is to be quiet, Beaunna thought. *I should make that a hashtag. #Momquote.*

"It is nothing, and none of yo damn business," Kenni spewed. "You just trying to make something out of nothing because yo punk-ass feelings hurt. Bitch."

"My feelings ain't hurt, but yo face gonna be hurt you call me a bitch again."

"Jeremy!" Beaunna intervened. "Don't talk to yo sister like that," she refereed.

"I ain't got no sister." He glared at her.

"Fuck you!" Kenni yelled at him.

"Fuck you!" Jeremy stated, staring into her eyes. "Why don't you tell Mama about that dumb-ass nigga you entertaining." He turned his attention to his mother and began running off at the mouth. "Mama, she tell you she dating a fuckin drug dealer and a gang banger. Nigga been all in and through the house and everything. You need to check and make sure yo jewelry still in yo room because I know the bitch steal, too."

Before his mother could answer, Kenni threw her glass at him. "Fuck you. Ronnie ain't none of that bullshit."

He threw the glass back at her.

"Stop! STOP!" Beaunna ordered, raising her voice. "Get out! Both of y'all. Separate until you ready to fix what's wrong. And Kenni, if another damn glass gets thrown or broke, me and you gonna have some problems."

"Then I'm out and I ain't coming back. That's fucked up. I'm trying to help you, mama, and you take her side like always. Cool, fuck it then. I ain't got no mama or no sister then." He stormed out, slamming the door.

"Kenni, what the hell is going on?" Beaunna asked, turning back to the kitchen table where she still sat.

"You told me to leave, remember?" She stood up. "Don't ask me nothing now," she jabbed, stalking out of the kitchen, punching in numbers on her cell phone.

*   *   *

"Thanks, Von," Kenni called out to one of her best friends as she exited her vehicle. She walked up the walkway of Ronnie's apartment and knocked on the door.

"Who is it?" a masculine voice called out over the music.

"Delivery!"

"Delivery?" Ronnie flung the door open, muttering, "I ain't order no damn food." She grinned. "What's up, baby? I thought I was picking you up in a lil bit. You all right?" She kissed her and stepped back so she could come into the apartment.

Kenni entered the apartment and her eyes bucked with surprise mixed with a tinge of anger. Shyna, Ronnie's neighbor, was lounging on her sofa with a blunt in her mouth and a controller at her bare feet. A hint of jealousy surged through her, looking at the curvaceous woman who was barely clothed. She pivoted around to face Ronnie.

"Why is she here? Can she leave?"

Shyna chuckled sarcastically and rose to her feet. Ronnie, facing Kenni, looked at her curiously. "Baby, what's wrong?"

"I just really wanna be with you right now," she stated, blinking rapidly.

"Ron, take care of yo girl," Shyna said, sauntering up to the pair. "I'm high as fuck, yo. I'll hit you up if I need anything else, aight?" Her hand clutched Ronnie's shoulder briefly.

"Aight, yo. Turn that bottom lock for me."

"You know I got you."

Reaching out, Ronnie pulled Kenni into her arms. She kissed her pouting lips. "What's wrong with my baby? Who I need to fuck up?"

"My stupid-ass fuckin brother," Kenni screamed, punching her in the chest.

"The fuck he do now?"

Kenni rolled her gray eyes and threw herself down onto the love seat in the living room. "He a fuckin bitch. You know I made dinner for my mama, and he made this whole big-ass scene in front of Mama because of you."

"What he was talking about?" she questioned, taking a seat next to Kenni, pulling her legs overtop her own.

"Dumb shit he made up. Talking about you sell drugs, gang bang, and you been in the house and gonna rob us."

"Well, he got one right," she laughed. "I do sell drugs. Not like how I used to, but yeah."

"But why he be on that soft-ass shit? Like, you gonna tell Mama, for real? And then he got mad when I cussed his ass out and threw a cup at him."

"You threw a cup at him?" Ronnie chuckled.

"Hell yeah, I threw a glass at his bitch ass. Twice. Then Mama kicked us both out of the house. Not for good, but to calm down. His ole dramatic ass like, fuck y'all, I ain't got no mama or no sister."

"I know that's yo brother, baby, but dude a whole-ass bitch."

"I know it! His fuckin bitch ass." She started to work herself back up. "He only mad because—"

"I know what will make you feel better," Ronnie commented with a smirk, cutting her ramble off.

"What?" Kenni asked.

Ronnie bit her lip and grinned at her, yanking her legs down further on her. She reached up to unbutton her pants. "I'ma eat that pussy until you cream in my mouth and forget about everything."

Her lips curved up wickedly into a smile. "Well, don't let me hold you up, daddy." She lifted her ass off the sofa so Ronnie could pull her pants down.

Every nerve ending in her body tingled with awareness as her pants were drug down her legs and tossed to the side. Her body ignited, overwhelmed with warmness when Ronnie pressed a kiss to her ankles and worked her way closer to her middle. By the time she'd marked her path between both legs, Kenni couldn't help but squirm with the tight knot of anticipation in her stomach.

"Oooohhh," Kenni moaned, shivering at the feeling of the tongue slipping between her pussy lips.

Instantly, her pelvis began to rock against the appendage, tripping over all of the pleasure switches, activating her yoni to coat itself. Pussy drenching with hard nipples, Kenni grinded in rhythm to the tongue lashes she received. Ronnie slipped a finger inside of her tunnel, making the pressure building within her intensify. Her eyes squeezed shut, pants turned to wheezing, and her stomach clenched at the immense orgasmic sensation rippling through her body.

"Fuuuckk," Kenni squealed, her thighs flexing around Ronnie's head.

One hand on either thigh, Ronnie spread them apart slightly and tossed her head from side to side, making breathing room for herself. In a languid motion, she traced out a W, her mouth pulling each lip into her mouth. She ran circles around her clit before wrapping her mouth around it, tugging it gently into her mouth while the tip of her tongue swiped furiously.

"Oh. Myfuckin…God, Ronnie! Shit… shit… shit…" Another orgasm threatened her.

Those fucking fingers darted back inside of her, only this time, with a pinky entering her back door. Kenni barely registered the sneak attack dipping in and out through the back. The three fingers assaulting both of her holes, actively demanding the ultimate burst of pleasure, compelled Kenni to chew on her lip, as she rode the wave, seeking her climatic ending as well.

Frustration lent to her hands digging in her own scalp just as an orgasm rocked through her body. "Dammit, Ronnie! Fuuuccckk!" Kenni screamed, climaxing again.

Lifting up to her feet, Ronnie smiled down at Kenni. She licked the cum off her face. "You still mad, baby?"

Kenni peered up at her curiously. "Mad about what?"

*   *   *

It was finally Friday, and all of the plans Kenni had made for the weekend could now begin. She eagerly pushed her way through the crowd after school to the parking lot, where Ronnie waited out front.

"What's up, baby?" accosted Ronnie, pressing a kiss to Kenni's lips as soon as she got in the car.

"Hey, baby. So, you gonna meet one of my friends at the game tonight," she revealed.

"Oh, shit, that's tonight. I forgot I got something to do."

"Ronnie!" whined Kenni.

The stud snickered. "I'm just playing with you, girl. I ain't got shit to do but put my mouth all over you."

"You so fuckin nasty," responded Kenni, leaning over and nibbling on her ear.

"And you love that shit."

"What? Girl, stop. You aight," she teased.

"Shiit. Remember that shit when you up in bed, talking about, 'Ooh, Ronnie… Fuck… Shit… don't stop," Ronnie mocked her.

"Shut up."

Upon arriving at Ronnie's apartment complex, they began their display of affection outside and continued into the apartment. The couple stumbled around the hallway of the apartment building, bumping into walls and others' doors as they hunted each other down, craving more. Across from Ronnie's apartment, a door opened, and Shyna exited. She watched them with a smile on her face. Ronnie had pinned Kenni against her front door with both wrists clamped in her hand above her head as the two kissed.

"Y'all almost there," Shyna joked to the pair with a chuckle, who were oblivious to having an audience.

Ronnie glanced behind her and laughed. She released Kenni's wrists and stepped back slightly from her. "What's up, Shy?" She spun Kenni around to envelop her from behind so the two feminine women faced each other. "What you about to get into?"

"Nothing as fun as y'all about to do," Shyna joked, moving past the two. "Y'all have fun, but be safe, though."

"Fa sho. You too." Ronnie kissed Kenni's neck and unlocked the door.

Kenni squirmed out of her grip and stalked into the living room. She plopped down on the couch with crossed arms and ankles. Hot on her heels, with her head cocked in confusion, Ronnie sat down next to her. She reached out to grab her, but her girlfriend huffed, rolled her eyes, and scooted away from her.

"What the fuck I do to you?" Ronnie exploded.

"I told you I don't like that bitch," Kenni spat back with a whipping neck.

"Who?"

"Yo ugly-ass neighbor you just had to speak to!"

Hiding a smile, but refraining from rolling her eyes, Ronnie told her, "Baby, Shyna cool peoples. She not gay, and her dude the police. We just smoking buddies when he not around. I only want yo cute ass." Ronnie unfolded her arms and kissed her cheek.

Folding her arms back across her chest, Kenni snapped, "I don't care. She can smoke outside. I don't like her ass."

Deep breaths, deep breaths, Ronnie cautioned herself, then began counting like her anger management class had taught her. Her temper demanded she check Kenni for even thinking she could control who she hung out with, but she squashed that desire. "Man, what's up? I know you got some homework, and I need my hair done before the game. Where yo bookbag at?"

"In the car," Kenni bit out. "I'll get it," she snarled when Ronnie bounded up from the couch.

"Fuckin women, man." She shook her head after Kenni left out. She went to her patio door and watched Kenni.

When she came back in, Kenni plopped down on the couch, slinging her bookbag down next to her. Ronnie rolled her eyes and came over to her.

When Kenni didn't open her legs so she could sit between them, she forcibly opened them.

"Don't be yankin' my fuckin head and shit because you feel some type of way, either," Ronnie ordered.

"I know," Kenni retorted, getting to work, unbraiding her hair.

Since Kenni had begun her hair, Ronnie pulled her bookbag towards her. She nabbed a notebook, along with her English work. Kenni reached into her bookbag and pulled out a folder and a book.

"We reading that stupid Shakespeare shit, *Romeo and Juliet.*"

"Dude a legend, shorty. People still imitating his work."

"So we need to read the new shit then, not this 'hast thou' bullshit."

Chuckling, Ronnie responded, "It ain't even that hard to understand. Do you even know what it's about?"

"No. I ain't even started reading that bullshit."

"It's about love and suicide. Two families don't want either of they kids fuckin' with the other 'cause the families been beefing for a minute. They keep fucking around and end up killing they self just to be with each other." Ronnie summed up her opinion of the world-renowned work.

"The fuck? Why we reading about that depressing-ass shit?"

"'Cause depression and suicide real, ma, especially with muthafuckas around our age. You never know what a muthafucka going through, and you never know what people can and can't handle."

"I guess. What you know about Shakespeare?"

"Girl, I'm smart as fuck. Don't let these golds fool yo ass."

"Yeah, whatever." She yanked Ronnie's head as she started to braid.

Ronnie smacked her leg. "Keep yanking my shit. You gonna ruin the surprise I got for you after the game."

Her hands fell away from Ronnie's hair onto her shoulders, and her eyes ballooned. "What surprise?"

Smirking, she replied, "Don't worry about it."

"Ronnie."

"Nope, you gotta wait to see if you can earn it."

In retaliation of her words, Kenni pulled her hair softly. "Whatever."

"What I tell you?" She smacked her leg again. "Read over yo questions real quick. I'm about to read this shit to you."

"Okay." Kenni peered over her shoulders, beginning to read the questions that went with the selected reading from the *Romeo and Juliet* play.

*   *   *

"I like her, she cool as fuck," Layla told her best friend after the game.

The two were standing under a shelter. The football game had been canceled due to heavy rain and lightning. They were waiting for Ronnie to pull her truck around to the front.

"You like her because she bought all our snacks. Fat ass." Kenni grinned and laughed.

"Girl, whatever," Layla laughed. "I mean, a nigga with money is always nice, but for real, though, I see how she be on it when you want something. She go get it for you even though it was only some punk-ass snacks. You could be walking to her car in the rain and shit," she pointed out, then voiced, "Shit, where her friends at?"

Kenni chuckled. "You know, I ain't even met her friends yet—"

"Oh my God, is that her truck?!" Layla's eyes ballooned at the sight of the vehicle pulling up to them.

"Yeah," she murmured, eyes on Ronnie, who had gotten out and was coming around the truck to open her car door with an umbrella already cast overhead.

Quickly, Layla snatched her into a hug. She whispered animatedly, "Bitch, don't fuck this up. She got some money."

"Whatever, Lay." Kenni pulled away from her, laughing. "Love you."

"Love you, too, boo."

Closing the door behind her girlfriend, Ronnie turned to face her friend. "It was nice meeting you."

"Nice meeting you, too," Layla smiled. "Where yo friends at? I know you got a friend for me."

One of Ronnie's eyebrows raised she knew which one of her stud brothers instantly would like the mocha toned female with the fat ass that wore a hat so beautifully. "I can set something up. Two of my brothers single and I got a fem sister."

"Ooh bet," Layla grinned with sparkling hazel eyes. "Tell Kenni to let me know when and where. I'm there."

Ronnie nodded at her. She hopped in her ride. "Baby, I—"

"Where's my surprise?" Kenni demanded to know at the same time she began speaking.

"Oh, you ain't forgot that, huh?"

"No, now what is it? We going somewhere? Is it a gift? I'm ready," she told her anxiously.

Chuckling, Ronnie rested a hand on her knee. "Just chill, lil baby. I gotta bust this move first."

"Okay, what you gotta do?" she said, not understanding her slang.

"I gotta run to the house and weigh out this quarter of cush for Shyna."

"Shyna?" Kenni grimaced and rolled her eyes.

Ronnie kissed her hand. "We ain't gotta stay, though. I usually just give her my keys to lock up if I can't kick it with her. So, that way, she can still smoke without her dude tripping."

"She never about to sit in yo house while we not there," Kenni objected, snatching her hand back. "And you never about to give her yo keys."

Deep breaths, inhale, exhale, Ronnie reminded herself while rolling her eyes. She pushed her temper down and gave her a side-eye. "You want yo surprise or nah?"

"I want you to quit hanging with that bitch, but obviously, I don't always get what I want."

"Listen, baby, I'ma get my money by all means."

"Well, let's get it then," Kenni sneered, throwing her car door open and stalking up to the entrance of Ronnie's apartment building.

*   *   *

Kenni's foot bounced rapidly as she stared daggers at her girlfriend. Her surprise had been postponed, she had to see her neighbor, Shyna, who she was sure liked Ronnie and who Ronnie continued to hang out with, and Ronnie had also decided to match Shyna, blunt for blunt. So, the assumed blunt and transaction Kenni thought would take twenty to thirty minutes had morphed into a full-blown smoke session for the past hour and a half. During which, Ronnie hadn't even spoken to her, nor did she speak to Ronnie.

Her phone buzzed in her pocket. Kenni pulled it out and checked the text message. "I have to go home," she snapped at Ronnie.

The conversation halted, and the pair looked at Kenni as if they had forgotten she was there. Ronnie smiled at her and Shyna stood, muttering, "Well, I guess that's my cue to leave."

"Could've been left," Kenni sniped.

Shyna's eyes slid over to her, running from top to bottom, but she didn't say anything to her. "All right, Ronnie. Get yo lil baby home. Holla at me when you get back."

"Aight, yo." Ronnie stood and pulled Kenni up with her.

She pulled away from her and stalked to the front door. Ronnie followed her, shaking her head and rolling her eyes. The ride to her house was silent. Ronnie pulled into the driveway and put the car in park. She leaned over to give her a kiss goodbye, but she turned her head.

"Baby, for real?" Ronnie finally said.

"For real my ass! Y'all just had to have a whole smoke session? And I expect my surprise tomorrow," she said, reaching out to open her car door.

Reaching out and grabbing her arm, Ronnie fired back, "And I expect my damn kiss before you get out my damn ride!"

"Kiss that bitch." Kenni rolled her eyes.

Chuckling softly, Ronnie jumped out of her truck and went to the passenger side. She pinned Kenni against her truck. "I don't wanna kiss her, I wanna kiss you." She kissed her lips. "All over." She kissed her again.

"Stop, Ronnie," Kenni protested weakly. "I'm mad at you. I don't like her," she pouted.

She kissed her forehead. "Baby, you ain't got nothing to worry about. I only want you." She put her lips on Kenni's softly, again and again, persuading her to kiss her back.

"I want my surprise tomorrow," Kenni told her, staring into her eyes as she separated them slightly, pushing her hands on Ronnie's chest.

"Whatever," Ronnie smirked with a playful roll of her eyes.

Kenni nipped her lip, prompting a grin from Ronnie, who then gave her a smooch. "You know I got you, baby." She eased off of her.

"You better." Kenni grinned and turned to walk into the house.

      *   *   *

Tomorrow never comes may be a true proverb, but surprise day damn sure did come quickly. Kenni buzzed with anticipation, wondering what the super secretive surprise was that Ronnie had for her. Patience was definitely not her strong point, so when her girlfriend pulled up to her house, she was in the car before the car was in park.

"Okay. I'm ready," Kenni announced.

"Ready for what?"

Kenni shoved her in the shoulder. "Ronnie!"

"Girl, what is you talking about?" Ronnie joked with a straight face. "The hell is you ready for?"

"Stop playing," she pouted and pinched her.

"Girl, we about to go back to my house and take a nap."

"Fuck yo nap," Kenni jested. "And we already passed the way to yo house."

Ronnie rolled her eyes dramatically. "And it's called taking the back way, with yo special smart ass."

"You get on my nerves." Kenni crossed her arms and slid down in her seat so she could lift her legs onto the dashboard.

"You get on my nerves, too. Get yo feet off my dashboard."

Silently fuming, but hoping this was all a

game, Kenni rolled her eyes. She looked out the window, vowing to herself not to speak again until she had seen whatever it was Ronnie had for her.

"Oh, you ain't talking to me now?" Ronnie reached over the middle console, and her fingers attacked her underarms. Kenni squirmed away from her, fighting off a smile and laughter. "Man, whatever then. Break that rello down for me, please, baby. It's in the pocket on the door at the bottom."

Sliding her hand down into the pocket on her car door, she didn't feel anything. She slid her hand back and forth again with the same result. Still not talking, Kenni caught her eye and shook her head no.

"It ain't nothing in there? Check the glove compartment."

Mock irritation dawned over Kenni's face. She opened the glove compartment and scanned its content. No cigarillo. She ran a hand inside of it, rummaging through the contents, and still no shell. The door to the compartment smacked shut to indicate to Ronnie that it was empty as well.

"Fuck!" She slapped her hand against the steering wheel. "Check in that bag behind the seat for me. It might be in there."

Expelling a sigh, Kenni reached into the back seat and pulled a bag up onto her lap. She opened the bag to find another bag. Uncovering that one, she discovered a package. Curious as a cat, she started to open it.

"Yo nosey ass! The rello right there," Ronnie spied, seeing the cigarillo package peeking out of the bigger bag.

"So, what's this?" she asked about the layer-wrapped package in her hands.

"Smell it. It's weed." When Kenni went to do exactly that, Ronnie snatched the bag back, laughing. "Don't smell it. I was fuckin' with you. Jay's dog took a shit in my car. You was about to get a nose full of shit."

"Fuck you," Kenni bit out. She threw the bag back into the backseat, and a small jewelry box tripped out. Instantly, she snagged it, a smile spreading over her face. "What's this?"

"That's for Mama. Put that back," Ronnie told her sternly.

Her face crumpled. She snatched the stupid bag from the stupid backseat and shoved it inside. Why she would even have her mother's jewelry in a bag was fucking stupid, Kenni thought.

Ronnie winked at the petulant expression she wore. "Baby, you know I'm just playing. That lil box for you."

Just like that, Kenni's whole being lit up once again. She turned around, damn near diving into the backseat to retrieve the box. Once she had it in her hands, she flipped it open to gaze at a modest, princess cut ring that made her heart sway. "Thank you, baby." She kissed Ronnie on the cheek.

"It's a promise ring," Ronnie told her. "I promise to always be here for yo lil crazy ass, not cheat on you, love you, one day marry you, and all that other shit."

"Oh, you wanna marry me? So it kinda doubles as an engagement ring, too, then, huh?"

"It could, but I would probably get you another one when that time came."

"Okay," Kenni grinned. "So, this just 'cause you love me?"

Pulling the car up to a restaurant, Ronnie stared into her eyes. "I love you, girl. Like, I really love the fuck out yo ass. This just me showing it." Their mouths met in the middle with one agenda: to devour each other.

"I love you, too, and I love this ring," Kenni told her honestly.

"Shit, you better, that shit wasn't cheap," Ronnie winked. "Now get the fuck out. I'm hungry."

"Fuck you," she smiled, opening her car door. "Race you." Kenni took off towards the restaurant's entrance with Ronnie hot on her heels.

Chapter 3

"What you doing, baby?" Kenni questioned Ronnie over the phone a couple of weeks later. "I thought you had to work today?"

"Fucking pissed," Ronnie snarled, throwing her game controller down onto the floor. It wasn't doing anything for her mood anyway. "My supervisor bitch ass sent me home early. I swear I'm trying not to go back to hustling, but this shit for the birds. Muthafuckas talk to you any kind of way at a job. I made more money in the streets, and muthafuckas knew better than to talk to me like how a job will. Shit, for one, I don't even need this damn job or have to be in the streets."

"What else would or could you be doing?"

"Shit, I could be at the club," she told her with a tone that inferred she thought Kenni should know. "I told you me and my niggas got a spot we all own."

"So, why don't you just do that instead of working at the shoe store?"

"Man, I almost feel like it's a handout type shit. My nigga brother passed, and he gave us the bread to start our own shit or do anything with as long as we kept our asses out the streets. For real, I ain't mooching or nothing, but, you know, a nigga wanna make my own way without no handouts, you feel me?"

Kenni let out a sigh, stretching back onto her bed. "Baby, you just said y'all all own it. It's not a handout."

"But my nigga brother gave us the cash to start this shit so—"

"So what?" Kenni interrupted. "To keep y'all out the streets!"

Ronnie smacked her lips together in annoyance. "Man, you just don't understand, shorty. You ain't never had or needed to provide for yoself. That's all the fuck I know. Shit, I jumped off the porch and started getting to the money early on the hustle side. Now I'm trying to do this shit legit and got all these cornball muthafuckas talking to me any kind of way. I made more money and had my respect in the streets. Yeah, the money was to keep us out the streets, but at least in the streets, I earned my shit. Shit wasn't given to me."

"So, earn yo shit at the club. Fuck that job and earn yo damn spot. What the fuck?" Kenni spewed as her anger began to build.

"Man, whatever, shorty. You just don't understand. Like, you not even trying to," Ronnie accused, picking her game controller back up.

"How am I not trying to, Ronnie? You want me to tell you to quit yo job and hustle full time? NO! I'm not going to. I fuckin love and care about you. I don't want you in danger or getting locked the fuck up."

"But what about what I want and how I feel?" The controller fell to the ground as she shouted into the phone, a vein in her neck flexing viciously. She took a deep breath. "Man, I'ma call you back," Ronnie spat out in frustration and hung up without waiting for a response.

She threw her phone across the room and kicked the game controller that was on the ground. She fished a bag of weed from her pocket and a pack of cigarillos. Ronnie immediately began the process of breaking the cigar and weed down in preparation for the blunt she was about to twist.

Rapid knocks pounded on the door just when she lit her second blunt. Ronnie ignored it, but the person persisted. She exhaled hard. "Who is it?" she finally yelled, only for the person to continue knocking.

Anger sparking at the no reply, and the presence disrupting the solace she'd found in her weed, Ronnie hopped up. Blunt still in her mouth, she wrenched the door open, ready to lay into whoever was on the other side for bothering her. A wailing Shyna collapsed into her arms, killing that notion. Her hands went around the woman awkwardly, attempting to comfort her as she snotted and cried on her shirt.

"They killed him," she cried, burying her face in Ronnie's shirt.

"Shit." Ronnie spun them a little so she could close her door. "Damn, Shy. I'm sorry for yo loss, yo." She extended the blunt to her, holding it at eye level.

Shyna sniffled, then released Ronnie. She took a step back and three deep, settling breaths before taking the proffered blunt.

"That was yo dude they been talking about on the news and radio? That officer?" Ronnie asked.

Tears streamed down Shyna's nodding face. "Yes and no," she whispered, hitting the blunt again. She passed it back to Ronnie. "I worked for Ill Will."

"Will Coors? Will Coors the Kingpin?" Ronnie questioned, eyes on her like she now saw her in a different light.

"Yeah. Will was like my daddy. He raised me and put me in this position so I could feed him the information I got from my fiancé. The officer who killed him and died, too, Officer Nathaniel Mostandfordt, was my fiancé." Cries burst forth from her again.

"Will knew that was yo dude?" Ronnie questioned, trying to make her story make sense. She hit the blunt, waiting for her to answer.

"Yeah," Shyna cried out. "He set us up. I was getting all the info out about the raids and shit from him and passed it on to Will. Will took care of me for that, like he looked out when I was younger. Now they both gone. I even fell for Nate. He took care of me in a way Will never tried. They both wasn't supposed to die at the same time! I could've dealt with one, but both? Both?"

"Damn, ma." Ronnie wrapped her arms back around her, attempting to quell the body-wracking sobs. "I'm sorry, Shy."

"What am I gonna do? They both gone."

"C'mon now, Ill Will was yo pops." She rubbed her back soothingly. "He been the man in our city for a while now. I know he taught you some shit. Take what you got and flip that shit. Shit, it's time to boss up, ma. And if yo fiancé loved you like how he was supposed to, he probably took care of you in case this type of shit happened anyway. Fuck crying, it's time to get it. I got you. I'm here for you."

"You right." A few more sniffles escaped, but Shyna took a deep breath after them and presented Ronnie with a watery smile.

"I know it," Ronnie grinned, reaching out to hug her again. She froze when Shyna's lips pressed against hers. Sexual attraction made Ronnie's lips react, causing her to kiss her back.

*   *   *

Kenni fumed and grumbled up the walkway to her girlfriend's apartment. She hated riding the bus, but Ronnie had hung up on her. So, here she was, stomping into Ronnie's apartment building. Kenni reached her front door and noticed it wasn't closed all the way. She pushed it open, stepped inside, and halted, her eyes trained on Shyna and Ronnie standing several feet apart.

"What the fuck is she doing over here?" Kenni exploded, glaring at Shyna.

Wide eyes left Shyna's and came to hers before going back and forth between the two again. Ronnie pinched her shirt, holding a piece of it out so Kenni could see the evidence of Shyna's crying episode. "Her dude died today, baby."

"So, she here for you to what, console her? You ain't got no friends? Yo peoples don't love you? You better go home," she fired at Shyna.

Shyna's eyes narrowed, but she didn't respond to Kenni. She turned to Ronnie and put a hand on her shoulder. Smirking, she said to her, "Thank you, Ronnie, for everything."

"Ronnie!" Kenni screamed in frustration.

The shrillness of her tone made Ronnie flinch. Shyna moved away from her, stepping towards Kenni. "Calm that shit down, shorty, I'm leaving." Shyna came closer to her and Kenni stood her ground, glaring harshly at her. Once the two were inches away from each other, to Ronnie's yards, Shyna whispered something for only Kenni to hear. In a louder voice, she moved passed her and called out to Ronnie, "Thanks again, Ronnie."

Silently seething, Kenni didn't reply to the other woman. She watched her saunter out of the door and locked it once it was closed behind her. Whipping back around to face Ronnie, she exploded. "What the fuck?"

That same indifference Ronnie had felt when they were on the phone earlier crept back up. She sat down, mentally rolling her eyes. "You blowing my high," she finally told her, lighting a blunt.

"Fuck yo high!" Kenni screamed, grabbing a cup off the counter, launching it at her.

Easily, Ronnie caught the cup in the air. "Quit throwing shit in my fuckin house!"

"Keep that bitch out yo house!" Another item flew towards Ronnie.

"What the fuck did I just tell you?" Ronnie erupted, shooting to her feet. She put her blunt out and tore her shirt from her body, throwing it over the couch, and snagged Kenni's arm. Ronnie dragged her out of the small kitchen, back towards the living room.

"Get the fuck off me!" Kenni struggled, attempting to pull her arm out of Ronnie's grip.

"You done fuckin' throwin' shit?" interrogated Ronnie, tossing her down onto the couch.

Her free arm backhanded the ashtray off the edge of the sofa. "You done kicking it with that bitch?"

Ronnie's fingers flexed into a fist, her lip curled up, and her jaw locked. "I swear to God, you picking all of that shit up."

"I ain't picking shit up," Kenni stated matter of factly. "You better call that bitch."

"No, I'm telling you! You gonna pick that shit up. You done making a fuckin' mess in my fuckin' house."

A raised eyebrow asked the question of, *am I really?* Kenni answered the silent inquiry by kicking the living room table over with her feet. She jumped up, swinging and screaming at Ronnie. "Fuck you and that bitch!"

One hit, two hits, duck, three deep breaths, four, and another hit landed. Ronnie's hand shot out, wrapping around Kenni's neck, squeezing tightly. "Keep. Yo fucking hands. To. yoself," she growled menacingly. "I fuckin' told yo stupid ass—"

"Ronnie! Let her go," her older sister, Arianna, commanded, rushing through the unlocked front door.

"No," Ronnie answered stoically. "How the fuck did you even get in, and why the fuck you here? Leave."

"The fuckin' door was unlocked," Arianna snapped. "And I'm not fuckin' leaving. Let that girl go."

Ignoring her sister, Ronnie increased the pressure she was applying to Kenni's throat, glaring at her harshly, not bothered by the scratches Kenni inflicted. "No," she said again, stubbornly.

Arianna took a deep breath. She walked to her sister and began rubbing her back while attempting to appeal to her conscience. "Ron, let her go. You know I love you, but you gotta let her go, aight? If you don't, we really gonna be in this bitch rumbling. Let her go, Ron. For me. I don't want you locked up."

Scowling deeply at both women, Ronnie flung Kenni away from her. Her sister immediately pulled her into a hug. When she didn't hug her back, Arianna gently slapped her face. "You gotta get a handle on that temper. What the fuck is even wrong with you? And don't get missing like this no more. I missed yo punk ass."

"Excuse me," Kenni called out from the other side of the room. She nabbed the remote off the TV stand. The siblings turned around to face her, and she launched it, clonking Ronnie in the forehead.

"The fuck?" Arianna hollered, grabbing Ronnie, who had lunged for her. She wrestled her further away from Kenni, towards the hall, and pushed her into her bedroom. "Don't punch yo

fuckin' walls. You got a bag for a reason, sis."
Ronnie turned around to face her, and Arianna
glared right back. "Go," she demanded and released
an exhale when the stud went into her other
bedroom, filling the apartment with the sounds of
skin on punching bag.

"Sis?" Kenni questioned meekly.

"Yes, sis," Arianna sniped. "Ronnie is my
fuckin' sister. Now, I'ma give you a pass because
you obviously young as fuck. But, if you don't want
my sister to fuck you up, you better learn to keep yo
hands to yoself. And quit throwing shit, too." She
looked around the apartment. "What the fuck was
y'all fighting for anyway?"

The original spark of Kenni's indignation
sprouted. "'Cause that stupid bitch from across the
hall was over here again and I already told Ronnie I
don't like her."

Her eyes rolled at the logistics of the teen
standing before her. "A muthafucka gonna do what
a muthafucka wanna do, and nine times out of ten,
there's nothing you can do to prevent it. Ronnie
gave you any reason not to trust her?"

"No."

"So quit being stupid before you lose her."

"Fine." Kenni's eyes narrowed at her. She
walked away from the older woman, headed to the
back room where Ronnie was assaulting the bag.
"Ronnie?" she said timidly, eyes wide at the speed
and intensity of which her girlfriend attacked the
bag. "Ronnie, I'm sorry."

"Ronnie," her sister prompted from the
doorway.

One last punch and she stepped back. Ronnie wiped the sweat off her forehead. She took a deep breath, facing the women. "Can you give us a minute, Ari?"

"Nope, I ain't got time for the theatrics." Arianna barged into the room. She grabbed her sister into a side hug and kissed her cheek. "Call yo mama."

"Aight," Ronnie agreed, wiping the kiss off her cheek.

"Remember what I said," Arianna told Kenni. "I ain't gonna say it's nice to meet you, but it would be smart to listen."

Kenni nodded. The sisters walked past her, headed back to the entrance of the apartment. Ronnie lingered at the front door after her sister left.

"I'm sorry, Ronnie," she apologized again, walking up to the stud.

Inhale through your nose, exhale through your mouth. "Uh-huh," Ronnie grunted, repeating her breathing exercises.

"Do you forgive me, baby?"

"Yeah," Ronnie murmured vocally. Mentally, distance pushed the two further apart. On the inside, an icy numbness draped over her body.

"You want me to stay the night?" she suggested with twinkling, suggestive eyes.

"Maybe next time. I'm about to go see what my mama want. You need a ride, or you got one?"

"I want you to drop me off."

Ronnie grabbed her keys off the counter. "C'mon," she muttered dryly.

*   *   *

"Have you talked to your brother lately?" Beaunna questioned her daughter, Kenni, who sat at the kitchen table, fiddling with her phone.

"I don't have one of those. I'm an only child," Kenni answered flatly, bringing the phone up to her ear.

Beaunna smirked and flipped her off. "Smart ass. I'll take that as a no." She dialed her son's number. "Jeremy Antonio, I have two children, and I always see my Princess Brat." She stuck her tongue out at Kenni, who rolled her eyes. "I have not seen your face or heard your voice in I don't know how long, and if that doesn't change here soon, I will find you, and I will make it so I only have one child. I brought you in this world, and I can take yo ass out." Beaunna hung up the phone and sat it on the table.

"Aarrgghh!" Kenni let out a scream of frustration and launched her phone across the room.

"And what the hell is wrong with you?" Beaunna frowned at her daughter. "I'm not buying you another one if you broke it."

"Ronnie won't answer the phone," she pouted. "And she already told me she on break."

"Well, maybe he had some things to handle," smirked Beaunna.

"So! That don't mean don't answer the phone. And it's been like that for a couple of days," she pouted, crossing her arms over her chest and tapping her feet. Kenni hadn't seen her since their argument when Arianna, Ronnie's sister, had popped up and broken them up. Even when she had dropped her off that night, Ronnie was cordial, but there was a bitter distance wafting from her.

"Did y'all have an argument?" Beaunna posed.

I swear she can read my thoughts, Kenni said to herself and narrowed her eyes at her mother. "Can I borrow the car?"

"Do I need to go with you?"

"I'm not a kid!"

"You are my child! And you're a stubborn brat. So, are you gonna behave, or do I need to go with you?"

"I know how to act!" Kenni fired back, standing and retrieving her phone.

"If the police call me, yo ass staying," Beaunna told her, throwing the car keys to her.

"Fine. I don't care."

*   *   *

"Fuck!" Ronnie rolled her eyes. She stared across the food court, watching Kenni stalk towards her. "Aye, Sean, can you let Robert know I may be a little late coming back from break?" she asked one of her male coworkers, who was sitting next to her.

"We got like ten minutes," he told her, checking his time. Ronnie jutted her chin at Kenni, who was almost near them. "Ohh." Realization dawned on his face. "You about to get fucked up," he surmised.

Ronnie cut her eyes at him.

"What? I'm just saying."

Kenni slid into the seat across from Ronnie, glaring at her. She flashed her gray eyes onto the coworker still hovering by the two. "Excuse us."

The coworker smirked at Ronnie. "Say less, sis." He walked away and mouthed for Ronnie to bob and weave.

She flipped him off. Kenni turned around to see who or what Ronnie was flipping off, but her coworker was gone already, disappearing into the store they worked in. Kenni whipped back around to face Ronnie.

"Why you ain't been answering the phone?"

"What is you talking about?" she began dismissively. "You know I was at work. You know I'm on break."

"So! You been all dry and barely texting and answering my calls, what the fuck?"

"Soo, you come up to my job and make a scene?" Ronnie sneered.

"Ain't nobody making a scene! I'm trying to have a fuckin' conversation with you."

"Well, try lowering yo fuckin' voice first," Ronnie hissed. "And what the fuck I been telling yo ass? Yo ass shoulda thought about all that and used yo fuckin' words before you thought to put yo muthafuckin hands on me."

Kenni blinked owlishly. "Really? Okay, well, I'm sorry. You happy now?" she asked with insolence.

Rage kindled in Ronnie's eyes. "No, I'm not fuckin' happy now! What the fuck? My muthafuckin' sister might not be there to save yo lil dumb ass next time."

"Don't call me no fuckin' dumb ass!"

"Don't act like one." Ronnie pushed away from the table. "I gotta go back to fuckin' work, I ain't got time to sit here and argue with yo ass. Congratulations, you made me late."

"Fuckin' sorry, all right!" Kenni screamed. "I'm sorry."

Ronnie leveled her with a look. "Keep yo fuckin' hands to yoself, and don't never stand in the way of my paper."

She strode away angrily, all the way back into her job, then into the back supply room. Ronnie was full to the brim with vexation. She pushed over a stack of boxes, then another. Her boss walked in, surveyed the room, and his scowl deepened.

"What are you doing to my store?" he hissed.

"Look, man." Ronnie battled to squelch the infuriation she carried. "My bad. I tripped coming back and knocked the boxes down. I'll get everything cleaned up."

"And what about the fact that you're late? Again."

"Sean told you I was gonna be late."

"So what? Sean told me this. Sean told me that. The fact of the matter is, you're late. When you get an hour break, I expect you to return on time, or we can go back to fifteen minutes."

Ronnie checked the time on her watch. She was six minutes late. "Man, fuck you and this gotdamn job!" she exploded, taking off her uniform shirt that had the store logo, a pair of shoes with wings, and tossing it on the floor. "I'm six minutes late, not no hour or some shit!"

"You're fired," he hissed, his Caucasian face turning red with anger as he picked up the shirt.

"So what?" Ronnie got in his face. "Fuck this job. Fuck you. Fuck you. Fuck you. Fuck you. Fuck you. Fuck you." She shoved him back into the lockers and stormed out.

"Yo, Ronnie!" someone in the store called out to her.

The bird finger was the only acknowledgment given on her way out of the store.

*   *   *

"What?" Ronnie yelled into her phone. "I'm at fuckin' home!" She hung up, jumped out her car, and slammed the car door. Ronnie lightly jogged up to her apartment, grumbling. She opened her mailbox, pulled out her mail, and slammed it shut. At her apartment door, she realized her key had fallen off her chain. She punched the front door and walked out. Stomping back to her car, Ronnie found her house key in between her seats.

"You aight?" Shyna asked Ronnie, leaning against her door frame, watching Ronnie charge in, still muttering to herself.

"I'm good."

"You not," Shyna stated, undeterred by the gruffness present in her voice. "I gotta bottle with our names on it, though. What's up?"

Ronnie stepped into her apartment. She didn't make any attempt to close the door behind her. Shyna shrugged, turning back around to go into her apartment.

"Nigga, is you coming in or nah?" Ronnie called out in exasperation.

"Yeah, let me grab the bottle," Shyna grinned, entering her apartment to retrieve the liquor.

*   *   *

"I'm gonna be cool. I'm gonna be cool," Kenni chanted to herself, exiting her mother's car hours later, in front of Ronnie's apartment. She took a deep breath, continuing her self talk. "She just lost her job. I'm not gonna spazz on her for yelling and hanging up on me," she grimaced. "Even though it was disrespectful as fuck."

Kenni walked up the walkway and cocked her head, looking at Ronnie's door once she entered the complex. She heard loud music, the sounds of her playing a shooting game, and over it all, Ronnie's good-natured voice. The weed smell permeating the hallway also seemed to be coming from her apartment. Kenni raised her hand to knock, then dropped it and twisted the doorknob.

"Really? Really!" she screeched, seeing Shyna and Ronnie on two separate couches, playing the game together with a big bottle between them that only had a swallow left.

Ronnie looked back at her and smiled. "What's up, baby?"

"What's up, my ass!" Kenni snapped, ignoring their childish laughter at her statement. "You know what, I'm not even about to do this with you." She turned to leave amidst Ronnie's calls. "I swear to God, I fuckin' hate you sometimes."

She took off, speed walking back to the car, ignoring Ronnie calling her name. Kenni jumped in and took off to her house with the music blaring, taking no heed to any of the traffic signals she passed. She made it to her house in record time and sat outside in the car, trying to calm herself.

"It's fine. It's fine." She took a deep breath. "She hasn't given me a reason not to trust her." She repeated Arianna's words to herself. Kenni got out the car as her front door opened and Jeremy walked out.

He smirked at her, seeing her scowl. "Yo lil dyke then pissed you off, huh?"

"Fuck you!" she snapped.

"Oh, you mad for real, huh?" he chuckled. "Mama went looking for you since you took the car without asking."

"So? Why is you even here?" Kenni asked him.

"Because you a brat and Mama can't deal with yo ass by herself," he joked with a smile on his face.

"Whatever. I ain't no brat."

"So, what you mad for then? Yo dyke-ass friend ain't ask how high when you told her to jump?"

"Fuck her," she spat and walked through the door.

Jeremy turned to follow his sister into the house but checked over his shoulder when he heard loud music approaching, along with the sounds of an engine. He turned around fully when a truck came to a stop in front of the house. Ronnie stepped out, and he smirked, watching her approach.

"Fuck you want?" Jeremy asked her.

"Bra, can you go get my girl?" Ronnie asked, hoping she didn't blow her buzz on the homophobic man in front of her.

"Ain't no dykes here," he sneered at her.

"Maybe not, but yo sister a lesbian," Ronnie scoffed, refusing to be baited into losing her temper. "So, can you get her for me?"

"Sis said fuck you. She cool on that dyke shit. So, get the fuck off my property," he snarled, looking her up and down.

"Man, listen, yo. I'm trying to be cool with you, my nigga. You my girl brother, so can you please go get her for me?"

"Fuck. Off."

"Aight, you know what, fuck it, nigga." Her temper flared. She started to jog up the stairs. "I'll go get my bitch my-damn-self."

"The fuck if you will," he stated, blocking her path to the door. "And my sister ain't no bitch."

Ronnie cocked her head back at him. "Nigga, I ain't call her no bitch, but I see who the bitch of the family is." The liquor and weed that had her mental calm and body relaxed had disappeared. With her temper swaying from him repeatedly goading her, she stepped up to him with a tense body, her fists balled up.

"Bitch, fuck you, dyke. Get the fuck off my property." He went to step back from her, but Ronnie popped off first with a quick three-piece.

He recovered, swinging wildly and missing. Jeremy took a few shots to the body and face before he was able to connect, and threw Ronnie off her game. He grabbed her, attempting to slam her, but

Ronnie fought and resisted. They tumbled down the porch steps, swinging at each other.

"What the fuck?" Kenni yelled, coming out of the house.

She jumped onto Ronnie's back, who was on top of her brother, pummeling him. Kenni grabbed her arms, wrapping her legs around her, and rolled them off of Jeremy. Jeremy jumped up, wiping the blood from his nose, and started towards Ronnie again.

"Jeremy, no!" Kenni shouted.

Refusing to be at a disadvantage, Ronnie wrestled Kenni off of her in anticipation of her brother's advances. Jumping to her feet, Kenni wasted no time going to her brother this time. Palms flat on his chest, she pushed him back repeatedly while glaring back and forth at them.

"Why the fuck are you here?" Kenni hissed at Ronnie.

"Yeah, bitch. Told yo dyke ass," Jeremy taunted.

Ronnie's eyes flashed to him. "Nigga, you a hoe. Bitch-ass nigga." She spat blood to the side of her and turned her eyes on Kenni. "Oh, word? For real? Yeah, aight," she nodded. "Fuck you, too, then!" She made moves back to her truck.

"Ronnie!"

*   *   *

Kenni sat in her room with her head in her hands. Her two best friends were sitting on her bed with her. They all listened silently as Kenni's phone call to Ronnie went straight to voicemail again. Tears seeped down her face.

"Girl, quit crying. Fuck her," Layla told her, handing her tissue. "Look at yo lip."

Sayvonne rolled her eyes. "She jumped in between two niggas fighting."

"So?"

"Lay, she didn't mean to," Kenni told her with a smile.

"Whatever." She rolled her eyes.

"Soo, what was they fighting for?" Sayvonne asked.

"I don't know. I had just left her house, mad as fuck," Kenni shrugged, dialing Ronnie's number again. "But they don't like each other anyway. They had got into it at the mall before we even started dating."

"Okay, so you was mad, left, and she followed you home?" Layla summarized.

"Nah. I wasn't even mad, mad. I ain't wanna trip, that's why I had left."

"You? Not tripping and acting a fool?" Sayvonne joked. "Let me find out you trying to chill out for Ronnie."

"Girl, whatever. I ain't that bad." Kenni grinned at her.

Layla and Sayvonne looked at each other, then to Kenni while simultaneously saying, "Shiiiitt."

"Fuck y'all," Kenni bit playfully at the two. "Her sister said some real shit the other day when we got into it. It's this bitch, her neighbor, that's like always the fuck around, and we got into a fight, like a real one."

"You mean, you spazzed and started hitting her?" Sayvonne surmised.

"Y'all know my temper. Anyways, so I was throwing shit at her, too, and her sister popped up, but I had never met her before, so I started tripping again, and her sister broke us up. I told her why we was fighting, and she asked me had Ronnie ever given me a reason not to trust her. And, you know, it just made sense."

Sayvonne smiled at her like a proud mother, while Layla asked, "Her sister ain't try to fight you?"

"Nah."

"She older?"

"Yeah."

"So, you was mad for what again today?" Sayvonne inquired, bringing the conversation back around full circle.

"Because that bitch was in her apartment again! Like, damn, every time I come over, I see this bitch, whether she in her apartment or in the hallway," Kenni snapped.

"Maybe they besties," Layla joked.

"That bitch can best these nuts. I'm the only female friend Ronnie need. I don't care what she say, that bitch like her."

A sigh escaped Sayvonne's lips at the same time she rolled her eyes. "How you know?"

"I just do."

"So, you do know it's not healthy to try to make your partner not have any female friends, right?"

"Fuck that bitch."

"And when Brandy alienated Layla from us because she ain't need no female friends, was that right?"

"Fuck that bitch!" the other two girls spat.

"That's why I got her ass locked up," Layla added about her ex.

"Exactly. That shit ain't right, and that shit ain't healthy," Sayvonne pointed out.

"All right, Oprah. So, what?"

"Keep an eye on that bitch until you got facts. You gonna fuck up y'all relationship with that 'you can't be friends with no other bitches but me' shit."

"Well, I would tell her all that shit, but she won't answer the phone."

"Me and Layla both here, and we both got cars," she stated matter of factly, like Kenni was dumb.

"Shotgun!" Layla hollered, standing up.

"Bitch," Kenni muttered as the trio headed out.

Fifteen minutes later, Kenni was getting out of the car at Ronnie's apartment. Sayvonne looked at Kenni with a serious face and said, "Don't have me out here waiting while y'all in there freaking."

"Aight."

Kenni squared her shoulders and went up to Ronnie's apartment building. She tapped on the door. No answer. So, again, she rammed on the door, only this time, a little harder.

*   *   *

Ronnie winced in her sleep, a noise in her background reverberating through her brain. It continued, and she gingerly peeled her eyes open. She blinked a few times, trying to come back to sobriety.

Did I drink last night? she wondered. The pounding sound continued on what sounded like the front door. Ronnie threw the covers off her to get out of the bed and cursed. "Fuck." She looked down at her strap, then over at the naked, sleeping woman next to her.

Pieces of the night drifted back over her. A quick recall of memory and she realized she had hit Kenni when she was fighting her brother. Ronnie searched her memories further. *We broke up,* she told herself firmly, staring at Shyna, but mentally replaying how they had parted. An empty bottle of Hennessey on her nightstand was her cue to what had transpired between her and Shyna. Her eyes perused Shyna's naked figure, and she looked away with guilt when the knocking on her door persisted.

Ronnie slipped her strap off and pulled on a pair of basketball shorts. She went to the door and peeked out the peephole. "Fuck," she said, seeing Kenni on the other side of the door. Ronnie took a deep breath and opened the door slightly. "What's up?" Ronnie greeted her gruffly, attempting to displace her guilt and latch onto the anger she'd held prior to all of this.

"Look, baby," Kenni sighed, "I'm sorry for everything. I'm not even gonna trip on that bitch no more. I promise."

"Okay," Ronnie agreed. "So, you wanna get back together then?"

Bewildered by her statement, Kenni cut her eyes at her. "We wasn't never broken up," she stated slowly.

Internally, Ronnie winced, but not physically. She plowed full steam ahead with her statement. "You said you hated me." A rustling in her room made her murmur, "You know what, it don't even matter, baby. Fuck it. I'm glad we talked, but I gotta do something for my sister in a couple hours, so I'ma pick you up afterward, aight?"

A warm feeling of contentment brought a grin to Kenni's relieved face. "Okay, baby. Can I have a hug?" Her girlfriend smiled and stepped out of the apartment to wrap her arms around her. Kenni asked again, just to be sure, "You sure you forgive me, baby? I am sorry."

She buried her face in her neck and squeezed her tightly. Ronnie placed a kiss on her cheek. "It's all water under the bridge, baby."

Behind the two, Ronnie's front door opened. "Ronnie?" Shyna posed.

Frozen like a deer in headlights, Ronnie didn't utter a word or move a muscle. However, Kenni's eyes raked over Shyna from head to toe. Her eyes flashed as she took in her half-clothed appearance. The shirt she wore, Kenni recognized as Ronnie's, and her hard nipples poked out, which meant she didn't have a bra on under that shirt, or probably anything else.

Kenni ripped out of Ronnie's arms and slapped her across the face. "Really!" She smacked her again across the other cheek upon seeing a hickey on her neck.

"All right, lil bitch, that's enough," Shyna stated casually with a smile like she was enjoying teasing the temperamental young woman.

Outrage clouded her vision, but her gaze focused on Shyna as if she were seeing through a tunnel. A fist smashed into her face. "Bitch!"

"Bra, y'all chill! Chill!" Ronnie yelled to the tussling women.

Her pleas fell on vacant ears as the two women were full-on banging in the hallway. Kenni wildly threw punches and attempted to pull Shyna's hair. Shyna threw shots and connected everywhere.

Unable to watch any more, Ronnie pulled Kenni away from Shyna to end the fight, but she lunged and managed to grab ahold of her hair. Her body suffered from jumping between the two women, and she was scratched and hit as well until she released Kenni. When her girlfriend finally let her hair go, Ronnie jumped in again. This time, she snagged Shyna, throwing her back into her apartment. She grasped the jingling door handle tightly so Shyna couldn't come back out. Her eyes went to Kenni, who stood in front of her.

Kenni's face was red, and a bruise was forming under her eye. Tears intermingled with the blood dripping from her lip. She held her ribs and stared Ronnie in her eyes. "Fuck you, Ronnie! You knew damn well we wasn't broken up! Yo fuckin' lying ass! Then you gonna go fuck that bitch! That fuckin' bitch!" she spat. "I swear to God I hate yo ass. I fuckin' hate you," she cried and turned to leave.

"Baby," Ronnie said.

"NO! Don't baby me!" Kenni screamed at her. "Nigga, we done. I'm fuckin cool on yo ass! Now, we broken up! I swear to God!"

"Fuck!" Ronnie yelled, still holding onto the door Shyna was still actively trying to get out of.

*   *   *

"Kenni, what the fuck?" Sayvonne shrieked, hopping out of the car when she noticed Kenni limping away from the apartment building. She ran up to her, trying to see the extent of the injuries on her face.

Both of Kenni's hands popped up, swatting away her prying hands. She went to the door. "Layla, unlock the door."

"Did Ronnie do this to you?" Sayvonne demanded to know, her hands glued to her hips.

"No!" Kenni denied. "Now, just get in the car, please. I just wanna leave," she mumbled dejectedly.

From the front seat, Layla glanced at Kenni but didn't say anything. Those hazel eyes scanned over her, taking note of her injuries. She reached a hand back to Kenni, which she squeezed like a lifeline.

"C'mon, Von, let's get up outta here," Layla said.

Sayvonne growled something incomprehensible, then got in the car. They peeled off fast, and she demanded again, "What the fuck happened?" Tears fell down Kenni's face as she rested it against the cool window. Sayvonne yelled at her again.

"Quit fuckin yelling at her, Von!" Layla snapped. "I wanna know, too, but give her a fuckin minute." She took off her seatbelt and climbed into the backseat. She pulled Kenni into her arms. "It's all right, sis. We got you. We here for you, baby."

The irate friend took a deep breath, self-regulating her emotions. She reached in the backseat and squeezed Kenni's hand once done. "I'm sorry. I love you, sis."

"I love y'all, too," Kenni whispered.

They made it back to Kenni's house in silence. Sayvonne cursed, however, as soon as they pulled up. Kenni's brother and mother were in the house, presumably in the kitchen or living room, due to the lights being on.

"Lay, take Kenni right upstairs. I'ma hit the living room and talk to Ms. B and Jeremy," Sayvonne directed.

"Tell them don't answer if Ronnie show up," Kenni sniffed.

"I got you."

Plan in motion, the three best friends proceeded up to the house. Sayvonne went in first, per the plan, clearing the way for Layla and Kenni to hurry in behind her. She stepped into the living room, where all eyes were on the stairs.

Beaunna cocked her head at Sayvonne, eyes traveling from the stairs and back to Sayvonne. "Everything okay?"

"Yeah, kinda." The warm smile she'd plastered on her face faltered slightly. "Umm,

Ronnie and Kenni broke up, so Kenni don't want y'all to answer if Ronnie show up."

"Okay," Beaunna sighed. "Well, I'm down here if y'all need me."

Nodding, she turned her eyes to an unnaturally silent Jeremy. "Nothing to say?"

"Nope," Jeremy said, turning the TV channels.

Curiosity coupled with a motherly instinct told Beaunna something wasn't right, and all of the kids were hiding it from her. She looked back and forth between the two, but no more words were exchanged. Sayvonne looked like she wanted to say something, but she turned and ran up the stairs. Jeremy didn't even look her way but appeared to be utterly engrossed in the movie they were watching.

Up the stairs, after a brief tour of grabbing ice out the fridge, Sayvonne walked into Kenni's room. Layla had cleaned her face off already. She had Kenni sitting on the edge of her bed while she applied makeup to her face.

"Lay, we need to put ice on it to keep the swelling down first," Sayvonne told her.

"I'll just redo it," Layla remarked, continuing to do what she was doing.

"Backwards bitch," Sayvonne mumbled at her teasingly and took a seat. "You ready to spill the beans now?" she gently asked Kenni.

Kenni sniffed and took a deep breath. "She fucked that bitch. Her neighbor, Shyna."

"Fuck her and that bitch," Layla countered.

"Why?" Sayvonne asked.

"She claim she thought we was broken up," she laughed, dispirited. "Fuck her, though. She knew we wasn't broken up. Then that bitch gonna come out her apartment in Ronnie's shirt, all giddy and shit," Kenni stated angrily. "So, I punched her in the mouth, and we got to hitting. Ronnie broke us up."

"At least she had the decency to do that," Layla muttered.

"Was y'all broken up?" Sayvonne asked for clarification.

"Von, do it matter?" Layla shot.

"No!" Kenni fired back. "We just had an argument
and her and Jeremy fought."

"Damn." Sayvonne shook her head sadly. "I liked
her for you."

"Me too," Kenni admitted.

"Fuck her now, though," Layla stated, but neither of the girls echoed her sentiments.

*   *   *

"What the fuck is wrong with you?" Ronnie exploded, interrupting Shyna, who was gloating over beating Kenni up.

"What?" Shyna asked defensively. "You know how much shit I've had to hear from that little bitch? How disrespectful that lil bitch is? Fuck her! She had it coming."

"I don't give a fuck about none of that shit you talking about, yo! I don't even know why I'm still arguing with you!" She grabbed Shyna's arm and took her to the front door. "Get the fuck out!" She slammed the door in her face. "Fuck!"

Ronnie went to her bedroom and picked her phone up off the charger. She dialed Kenni's number and didn't get an answer. She redialed and got the same result. Ronnie grabbed her keys and dialed again. The entire ride to Kenni's, she called but didn't get an answer. The driveway was full, and the lights were on when she pulled up. However, no one answered the door when she knocked.

"Fuck!" Ronnie said, kicking at the porch before making her way back to her truck.

*   *   *

"My nigga, do you know what time it is?" Chantel questioned, finding Ronnie sitting on her front porch steps.

"Yeah, nigga. It's after midnight." Ronnie heaved a sigh and dropped her head in her hands. "My bad, bro. Shit, I been driving around for a minute, and I just ended up here. I hope I ain't wake Dreamz up. I fucked up, bra," she stated.

Chantel glanced behind her, into the open door where her girlfriend, Mya, stood. "Baby, will you call everybody—"

"Nah, bra. I just wanna talk to you, or you and Mya, man," Ronnie interrupted her stud brother.

The couple shared a look before Mya widened the door. "Come in, Ronnie. Dre sleeping," she stated to Chantel, referring to her son.

The two studs walked through the door and took a seat in the living room. Mya went into the

kitchen, coming back with beers for both of them.
She opened them and placed them down in front of
them. Mya retreated from the room again, this time
coming back with a blunt already rolled, a bag of
weed, and a few packs of cigarillos, which she
passed to her girlfriend.

"Thank you, baby," Chantel murmured,
kissing her cheek.

"You're welcome, baby," Mya answered
back, turning the TV on low.

"So, what happened?" Chantel wondered.

"Shit, where do I even fuckin' begin?"
Ronnie exhaled smoke rings from the blunt Chantel
had passed her. She hit the blunt again and passed it
back. "I got fired. Well, I quit, so I quit-fired my job
today."

"What?"

Mya cast her a disapproving glance but
remained silent.

"Wait, hold on, before that. You know the
bitch who live in my apartment building? Her dude
the police and she thick as fuck?" Ronnie
backtracked.

"Yeah."

"Aight, so you know me and her cool like.
She get weed from me and shit since dude don't
know she smoke. We usually end up smoking
together and shooting the shit, you feel me? So, my
girl—"

"The young girl that got yo nose open?"

"Yeah. I don't know why, but she ain't
never liked her from the first time she met her."

"What you mean? It gotta be a reason."

"I don't know, but shorty a firecracker like, so she been throwing shots at her. Then she started with that 'I don't want you around her, she like you' bullshit. I brushed her off, you feel me? Me and Shyna always been cool, no bullshit. She one of the homies."

"And then you fucked her?" Chantel summed up.

"Maann! Nigga. Check dig. Shorty fooled on me one day because Shyna was there, but we was just kicking it. Her dude had just died, you feel me?"

"You fucked her after her nigga died?"

"Nah, but she kissed me, though. I chalked it up to grief, you know? I pushed her up off me and made some space, then here come Kenni fooling. She leave, I go after her, and her brother there on bullshit, so we get to rumbling. Nigga, swear to God, Kenni break us up, hollering she hate me and why the fuck am I there. Like, what? What that even mean? So, I go back to my spot like, fuck that bitch, too. Shyna come over with a bottle, we drinking and kicking it." Ronnie paused to lick her lips and rub her hand across her face. "Sometime during the night, we end up fucking, and I passed out. Man, I don't even remember fuckin' this bitch. I just woke up with my dick on and shorty naked, laying next to me. Nigga, I don't even know if the pussy was good or ass. Tight or no walls. I don't know.

"So, we passed out, right? How about somebody come knocking on the door. I get up, and it's Kenni. So, we talking, and I'm like cool, you wanna get back together, I'm with it. She like, we was never broken up. So, I'm telling her, you can't say shit like you hate me and expect me to think we still go together. We end up moving past that lil shit. She about to leave and muthafucking Shyna pop out from my room with nothing on but my shirt. Words got exchanged, then I had to break them apart. Shorty crying and screaming she hate me, then she left and ain't answering my calls, texts, or coming to the door now. I'm salty, bra."

Chantel chuckled. "Yeah, you fucked up, my nigga."

"But, bra, come on, man—" Ronnie interjected.

"Nah, nigga. And you beat up her brother," laughed Chantel. "Who won the fight between the girls?"

"Nigga—"

"Not yo girl," joked Chantel, laughing again.

A ghost of a smile finally appeared on Ronnie's face. "Fuck you, bra."

"You had a hell of a night," cracked Chantel again. "Fucked Shyna, don't remember, but hey, you still fucked, though, said fuck that job, finally, lost yo girl, and beat up her brother."

"Man, you feel me? Fuck that job, though. I'ma get money regardless, and I know I can do it now. Fuck Shyna because that pussy was probably garbage anyway. I'm getting my baby back, though," Ronnie stated, pulling her phone out her pocket and calling Kenni's phone.

"Ronnie, you have to give it time," the soft-spoken Mya voiced.

"Why? She shouldn't even be mad. One, I don't remember fuckin' that bitch, and two, I thought we was broken up," Ronnie rebutted.

Mya chuckled softly. "And if she slapped you then said I didn't mean to and then did it again and said sorry, would you still be mad?"

"Hell yeah. I told her to keep her fucking hands to herself, but what the fuck that got to do with anything, Mya?"

"Bra, she saying shorty still hurt, even though you thought y'all was broken up," Chantel interpreted.

"So, like, how much time to give her?"

"Only you and her know that, Ron. You know her better than we do. Do you even think she can move past this? In her eyes, you cheated, and with someone she already didn't like."

Ronnie's eyes furrowed, and her jaw tightened stubbornly. "She gonna have to get over it, we getting back together. I'ma just buy her something."

"She's young," Mya pointed out. "You'll start a pattern of buying her things when she gets mad."

"So? I don't mind buying her shit," Ronnie countered, redialing her number for the fourth time.

Mya placed a hand over Ronnie's hand and ended the phone call. "Ron, just give her a little bit of time and explain your feelings for her and what happened."

"And apologize," Chantel added.

Ronnie was beyond frustrated after not receiving the answers she wanted to hear. These two had been together forever, though, and had been through a lot. If anybody knew what to do to help her get Kenni back, it was definitely them. "Fuck, all right," she agreed to what Mya had told her.

Chapter 4

Tears slipped down Kenni's face as she read one of Ronnie's longest text messages she'd sent since their break up. Her heart clenched, and she ached for Ronnie's touch as she read the words I love you and the description of what it felt like being with her. The apology definitely made her heart lift a little, but, *It don't matter,* she muttered to herself. Fresh water leaked from her eyes when Ronnie stated how she was drunk, too drunk to even remember having sex with Shyna. She flung her phone away from her and collapsed onto her bed. She clutched at a teddy bear drowning in Ronnie's shirt and buried her face in it.

"What's up, brat?" Jeremy barged into her room. "What you crying for? Mama told you no about something again?" he teased her, and his sister didn't reply. "I'm telling Mama you stole her vibrator," he joked again.

Shooting off the bed, into a sitting position, Kenni glared at him. In addition to the new waves making paths down her face, the wetness that had seeped from her eyes still stained her cheeks. The mental hand she felt digging its claws into her heart and crushing its palms together rendered her unable to speak.

"Damn, sis," Jeremy said gruffly. "C'mere." He held out his arms.

A spurt of hot anger shot up her spine. The pain in her heart made her gray eyes narrow. "Get out," she said. "Get out!" She threw a pillow at him. "Get out! Leave me alone!" All of her animosity fled, crippling her back to containment on the bed while her body shook from the body-racking sobs.

Not one to listen to commands, Jeremy stepped further into the room to sit on the bed and pull his sister into a bear hug. He kissed her forehead. "Damn, sis. I'm sorry you going through this."

"Why do it hurt so bad?" she puffed out amidst the wheezing.

An unexpected lurch made his heart jump at her words. Jeremy stroked her hair. "Love hurts, sis."

The two mused silently, lost in their thoughts. With the absence of words, Jeremy squeezed his arms tighter around her, swaying her gently to make the cries subside. Due to these moments between them being rare, Kenni felt her body slowly beginning to relax in the comfort her brother provided. Her sobs dwindled away to sniffles, and she wiped her nose on his shirt.

"Should I take her back?"

On first thought, a plethora of derogatory words wanted to pop out, but when Jeremy tuned into the pain she was broadcasting, he answered without pride and ignorance. "Only you can answer that, sis. It don't matter what I say, Ma, or anybody else."

Could I even take her back? She cheated, but I love her. How can we even move past that if I wanted to? "Thanks, Jeremy," Kenni said, wiping her face off with her hands, unwilling to answer the questions she'd asked herself.

"You welcome, brat." A half-smile graced his lips, and he stood, exiting the room.

Phone back in hand, Kenni read the message again. Those questions popped back up. No answer came to her, only the pain in her heart from the betrayal. Unwilling to succumb again, she turned the phone face down and fell back on her bed.

*   *   *

"Fuck!" Ronnie smacked her phone off the counter, sending it sailing into the living room.

No text back from Kenni had her temper flaring. The advice given to her from Chantel and Mya hadn't done anything. Two weeks apart, an apology and explanation yielded to fucking nothing. *Fuck her then*, Ronnie grumbled. Justification dictated she wasn't going to keep apologizing and bending over backward for her.

"What the fuck I do with my lighter?" She patted her pockets, only to retrieve it from her sports bra. "Who is it?" Ronnie yelled at the door where someone was knocking.

"Shyna."

For the last two weeks, there wasn't even contact with Shyna, and she was bound to run into her! It didn't hurt her pockets, but it was an effort to show Kenni she didn't want the woman. *Fuck her.* Ronnie flung the door open, blowing smoke in Shyna's face. "What?"

"Nigga, I need some fuckin' weed! You been ignoring my calls and shit. What the fuck, yo? I thought we was better than that."

Stupid, meaningless words from the bitch she'd fucked but couldn't even remember doing the nasty to. She couldn't care less about her needing some weed. All this shit with Kenni had started because of her. Ronnie continued to puff, eyes perusing her body. It didn't even count if she didn't remember. Hell, how was she supposed to know if her juicy lips had sucked on her neck, or if their tongues had played together? Did she even hit her from the back? Did she take the entire dick? Kenni was skinny, but Ronnie wondered about the difference in feel with Shyna's lower appendages being thicker, and how it felt having them wrapped around her hips.

"So, you not even gonna speak?" Shyna snapped. "Wow, okay, that's what's up. Look, I need to smoke. I'm sorry, not sorry for coming in between you and that lil thing you was fuckin with," Shyna snapped.

Just a general mention of Kenni reinforced her feelings. "Fuck that bitch." She extended the blunt to Shyna and walked off into the living room, fully expecting her to follow.

"Fuck that lil bitch," she puffed, maneuvering herself between the legs of the stud, who had sat down on a bar stool.

I know I can fuck again, Ronnie's delighted thoughts declared with confidence. All of the nerve endings in her tingled in a state of hyper-awareness with Shyna between her legs, her hands on her thighs. Not one to be accused of being too thirsty, she played it cool, pulling on the blunt while allowing her eyes to convey the pool of desire that had begun to build within. Shyna took one of her hands, moving it to rest on her rump.

The woman made another move, stroking Ronnie's chest and kissing along her neck. "Fuck me again," Shyna purred in her ear in a sultry tone.

Yipping internally with excitement, Ronnie relaxed into the arms that had wrapped around her shoulders. She pulled Shyna closer with both hands grasping her ass. For the first time, she initiated the kiss, nipping at the succulent lips. Ronnie slid off the stool, hoisting Shyna's legs around her waist.

In the bedroom, she threw the feminine woman down onto her bed and disappeared into her walk-in closet. She pulled on her chocolate, nine-inch strap-on and walked back to the bed on full mast to find Shyna, legs spread on the bed, playing with her clit. The sight of her finger kneading against her pearl and dipping in her middle had Ronnie licking her lips unconsciously. The moans started to intensify, gradually becoming more vocal. At the peak of her orgasm, Ronnie thrust her toy deep inside of her.

Balls rammed against Shyna's pussy lips, and she shattered. Ronnie shifted her legs so that her feet were planted on her chest. She stroked her pussy relentlessly, retreating to the head of her dick and pounding her dick back inside of her. Legs shaking, toes curled, Shyna reached for Ronnie's hands but settled on scratching her midsection. Another orgasm started to creep up.

"Fuck, Ronnie! Yes! Fuck, shit!" Shyna shouted, lips tingling at the assault.

Smacking one of Shyna's hands away from her nipples, Ronnie clutched her throat, flexing her fingers. She allowed her feet to fall from her chest and one arm curled under the small of the woman's back. Ronnie grunted, pounding inside of her.

Hands on her own nipples, twisting them harshly, Shyna's eyes rolled back in her head, another climax rushing through her. Incessantly, she tapped on the hands around her neck. She wanted her favorite position. When her request went ignored, Shyna pushed her feet into the stud's chest.

Acquiescing the subtle demand, Ronnie let go of her neck. Shyna held up one finger to indicate one moment, then slipped the strap-on out of her with a wet plop. She flipped over on her stomach, taking it into her mouth, bobbing up and down the length.

Eyes locked on the movement, the visual of a plump set of lips sliding down her dick brought about a rash infection of lust, spreading throughout Ronnie. Throaty sounds of choking filled her ears. She smiled when Shyna gagged but continued. Her hips jerked on their own accord, forcing the head artist to take all of it. A surge of something shivered through Ronnie's body, making her breath begin to labor. She tangled her hands in Shyna's hair. A sense of urgency implored her pelvis to lunge, her hands to thrust harder on the head, making it move faster, up and down.

"Fuck," Ronnie groaned at the climatic feeling of fireworks shooting off through her body.

Shyna slurped on the head, grinning broadly. She sat back on her haunches, staring at Ronnie, whose chest heaved. Winking at her, she flipped around and put her ass in the air.

The sight of that candy apple ass in the air filled Ronnie with lust. Hands went straight to cheeks, splitting them apart and dropping a glob of spit in between. A finger dipped in her anus, her strap digging into her pussy from the back. One hand blistered her ass cheek, starting the stroking game, finger and strap in competition, both running the same repetition, in and out.

Jiggling her ass cheeks, Shyna threw her head back in the air. Back arched, down on her forearms, she slammed her apple backward, intent on making Ronnie back up. Her finger came out, hands grasped her hips on both sides, and her mouth formed an O, silently screaming at the hot zap creeping up the base of her spine while that dick pistoned inside of her.

"OH... MY... GAWD," she finally cried out, overwhelmed by the aroused state of culmination. "DADDY! FUCK! YES! YES! SHIT, DADDY! OOOHHH," Shyna shivered, collapsing forward on the bed, devoid of energy.

Shyna's pussy jumped again when Ronnie eased the strap from between her lips. Ronnie stared down at her body glitching. She smiled and leaned forward, burying her face between her legs, giving her inner folds a slow, languid lick.

"Fuuuccck, Ronnie," Shyna whimpered, body trembling uncontrollably. "Ooh, shit, daddy," she heaved out shakily, pulling her head deeper into her center. "Yes, baby… Fuck… oh my God. I'm about to cum again. Fuck, daddy… fuck."

Juices barreled out of her into Ronnie's mouth, which the young stud swallowed with her tongue curled around her clit. Her tongue lapped up all of her nectar, sucking each lip into her mouth until it was dry. Once she was satisfied, Ronnie leaned back, grinning.

"I would lick yo face, but I can't move," Shyna panted.

Proud that she couldn't, Ronnie ignored the prickling in the back of her head. Finally, she could say she had fucked Shyna. And that damn session was unlike any other times she had fucked a bitch. Just gazing down at her naked, sweating body had her feeling like fucking her again. They fucked like champions together. *It don't get much better than that.*

"You know, Will never tried to take advantage of me. He took me right out the system, but even when I was a kid, he steered me right, you know? Taught me what a woman was supposed to know about her body, I mean," Shyna yawned. "I watched plenty of porn, but my fiancé was the only partner I ever had. Will might've groomed me for that role, but I fell for Nate, too. But Nate ain't never did *half*"—she stressed the word—"of what you do to my body. Since that first time, I just want you all the time now."

I got good dick, Ronnie proclaimed joyfully in her head, proud as a rooster at the crack of dawn. She grabbed her phone to spill the beans to one of her friends and remembered how they had ended up in bed together. Kenni. No notification meant she still hadn't texted back. Disgust rolled through her body. Shame made her drop her head. They were broken up because of Shyna, and what had she done? Fucked Shyna again. Anger toward herself started to blaze forth from her. She quelled the rudeness demanding her to tell Shyna to get the fuck out and sent Chantel a text message.

"You want a wet rag or something to wipe off?" Ronnie questioned.

"Aww, look at you. You so sweet. Yes," Shyna murmured in a thick voice.

Bounding up, Ronnie retrieved a rag for her and threw it on her. She went back to the bathroom and cleaned her strap off. When she came back into the room, Shyna hadn't moved. Her eyes were closed, rag dripping water down her thigh, onto the bed.

Aww, nah, she gotta get the fuck up outta here, Ronnie thought. On cue, her phone rang. She answered it, smiling at Chantel's number. "What's good, Lil Buddy? What? Aww, nigga… Chill, bra… Nigga…" She invented pleas of logic to her friend's fake situation. She shook Shyna awake. "Aye, get up! Get up! Get dressed. I'm about to make moves."

In a daze, Shyna dressed while Ronnie paced in the background, dressing also, attempting to calm her perceivingly troubled friend down on the phone. Shyna kissed her and stumbled out of the room, towards the door. When Ronnie heard Shyna's door open and close across the hall, she laughed into her phone.

"Aye, good look, nigga," she chuckled, thanking Chantel.

*   *   *

"The fuck is you looking at?" Kenni spat at one of her classmates, who she'd bumped into, walking down the school hallway.

From behind her, Layla rolled her eyes. "Period time, sorry." She clamped down on one of her friend's arms, steering her towards their class. "What the fuck is wrong with you today?"

"Nothing. What's wrong with you?"

"Bitch, you don't smoke, and our periods synced. What the fuck is wrong with you?" Layla repeated again, entering their class.

Plopping down into a seat after yanking her arm out of Layla's grasp, she admitted, "I ain't wanna come to school today."

"So, go home."

"I fuckin would, but my mama made me come."

"Yeah, whatever, that ain't what got yo ass acting up," Layla commented quietly as the teacher came into the room. "You then started fucking, now yo ass going through withdrawals. You need to bust a nut," she diagnosed with a chuckle.

Not bothering to lower her voice, Kenni sniped, "Fuck you, and fuck Ronnie, too." A sharp look of promised retribution came from the teacher. Undeterred, she stared back at him, mouth twisted up, chin raised defiantly.

When the teacher looked away, Layla murmured softly, "Girl, quit playing like you don't want her still and go get some act right. Y'all ain't gotta be together for you to get a nut."

"Fuck her and fuck you, too, Lay."

"Kenni, do you plan on joining the rest of the class?" implored the history teacher from his position at the front of the classroom, placing projections on the projector.

All of their classmates turned to face either of the two. A surefire way to kill time in this class was to pit the two against one another. The heated arguments that ensued made all of the high school gossip of the day.

"Do you know you being rude?" she shot back at him.

"So, I take it that's a no?"

"You being nosey and acting brand new, *Eric.* I ain't bothering you, and you can't hear my conversation, so teach yo class and leave me the fuck alone."

Laughter rippled throughout the classroom. She'd called him by his government name. A few instigative 'oohs' sounded from several boys.

"Get out," he hissed at her, projection sheets shaking in his hand. "Take all of your things with you and don't come back."

"No! Don't tell me what to do because you know I'm right. You got yo panties in a bunch. I wasn't even bothering anybody, and you not even ready for class to begin anyway, so like I said, leave me the fuck alone."

"Get out!" the teacher thundered again, his face contorting with the barely controlled rage making a vein pop out on his forehead. He strode over to the wall and pressed a button for security to come to the classroom.

"Kenni, just leave," Layla advised her.

"No. Fuck him. I'll leave when I want." Stubbornly, she folded her arms across her chest, glaring at the man who glared right back at her.

"Mr. Vince work today. You know he ain't got no problem dragging anybody up outta the class," Layla told her, mentioning the security guard with the no-nonsense, no-bullshit reputation.

Exhaling, Kenni grabbed all of her stuff and stomped all the way to the office. She barged past the waiting area, into her principal's office.

"Kenni, wh-what are you doing in my office?" her principal sputtered. "And why didn't you check in and wait first?"

"*Eric* sent me here."

"Eric?" the principal parroted, then caught sight of her history teacher. He closed his eyes for several seconds. "Mr. Jackson sent you here, you mean."

"No, I mean Eric. If he don't respect me, then I ain't gotta respect him."

"I want her out of my class. She's rude, disrespectful, insubordinate, and disrupts the class," the history teacher stated angrily.

"How was I disruptive if you wasn't even ready for class?"

"Kenni," the principal rebuked. "What started everything this time?"

"Nothing. I told him to leave me the fuck alone. I wasn't bothering him, he wasn't ready for class. I can't talk because he ain't ready? Miss me with that bullshit. He could've taught his lil class, I ain't disrupt nothing."

The history teacher walked out with a smug smile of contentment at her words. Her principal, however, shook his head. He reached for a stack of suspension slips. "You know better. Fix that attitude. I'll see you in three days."

She snatched the slip from him and jumped up out of her seat, stalking out of the office.

*   *   *

Music on blast, Ronnie cruised down the street, away from Chantel and Mya's house. They'd berated her. Well, Mya had for fucking Shyna again when she really wanted Kenni. Chantel understood. Niggas had needs. Niggas liked to fuck, and Shyna was stacked with hips, tits, thighs, and an ass so big, you could see it from the front. She'd already fucked her once; hell, at least this time, it was worth it. Well, kind of. The sex was great. The guilt gnawing at her and the desire in her loins to fuck her again, not so much. *Damn, fucking her was fucking great, though,* Ronnie quipped, smiling at the thought and allowing her mind to wander to fucking her again. They definitely fucked very well together.

From behind her, a horn beeped, snapping her out of her reverie. "All right," she muttered, glancing in her rearview mirror to see a man gesturing impatiently at her. "My bad." Her eyes roamed away from the road when the impatient driver zoomed around her. She spotted a feminine figure walking a distance ahead, and her eyes roved over her backside.

"Kenni!" Ronnie shouted when she'd passed the female walking and checked the rearview mirror to see what her front looked like. Immediately, she threw the car in park and hopped out. "Baby." She was ignored, so she called out to her again. "Kenni, why you out here walking? Why you not in school, baby?"

"I'm not yo fuckin' baby!" Kenni snapped. "You fucked Shyna, remember that? So, whether I'm walking or supposed to be anywhere is none of yo concern." She walked around Ronnie, continuing down the street.

"Fine, stay mad. Don't be my girl, but you know yo ass don't wanna walk nowhere, so get yo ass in the fuckin truck."

Whipping back around, she screeched, "Don't cuss at me!"

"Get yo ass in the truck then and tell me where you going."

"Fuck you. I'm going home."

"Aight, good. Thanks for sharing. Now, that's a long-ass walk and you not even close, so get yo ass in the damn car and quit being stubborn 'fore I pull the fuck off."

That got her. She stopped walking but didn't face Ronnie. For a moment, Kenni stayed motionless. Abruptly, she spun on her heel, stepping towards the truck. "Open the door."

Ronnie opened the car door for Kenni and hopped in on the drivers' side. The drive started off silently with Kenni directing all of her attention towards her phone.

"Kenni, when this shit gonna stop, baby? Like, what the fuck do I gotta do to show you I'm sorry and you ain't gotta worry about no bullshit like this again?" Ronnie asked sincerely.

The queen of ignoring someone, Kenni didn't reply. She rested her head against the glass of the window with her arms crossed over her chest.

"So, you ain't gonna say nothing?"

"I just wanted a ride home."

"Bra, answer my fuckin' question."

"Ronnie, I don't fuckin' know!" she exploded, opening up about the confusing feelings she felt. "I know you sorry, but you fuckin' hurt me! I love yo stupid ass, but that shit still hurt."

"I love you, too, and if you just give me a chance, I can show you. I won't hurt you again. I'll make everything right. I love you, Kenni," Ronnie told her earnestly. Hope bloomed in her chest. Talking was key. She had finally gotten to know how Kenni felt, so that was a start, and they could move past this now.

"Yeah… well…" Kenni grumbled dryly, eyes catching sight of her home. "Here's my stop." She popped her car door open, jumping out at a stop sign and not responding to Ronnie's last words.

Bewildered, Ronnie stomped on the brake to come to a full stop instead of her usual rolling stop. "Kenni, for real?" she yelled at the retreating figure crossing over three front yards to get to her house.

All of that fucking optimism Ronnie had felt vanished. Not only had she not even said any more on the subject of them getting back together, but her ungrateful ass hadn't even said thank you for the ride. No wave goodbye or anything.

She always want somebody to kiss her ass. Don't nobody owe her shit. "Fuckin' bitch!" Ronnie's temper boiled over, and her hand slammed against her steering wheel.

*   *   *

Arriving outside of her apartment building, grumbling to herself, she hopped out of her truck, slamming the door. The door rebutted, flying back towards Ronnie due to the seat belt being in the way. "Muthafucka." She began kicking at her door until it closed even with the seat belt still there.

Keys in her apartment door, Shyna emerged like she'd been listening out for her.

"Hey, you trying to kick it? I got yo favorite. I just wanna drink and be happy. I'm kinda fucked up right now, so, please?"

Flashes of their sexual meetings rolled through Ronnie mentally, heightening the need to do something physical. She pushed the sensations down, trying to placate her anger. After all, Shyna hadn't done anything to her. "I really ain't in the mood either, yo."

"Exactly. So, we'll drink and bullshit until we both good," Shyna suggested. "Bring yo ass, don't bitch up now."

Chuckling to herself, Ronnie had made up her mind that quick. One thing she was never was a bitch. *It ain't no bitch in my blood.* "What-the-fuck-ever. Come on, let's drink up." Her keys went to her pockets, and she headed over to the other woman's home. "This nice," Ronnie stated gruffly about the layout of her apartment.

"Thanks." Shyna placed two shots on the table and poured up. Together, those went down the hatch. More liquor filled the glasses, disappearing like she hadn't poured them. "My fiancé left me some stacks."

"That's what's up," Ronnie murmured, watching her pour them another round. "Slow down, yo. The bottle ain't going nowhere."

"You gonna bitch up or keep up?"

"Yeah, you gonna get enough of that bitch word when you talking to me." She tossed her shot back before Shyna was finished pouring her own. Reaching out, she snagged the bottle, splashed some more in the shot glass, and quickly swallowed. "Catch up." The shot glass in her hand slammed down on the center table.

An hour and an empty bottle later, the music was up, blasting old school 90s music. The two were up, singing and dancing together while passing a blunt back and forth. The music slowed down to a sultry tone as TLC sang about giving a Red Light Special blared out the speakers.

Performance time, Shyna pushed the stud down on the couch, swiping the liquor bottle off the floor to act as her microphone. In character, body doing the TLC creep dance, she slapped the stud's hands away from her. Prancing around the seated woman, she bent over, shaking her bountiful ass, trailing hands over her chest.

Marijuana intermingled with all the liquor she'd consumed bred the start of her arousal. Light touches and visual stimulation stirred her wanton state into a storm. Unable to remain in her seat, Ronnie rose, slinking behind the teasing woman, matching her body rolls. Lips dashed to her neck, grazing across the hot spots. Refusing to accept anything other than what she wanted, she pulled Shyna's ear into her mouth, making her turn her head, latching onto her lips. Her hand crept around her hips, beneath her pants, to manipulate her clit with her fingers.

"Ooh, fuck." Shyna's legs buckled in pleasure.

A spark of horniness fissured through Ronnie. Smooth and quick, her other hand unbuttoned and unzipped her pants, tugging them down her legs. That same hand bent Shyna forward, so her ass was in the air. When the woman attempted to come back up, she left a blistering smack on her ass cheeks and shoved her strap inside of her.

"Oh my God," groaned Shyna, stretching her hands out to grab hold of her ankles.

Fingers digging into her hips, Ronnie growled. "Yeah, talk that shit now," she urged her, lost in the moment. In reality, balls deep, battering away at the pussy, but subconsciously, speaking to the young woman she really wanted to be with. "Fuckin' bitch." One of her hands yanked Shyna's head backward by her hair. "This my pussy! You hear me? This my shit!" Another blow landed on her ass cheek.

"Yes, daddy! Oooh... yes, baby... it's yours. Fuck, it's yours, Ronnie," her voice cut out, fingers tensed around her throat.

Unrestrained and relentless, Ronnie thrashed away. This was therapy. All of the anger she felt towards Kenni, the desire she still had for her, even the dejected feelings of rejection were poured into the motion of banging in and out of Shyna. She might not ever get her back. I'ma get her back, Ronnie promised herself.

"Fuck," Ronnie bit out, watching the shaft of her dick disappear and pop back out of Shyna's pink. The way the base of the toy was positioned, coupled with the way she was stroking, sent shivers of delight fluttering through her. Riding the wave of an orgasm, she gripped her hips, ramming her strap within her until the aftershocks of her climax faded away.

"Damn," Shyna panted.

Wheezing slightly, Ronnie dropped down onto the couch. She looked around, attempting to clear the sexual haze. Her eyes focused on Shyna, curled up on the floor with her hands between her legs. A niggling at the back of her mind threatened to become more pronounced, prompting Ronnie to stand, pulling her clothes back up. The two women's eyes met briefly, but a filling of remorse only allowed a curt nod in Shyna's direction before exiting the apartment.

*   *   *

After an unceremoniously quiet dinner full of general scowls and an unpleasant aura about her daughter, Beaunna finally questioned her about what she knew was the cause of her demeanor. "Have you thought about getting back with Ronnie?"

"No!" Kenni snapped. "Fuck her."

Smirking, Beaunna rolled her gray eyes,. "What did she even do? You never told me why y'all broke up."

"Is it yo business?"

"You wanna get popped?"

Huffing and foot tapping, Kenni spat out, "Because she cheated on me with that trifling-ass bitch I told her I ain't like her talking to anyway. Talking about she was drunk and didn't even remember, and she thought we was broken up anyway. Like that make any difference. If we was or wasn't, that don't mean you go fuck that troll."

Slightly amused, and knowing her daughter's temper, she had to ask, "Kenni, was y'all broken up?"

"No!" Kenni shouted. "Why do everybody keep asking me that? She knew that shit."

"Because we all know how you are when you get mad. You say anything. So, why did Ronnie seem to think y'all was broken up? Did you say something to imply that you didn't wanna be together anymore? Or that you wanted to break up?"

"No, we had an argument because she was kicking it with that troll. And when Ronnie followed me here, I asked her why and said fuck you, leave, like why are you here at my house?"

Beaunna laughed softly. "Yeah, because that's how you talk to your partner in anger, but not mean that you wanna break up," she told her sarcastically. "Jeremy," she called out to her son, who was walking through the front door.

"What's up, mama?" he asked, coming into the kitchen, finding his two favorite women at the table. "It's some food left?"

"You know where it is if there is. Let me ask you a question." Kenni's head shot up, scowling at her, but mother rank deemed her to ignore it. "If you had an argument with your girlfriend, she walked out and went home, and you followed her, and she said fuck you, told you to leave, and questioned why you had even come over to her house, what would you do?"

Immediately, his eyes went from Kenni to his mother. Of course, he knew the situation she was referring to. Unbeknownst to his mother, his altercation with Ronnie had helped propel his sister into the pain that now shone forth from her eyes.

"Jeremy, be honest. If that was you and your partner, what would you do?"

"Say fuck her too and leave."

"Would you think y'all was broken up?"

Again, his eyes traveled from sister to mother. "Yeah—"

"Fuck you, Jeremy!" Kenni fired at him, pissed that once again, he wasn't taking her side.

"You ain't let me finish! If that was our relationship and how we argued, then nah, but our first real argument… yeah."

"Fuck you."

"Kenni, shut up. I'm trying to teach yo ass something. Every relationship is built or broken with communication. When you first meet someone, you have to learn not only the other person's likes and dislikes but their behavior and ways. You have to know how each other communicates. Have you ever argued with Ronnie like that? If not, how the hell was Ronnie supposed to know that you were just running off at the mouth?"

"That don't even fuckin' matter!" Kenni hollered, standing up from the table. "Y'all taking her side! Like, damn, I got cheated on. Your daughter, yo sister, and y'all just want me to put my pain to the side and take her back."

"No, you're entitled to feel hurt and do whatever you want to in regards to your relationship. As your mother, it's my job to correct you when you're wrong, praise you when you're right, and love your spoiled ass no matter what. This is me attempting to guide your bratty ass on how relationships work and advice for the future, not necessarily for in this situation with Ronnie."

"I don't wanna hear none of that! Why can't you just take my side and say fuck Ronnie! She hurt me!"

"No, I'm not going to just tell you what you want to hear. I love you, so I'm going to tell you what you need to hear—"

"Whatever."

"And it's not about sides. I understand you're hurt. I can feel your pain—"

"Then stop preaching to me to get back with her! Fuck her!" Kenni ran to her room, tears streaming down her cheeks. She brushed them away furiously, flinging herself down onto the bed.

Landing on the suspension paper, her fingers instantly began to shred it, provoking growls of discontentment.

"Aye, sis." Jeremy pushed into her room, taking a seat on the bed.

"What?"

"Listen, you my baby sister, and even though we fight like cats and dogs, I love yo punk ass. That nigga hurt you. Fuck that nigga."

A watery smile dashed across her face. Relieved that someone understood she muttered, "Thank you."

"But like I said you my baby sister, and I don't wanna see you hurting, especially when it's nothing I can do to help. Maybe it was a miscommunication. I know I hyped the situation, and don't none of that change that she fucked somebody else, but you know you could take mama advice. She right, communication is key. With the right communication, y'all could get back together again."

"Nigga, you don't even fuckin' like her!"

Winking at her, he grinned. "You right, I don't. So? You like her. Shit, you love her. You my baby sister, and I want you to be happy."

Lips twisted up in disbelief at what she was hearing, her hand shot to his forehead, checking for a fever. "So, you don't care that I like girls now?"

"Nah."

"Why?" she questioned. "Ooh, you talked to what's her name? Y'all back together?"

"No, fuck her."

"So, what the fuck sparked this lil revelation?"

"What the fuck I been saying, yo! Regardless of how I feel, I want yo spoiled ass happy because you my sister. I'm about to quit talking to yo ungrateful ass."

"Man, whatever, you high." She dismissed his statement, rolling away from him.

"Man, whatever. Look, you heard what I had to say, and we both know Mama right. You make a decision on what the fuck you want. We gonna love you no matter what." He walked out.

For a few moments, Kenni didn't move. She digested the conversation with Jeremy. Aimlessly, she grabbed her phone, scrolling up to the beginning of the text history with Ronnie. Reading from the beginning made butterflies take flight in her belly, a permanent smile etched on her face. The last message Ronnie had sent ended with I love you, I'm sorry, and wishes of wanting to talk and work things out so they could get back together. She took a deep breath. Decision made.

*   *   *

"Ronnie!" Shyna knocked on Ronnie's front door.

Ronnie paused her game and herself, wondering if Shyna would go away if she didn't answer. No such luck when her ears registered her knocking again. She set her joystick down with a roll of her eyes, relit the blunt perched on the end of her lips, and hollered, "Hold up." Ambling towards the door, she praised herself on the other successful attempts of dodging interactions from Shyna.

Ronnie had a theory that the woman watched from her window to see when her truck pulled up and left, due to her living room window overlooking the parking lot. The last few days, Ronnie had started parking in the back parking lot. She opened the door. "What's up?"

"You hungry? I just made chicken alfredo, garlic bread, and vegetables."

"Man, hell yeah. That shit sound good as fuck."

"Come on over, I'll make you a plate," Shyna told her, walking back towards her apartment.

"Bet. Good looking." She went back into her apartment, grabbed her phone, and slid it into her pocket.

Food happy, Ronnie went back to the woman's apartment with her mouth drooling in anticipation. Shyna had already set up a place for her at the head of the table, complete with food and drink. Not waiting for her to finish getting herself together, Ronnie dug in.

"Thanks, yo. This shit good as fuck," she mumbled between bites.

"You welcome. Anything for you, daddy," Shyna smirked impishly at her.

Proud as a peacock, Ronnie continued to eat. She allowed her to refill her plate and drink, happily smashing. Once finished, Shyna collected their dishes and set a blunt down next to Ronnie. Elation rippled through the young stud, but street rules dictated, if you didn't see it rolled or hadn't rolled it yourself, don't smoke it, so she sparked her own blunt that she had come over with.

"Yo, I ain't know you could cook that damn good. That shit hit the spot," Ronnie complimented.

"Well, you know my door and this pussy open for you anytime, daddy."

"Oh, word? True."

"Speaking of," Shyna began, leaving the dishes in the sink. "I did something for you to show my appreciation."

Suspicion clouded Ronnie's brown eyes. She asked, defensively, "You did what?"

"I paid your rent up for the next few months."

"You did what?" Her jaw dropped. *Damn, I fucked her so good, this bitch paying bills,* Ronnie thought. *Ooh, I'm about to have her cash out for me on everything.*

"I paid your rent up for the next few months," she parroted. "That way, you can rent your spot or something. We can move into one of the apartments, or just get a new place together."

The bubble of pride burst dramatically in Ronnie's mental. She shook her head, trying to process what she had just heard, if she had heard correctly. "Shy."

"I know, I know, our relationship is still fresh with you still getting over that lil bitch and me still grieving."

A buzzing in Ronnie's pocket demanded her attention. The phone notified that she had a new text message. When she unlocked the phone to see from who, her heart skipped a beat, and a grin stretched from ear to ear. Kenni had finally hit her up.

"I'm happy you as excited as I am," Shyna told her, diverting her attention back to her.

"What?" She looked at her, puzzled. Eyes went from her phone and back to Shyna. "Man, nah. Shy, come here, man. Come sit down."

Obediently, Shyna took a seat at the kitchen table with her, a look of expectation on her face.

"First off, like I said, the food was banging, ma. I'm really glad we friends and all, but this ain't that."

Ice took over her features, and her smile chipped down into a frown. "What you mean?"

"I'm saying, ma, you cool peoples and all, but…" Her phone notification alerted her to a new message from Kenni. She quickly read the contents, seeing that she was stating everything she already knew: she missed her and wanted to get back together. "You catching feelings. I thought we was just fuckin' and to keep it all the way funky with you, I still got feelings for Kenni. Shit, she the only person I wanna be in a relationship with."

"So, so," Shyna began stammering, recoiling as if she had been struck. She bit her lip. "So, basically what you telling me is, this whole time we been fucking, it didn't mean shit to you?"

"Shy—"

"Nigga, I just paid yo damn rent!" she erupted.

"You act like I asked you to!"

"Muthafucka, fuck you!" She threw a glass at Ronnie. "Fuck you! You can be in a relationship with that bitch, fuckin' me but pining away for that lil bitch when you got a real one in fuckin' front of you! You stupid muthafucka! Get the fuck out!"

"Fuck you, at least I was honest," Ronnie huffed, making her way towards the door.

"Shut the fuck up and get the fuck out!" she hollered, hurling another glass at her retreating back.

"Man, whatever. Fuck you, too, then, bitch," Ronnie bit out, slamming the front door shut.

Chapter 5

"So, clue me in as to why I'm riding past the tattoo shop and see yo fuckin' truck and you ain't called and told a nigga shit about getting some new ink," joked T, one of Ronnie's stud brothers.

"What's good with you, too, nigga?" she greeted her.

"Nah, fuck all that, nigga. What you getting?" the deep baritone questioned her.

"My girl's name," she declared proudly. She and Kenni had been talking a lot over the past few days. They weren't officially back together yet, but she knew this was a surefire way to prove her love for Kenni.

"Nigga, what? Say that again. I know I ain't hear you right, lil bra?"

"Fuck you, T. You heard what the fuck I said, nigga."

"I did, I just ain't wanna believe it. I thought I had taught you better. We don't love these hoes."

"Hell nah we don't, but I love my bitch."

"Aww, you on that Lil Buddy shit, man. I guess you gotta ask permission to step out tomorrow night, huh?"

"Fuck you, nigga. I do what I want," she bragged, checking out her neck tattoo.

"Yeah, whatever. Call and ask if you can come through then."

"Fuck you, fool. I'll be there," she muttered, leaving the shop and texting Kenni, letting her know she had a surprise for her whenever she was ready to see her.

"Yeah, aight. Let me find out you got a young girl putting a leash on you. That is who you talking about, right? Yo young girl?"

"Yeah, she my only girl, but aye…" She read another text message from Kenni and muttered, "I'ma hit you back, bro."

"You getting cussed out for even asking, huh? I heard yo keypad, nigga, don't deny it."

"Man, nah, nigga. I'm about to slide over to my shorty house. I'll hit you back when I leave."

"Yo sprung ass," T jabbed playfully. "Aight, be safe, bra."

Ending the call, cranking her engine and smiling to herself, she admired the bold font of Kenni's name on her neck. She sped off, excited to be back on good terms with Kenni. A rush of exhilaration filled her just thinking about seeing her again. In no time, she was parking and walking up.

From the doorway, Kenni stood with a huge Kool-Aid grin. Hesitation due to the time away made her watch Ronnie walk up. Excitement won, and she took off running, launching herself into Ronnie's open arms.

"Oh my God. I missed you so much. I'm sorry, baby. I want to be with you," Kenni admitted.

"I'm sorry, too, baby, and you know I wanna be with you. You the only girl I want." Ronnie kissed her lips.

Words ceased to form with the two on the porch, rediscovering each other's lips and tongues. Torrents of jubilation flooded their touching bodies. When Kenni moved to kiss her neck, she squealed.

"You got my name tatted!"

"Surprise."

Laughter trickled out of Kenni. One of her hands fell down to the front of Ronnie's pants, patting to see if she was strapped like she always was, and of course, she didn't disappoint. She gripped her package. "Fuck me with this. Right now."

"You sure, baby?"

Not a doubt clouded her mind. The only thing present in her mind was to solidify the relationship and to make up. "Yes," she moaned, kissing her lips. "I want you to be my first."

Picking her up by her waist, Ronnie carried her all the way into the house. In the house, Kenni scrambled down off of her and pinched her ass, saying, "Catch me if you can," running towards her room.

Sprinting after her, Ronnie discovered her lying naked in the bed. Her eyes roamed over the butter yellow figure spread out before her. Dusky brown nipples stood up, begging for attention. She began to strip, eyes trained on the motion of Kenni's fingers entertaining her center. Wetness coated her bare lips that would soon be in Ronnie's mouth.

Fully naked, besides her strap-on, she climbed on top of the young woman. "I love you," she told her tenderly.

"I love you, too, baby."

Their lips clashed against each other. Mustering every ounce of self-control she possessed, Ronnie teased her lips, played on each of the nerve endings of her neck, and seduced her tongue out of her mouth. Hand wrapped around her strap, she slowly guided the tip in, reminding herself that Kenni was a virgin.

The girth of the strap pierced her, stretching her walls to a new capacity. "Oww, baby, it hurts," Kenni whimpered.

"It's only gonna hurt for a second, baby. I got you. You know I would never hurt you on purpose, right?" She kissed her lips without waiting for a reply.

She bit down on her bottom lip. "Okay, okay." Kenni moved her hands to Ronnie's ass and rocked her inside slowly. "Ooh, fuck." A tear slipped out of her eye that was kissed away. The pain started to give way to pleasure, stealing her breath away.

Enraptured by the flittering faces of ecstasy consuming every molecule of the young woman pulled at Ronnie's heartstrings. On a whimsical level, it felt like something was tying them together. She pushed deeper inside of her, seeking the scream of a climax. Plodding away at her inner parts, her walls were forced to constrict and expand every time. Ronnie took her to another realm where only the two of them existed in the passionate throes of sexual stimulation. Fingers twisted her nipples alternatively, imploring her to orgasm.

"Harder," Kenni gasped, loving the feeling of being full. Her hips wound feverishly as her need rose. She latched onto Ronnie's neck with her teeth, back arching, legs tensing, and toes curling, and a load of cum shot out of her. "Fuck, baby... Yes... ooh, fuck."

Shifting gears, Ronnie increased the tempo. In each hand, she grasped an ankle and thrust them apart. Body rolling, pistoning her dick back and forth, in and out of her pussy, Ronnie claimed her body. She pushed her legs back.

"OH! My... gawd," Kenni stuttered. Failing to maintain a grip on her sheets, she scrambled backwards on the bed. "Fuck, baby," she cried out, unable to retreat. "Fuck... yes, daddy. Oh myfuckin God! Ooh, shit, baby... Ooh... ooh... I'm cumming... I'm cumming." Juices charged out of her.

Jumping out the coochie, Ronnie slurped up her liquids, making her box buckle. Legs convulsed around her head, another orgasm headed her way. Flicking her tongue against her sensitive spot, she dared her to climax. Lips wrapped around her clit, beckoning it into her mouth, the tip of her tongue attacking her sweet spot.

"OOH, FUCK!" Kenni sat up, staring down at Ronnie, hands glued to her head, grinding against her face.

Oblivious to anything outside of their sex cloud, neither female heard a knock on Kenni's bedroom door. Neither of them registered Beaunna entering the room, saying Kenni's name. Beaunna's mouth fell open when she took in the scene of her daughter getting her pussy eaten.

"What in the entire fuck? Kenni!" Beaunna screeched.

Attempting to pull away, Kenni locked her in position. She rose from the bed, body spazzing, and squirted in Ronnie's mouth.

"Kenni!"

"Ooh… yes, baby… Fuck," she panted, grinding out the last wave of her orgasm. Her mother yanked a pillow off the floor and whacked her in the face with it. Kenni opened her eyes, releasing Ronnie. She smiled at her mother. "Hey."

"Hey my ass." She hit her again with the pillow. "What the fuck happened to a sock on the door?" Beaunna demanded.

"I mean, I'm pretty sure I wasn't quiet, mama," Kenni joked, eyes drifting shut.

"Shut up," Beaunna shot at her. Her eyes shifted over, focusing on Ronnie, who was dressing. "Did y'all even use protection?" She winked at the stud. "You better not had got my daughter pregnant. Go wash your face and hands and introduce yourself properly. You"—she smacked a snoozing Kenni with a pillow again—"put some damn clothes on. I'm coming back in," Beaunna warned her, leaving the room.

A sigh of slight frustration, but more contentment left Kenni. Her eyes twinkled when Ronnie came back in the room, grinning and laughing. She signaled Ronnie into bed with her for a kiss.

"That was… that felt great, baby," Kenni admitted, laughing at the wet spot they were avoiding.

"Girl, where is yo clothes?" Beaunna said, coming back into the room.

Throwing herself backward and groaning because Ronnie had gotten up, she told her mother, "Ma, I need a minute."

"I bet you fuckin' do." She threw a pillow at Kenni, who didn't attempt to prevent it from hitting her in the face. "Lil nasty ass didn't even stop."

Kenni pulled a cover around her. "You gave birth to me, so why do I even need to put clothes on? And Ronnie has seen me naked."

"Obviously," Beaunna sneered. She turned to Ronnie, feigning ignorance. "And you are?"

Ronnie grinned and extended her hand to Beaunna. "Ronnie. Nice to meet you, ma'am." She played along as if they hadn't had a conversation in the hallway and agreed to respect Kenni's wishes until she popped out of the closet and admitted to her mother she was a lesbian.

"Uh-huh. Did you use soap?" She eyed Ronnie's outstretched hand.

"Yes, ma'am," Ronnie chuckled.

"Umm-hmm. I'm Kenni's mother, Beaunna." She shook Ronnie's hand. "I guess it's nice to meet you, though I would've preferred it had been under, you know, normal circumstances, not with your face between my daughter's legs."

"Yes, ma'am. I apologize."

"Unh-huh. No, you don't. You know about

the sock on the door rule?"

"Yes, ma'am," Ronnie laughed.

Beaunna smacked her lightly against the back of her head. "Well, next time, put a sock on the door."

"Yes, ma'am."

"So, y'all back together now?" Beaunna questioned, eyes peering between them.

"Yes, ma'am."

"Yes, Ma."

"Good," she smiled. "So, Kenni, yo hot ass on punishment. Ronnie, let me walk you to the door."

"Ma, is you serious?" Kenni whined.

Her mother walked out without replying, waiting at the door for Ronnie, who pressed a kiss to her cheek, whispering that she'd call her later. Ronnie, unable to wipe the smile from her face, walked without words. At the door, a hand on her shoulder demanded her attention.

"Don't break my baby heart. She really like you."

"I love her, too."

"Yeah, you better. I better not walk in on y'all having sex no more." She stared pointedly at the stud. "Sock on the door. Sock on the door."

Chuckling, Ronnie repeated, "Sock on the door. Yes, ma'am, I got you."

"Okay, now you be safe going home."

"Yes, ma'am."

Driving away from her girlfriend's home, Ronnie fumbled with her phone. She chuckled to herself about her mother-in-law while waiting for T to answer the phone. "Aight. So, we all going out tomorrow night?" she questioned, resuming their conversation from earlier.

"Well, hello to you, too, muthafucka. And now that you have permission, yeah, that's the move."

"Man, fuck you, bra. Aye, why my shorty mama just walk in on us?" she chuckled. "I was giving her head, and her mama came in, like, the fuck. Aye, shorty ain't even stop. She was gonna get that nut."

T guffawed on the other end. "So, tell me about yo lil shorty, man. I heard a lil bit from Lil Buddy, but yo ass been MIA."

"Man, shorty everything, yo." Just talking about her painted another grin on her face. "Bad lil redbone. She got goals to be young, for real."

"How old is she?"

"Sixteen. She'll be seventeen next month, though."

"Aww, you fuckin' somebody daughter for real," jested T, calling out for another one of their friends in the background to tell her.

Paying no mind to the shit talking and banter, Ronnie continued. "Yeah, but her mama cool as shit. Her brother a bitch, though. I had to flash my piece at him the first time I met him. It's funny, though, because us getting into it led to me and Kenni meeting," Ronnie mused. "Nigga, why I have to put hands on dude, too! Nigga had got mad disrespectful when me and shorty had an argument."

"Did you win?"

"Come on, man, act like I wasn't the hood Golden Gloves winner. You know I beat his ass. Baby got in the way, though, and I ended up hitting her in her shit. Aww, bra!" she said excitedly, remembering a key piece that T had to know. "Nigga, you know my neighbor, Shyna? The thick lil bitch that fuck with the police officer?"

"Yeah, her lil sexy ass."

"Nigga, I hit that."

T smacked her lips together. "Nah the fuck you didn't! Quit lying on yo dick."

"Nigga, on my mama," Ronnie promised. "I then fucked her ass a few times now. Bitch got some good-ass pussy, yo. Her lil freaky ass a lil crazy, too. 'Cause, na mean, the first time I hit, I was drunk. I don't really remember, but me and shorty had broke up and shit. But I hit a few times later before me and shorty got back together, and nigga, she started trying to talk to me about her life and shit, like I give a fuck. I had to tell her we just fuckin', that's it. Nigga, she flipped on me on that rah rah shit, like, I'm good enough to fuck, but that's it? She was throwing shit and everything."

"Yeah, well, you know what they say," T laughed. "Crazy hoes got some good-ass pussy."

"And, nigga, she definitely do," Ronnie agreed with the myth. "And her ass sexy as fuck, too, yo. Aye, why my lil shorty and her end up hitting, too. This was after we fucked the first time and shit. I had passed out on that drunk shit when shorty popped up. Nigga, we squashing everything and muthafuckin' Shyna come out of my room.

Nigga, when I say they got to fighting, they got to rumbling."

"Yo shorty win? She got hands?"

"Nigga, I ain't even gonna lie to you—"

"Aww, she got beat up," cracked T. "Let me find out you let yo main get beat up by yo side. You a piece of shit, bra bra."

"Nah, nigga, my baby ain't get did dirty. Like, she ain't get dog walked, but shit, lil baby can't fight. She got hella mouth, though. It is what it is. I stepped in, you know, before it got too bad. Man, if I wouldn't had, Shyna was gonna give her her issue."

"Damn, so you beat up her brother, she got beat up by yo side piece, and she still want yo lil ugly ass?"

"Lanky bitch, yeah, that's my lil baby." Ronnie got out of the truck and walked up to the front entrance of her apartment building. "What's good with you, though, nigga?"

"Hey, Ronnie." Shyna stepped out of her apartment. "I just wanted to say I'm sorry for the other night."

"Bra, what the fuck? Do you watch me coming and going? That shit weird," Ronnie commented. When she didn't respond, Ronnie nodded. "Nah, nigga. Shyna just stopped me in the hallway," she told T.

"You wanna match?" Shyna asked.

"Nah, I'm good." Ronnie turned to her door. "Aye, T, I'll see y'all tomorrow at Colorz. I'm about to go play the game." She unlocked the door and walked in, leaving Shyna in the hallway, staring at her.

                    *   *   *

"Aww, look who finally brought they ass!" Chantel hollered, smiling jovially at Ronnie from behind her girlfriend, Mya, who sat on her lap.

A middle finger flipped up in Chantel's direction. Ronnie's eyes scanned the crowd in the VIP area of their nightclub, Colorz, that the rest of her gay family was scattered around. "Where big bro at?"

"She was downstairs wit' Meeka," stated Kim, the only fem of their crew.

"She finally pulled you in, huh, ma?" another one of her stud brothers, Jay, said, squinting slanted, green eyes at a woman behind Ronnie.

Eyebrow raised, Ronnie whipped around, and her jaw almost dropped seeing Shyna smirk behind her. "The fuck?" she finally questioned. "What the fuck, is you following me now?"

"Don't flatter yourself." Her eyes ran up and down Ronnie, then away like she wasn't impressed. "I been here since eleven. I'm here to kick it, let loose, and have fun, none of which you can handle. None of which is about you. Mind ya business." She sauntered away towards the bathroom, ass barely covered and rocking side to side, hypnotizing the eyes that fell upon it.

"I can handle it! Shit, what you need, baby?" Jay hollered.

Checking over her shoulder, Shyna quickly perused the green-eyed, Caucasian and Latino stud. "I'll be back to see you, daddy."

Jay winked at her. "Ron, good lookin' bringing that to me."

"What's good, lil nigga?" T greeted Ronnie, draping an arm over her shoulder. "I see you was able to get out the house with no punishment, huh?"

Pushing the taller stud off of her, she laughed. "Fuck you, bra. Where yo other half at? I ain't seen Meeka ass in a minute."

"Other half? Shit, nigga, right here. Never leave home without it. I'm something like a boy scout, always prepared." T grabbed her crotch, laughing.

"Preach!" Chantel agreed, holding up a shot glass.

"Man, where yo girl, nigga?" Ronnie rephrased with a roll of her eyes.

"I just sent Meeka home to Rachel so they can wait on me." She began counting off on her fingers. "Tsoi, my Asian girl, won't be back here for like three more Saturdays, Tricia fake mad at me, my young girl can't stay out this late, and Yolanda gotta work late, but I'm going over there for overtime. Where yo girl at? Shit, which one you bring?"

"Fuckin' neither. I got one bitch. Yo, why the fuck Shyna ass just popped up behind me like I told her to come here. And fuck you, Jay. Shit, you can have that crazy bitch."

"I told you dope dick make 'em sick," T told her, surveying the main area of the club from their upstairs VIP section. "I think she trying to bring her ass up here, too. Damn, that ass fat."

Sure enough, when Ronnie looked over the balcony railing, Shyna had eyes on the VIP area. She weaved through the crowd expertly, smacking hands down that tried to grab her, and shooting stank faces to people. "See, Jay, you just had to bite, now she coming back."

"Nigga, you see all that ass? Her body stacked, fool. I'm trying to bend that bitch over *tonight*. Shit, she just might be a team player. I'ma find out, dammit," Jay chuckled.

"She do got a point," jested T, licking her lips, admiring the voluptuous, barely-clothed woman. "What you wanna do, though, bra?"

"Man, you know I just got my baby back. I ain't about to fuck that shit up entertaining that bitch. I don't even wanna be around her, and my shorty see it type shit. I'm about to just go beat her ass for pulling this lil shit," she spewed, turning to go down the stairs.

"Hold on." T dropped a hand on her shoulder. "Chill, lil bra. Let's do this. Aye, Stacey," she called out to one of her employees assigned to the VIP section.

"What's up, big daddy?" Stacey called back.

"You been checkin' the list? Is there a Shyna on there?" she asked, referring to the list of people allowed in the VIP area.

The woman checked her clipboard. "Marlowe? There's a Shyna Marlowe who paid for VIP and bottle service."

"Aight, never mind," T called back to her.

"See, she on that bullshit. I'ma just fuck her up when she get up here then," Ronnie stated.

T nodded, watching Shyna make her way back over to the steps that led to where they were. "Don't make a scene. Invite yo young girl up here. She wanna play, we can play, too. This our shit."

"Or else I can get her," voiced Kim, always the one itching for a fight. "It ain't no problem."

"Nah," T dictated with a shake of her dreadlocked hair. "Let shorty come up here."

"Hell yeah, I like that," declared Jay, licking her lips at Shyna climbing the stairs. "Then ole girl can come cry to me, and my arms gonna be open for that hoe."

"Diss and dismiss that trick," concurred Chantel, making her way to the dancefloor with her girlfriend, Mya.

Ronnie smiled. "I think I will."

*   *   *

Perched on the edge of her mother's bed, who sat watching a Lifetime movie, Kenni played with a seam in the comforter. "Mommy?" she said in a little girl's voice.

"Yes, Kenni? What do you want?" Beaunna inquired with a hint of vexation.

Still in a little girl's tone, which she hoped to persuade her mother with, Kenni questioned, "Can I go out?"

Beaunna yawned, "No, it's too late." She turned the television volume up.

"Mommy, please."

She turned and locked the evil eye onto her daughter. "What did I just say?"

Instantly, her demeanor changed, sapped from baby girl to her normal, pampered attitude.

Kenni stalked out of the room, sucking her teeth. Inside her room, she selected an outfit to wear: a pair of jeans that hugged her legs, an off-the-shoulder shirt, and a pair of stiletto heels. Fresh out the shower, thirty minutes later, praying that her mother was sleeping, she crept downstairs. Snatching the keys off the key rack, she tiptoed outside. Backing the Jaguar out onto the street, she heard her mother's window open.

"Kenni! Put my damn car back!" Beaunna hollered.

Kenni beeped and kept driving, driving to Ronnie, to Colorz.

*   *   *

"So, what is this now? Her trying to make you jealous?" Kim questioned, staring at Shyna, who had draped herself all over Jay.

"F for failure!" T hollered. "My nigga gives no fuck."

The group laughed at Shyna's expense, and even Jay smirked. When Shyna had come back to the section, she'd attempted to talk to Ronnie under the guise of needing weed, but Ronnie had pretended like she wasn't even present. Shyna had gone to Jay, dancing seductively, rubbing on her, allowing the stud's hands to roam over her body, all while shooting glares in Ronnie's direction.

"Yo, when is yo shorty getting up here?" T questioned Ronnie.

"Right. It's time to diss and dismiss that trick," cracked Kim.

"Aye, I'm having fun," Jay admitted, grinning devilishly, free from Shyna, who'd gone to get drinks.

On cue, Ronnie's phone screamed for attention from her pocket. Pulling the phone from her pocket, she directed Kenni to where she was waiting for her, tracking her progress from over the balcony railing. Her nostrils lit up with the scent of perfume tickling her nose hairs, eyes engulfing the beauty Kenni possessed.

"Hey, baby." She kissed Ronnie's cheek, looking at the group surrounding them curiously.

"Kenni." Ronnie held her hand up for her family. "That's Chantel aka Lil Buddy, her girlfriend, Mya, the oldest of us, T, ugly-ass Jay, and Kim short ass." She gestured to each person introduced.

Amidst everyone murmuring greetings and exchanging smiles, Jay divulged, "Aww, Ron, I'm proud of you. Yo ugly ass pulled in a diamond."

Everyone laughed, and Kenni smiled at their repartee.

"Fuck you, Jay."

"Damn, you must really want me, bra. That's the second or third time you then told me that tonight. So, once again, for yo hard of hearing ass, only fems. I only fuck fems, G."

The crew erupted in laughter. Ronnie turned Kenni away from them. Facing her, she whispered in her ear, "Baby, I need you to trust me, aight?"

"I do, baby. That's why I'm here."

"Well, listen, like I been telling you, you all I want and need, but some muthafuckas just don't get that shit." Ronnie nodded at Shyna, who was coming up the stairs.

Kenni's eyes narrowed, but before she could say anything, Mya brought her over a drink. Her eyes twinkled. "It's nice to finally meet you. You keep my brother on her toes, and you got her nose open. Cheers to you." She clinked their glasses together, and the two had a drink.

"Thank you," she beamed. "She got my nose just as open."

"Aye, sis!" T hollered. "Sis! Kenni," T called her loudly again. "You drink?"

Her voice carried over the music and light VIP chatter. The group of friends watched Shyna pull away from her conversation with someone in VIP, eyes darting to Kenni, who was oblivious, smiling brightly at T.

"Just a little bit. It's good, whatever it is!" Kenni hollered back.

"It's only a virgin daiquiri. I don't drink," Mya told her quietly with a smile.

The group burst into laughter, tapering off when Shyna stalked over to the group. "Oh, so you was dead ass, huh? You really back playing with yo plaything," she fumed.

"Don't come at me like that, hoe," snapped Kenni.

"Lil bitch, I'll come at you any way I want because you can't do shit about it. You trying to get yo ass beat again, sweetie?" Shyna stepped to her. "This will be what, the second time?"

Jay snorted, turning away from the feuding ladies, the rest of the squad biting back smiles and giggles. Ronnie's body tensed. If anybody was going to get beat the fuck up tonight, it was definitely going to be Shyna.

"Ain't nobody scared of you," continued Kenni.

Snorting, Jay walked away from the group, shoulders shaking.

"Shit, after this one, please believe you will be. Keep talking shit, I'ma crush yo lil heart and fuck yo nigga again."

"Damn, Ronnie." Jay strode back between the two women glaring at each other. "You got girls fighting over you and shit."

Ronnie scoffed. "Nah, I can't have my baby hanging in here." She stepped in Shyna's personal space, snarling. "Bitch, I wouldn't fuck you again with a homeless nigga's dick. You don't measure up to my bitch in no categories, but I will present you to my brother since you wanna be a team player." She laughed in her face with an arm thrown around Jay.

Grinning broadly, T draped an arm around Shyna's shoulder. "Damn, cuz, Ron say sayonara, too bad for ya, but she got a couple brothers for you. What's up?" She licked her lips, eye fucking her.

"Ump, I knew you was a fuckin whore. That's why don't nobody want yo ass," Kenni hissed. "Dirty bitch."

Shyna ripped out of T's grip, running up to where Kenni stood, next to Ronnie. Cocking back to punch her in the face, she dropped when Ronnie's blow landed first.

"OOOOH!" T hyped, jumping up and down. "She came"—she pointed to Shyna—"and I saw," she added, gesturing to herself. "And she hit that bitch"—finger pointed back to Shyna—"right dead in the jaw." T laughed, using the line from rapper Ludacris' "Get Back" song.

"Bitch, stay the fuck away from me and mine. I don't fuckin' want you," Ronnie spazzed. "You wanna do something?" she fired at Shyna, who stood with fire burning through her brown skin. "Bitch, I will fuck you up in this club and reunite you with yo punk-ass fiancé and daddy, nigga. I don't give a fuck. Fuck Will Coors. Fuck you." She lunged for her again, but Chantel restrained her.

"I think it's fair to say that you have been..." Kim glanced around her group.

"Dismissed," they told her collectively.

"And if you jump towards my brother or sister again, I'ma fuck you up, too. I like fighting," Kim threatened with a smile.

"I think it's best you leave, ma," T prodded.

Body rigid, steps stiff, Shyna heeded the advice given. Being outmanned was a guaranteed losing battle. She started to march away.

"You are the weakest link, goodbye!" Kim hollered.

"Na na naa na... na na naa na, hey hey-hey, goodbye!" shouted Jay.

The set of friends cracked up in laughter again.

*   *   *

"Ronnie, what you doin'? What's all that damn noise in the background?" Kenni questioned her girlfriend, holding the phone away from her ear.

It had been a fast two weeks since their night at the club. True to her word, her mother wouldn't let her go anywhere or do anything. True to being a teenager, regardless of how many months shy of eighteen she was, Kenni rebelled, sneaking her girlfriend in the house whenever her mother was gone. Today, her mother had given her the green light that she was off punishment.

"Who it sound like, baby?" Ronnie laughed. "T dumb ass and Kim. They arguing and Jay instigating," Ronnie responded, laughing at her friends.

Before Kenni could say anything, she heard T yelling at Kim. "Nah, fuck that! Ron, gimme the phone, let me ask lil sis what she think." A smile flitted across her face. "What's good, sis?"

"Nothin'. What's going on?" wondered Kenni.

"Hold on, let me put you on speaker phone so Kim can feel stupid," replied T, fumbling with the phone. "Aight. Yo, answer me this, right?" T began as silence fell across the room. "We too old to go to laser tag?"

Kenni burst out laughing as they all waited for her answer with bated breath. "No. I wanna go. Ronnie, come get me."

"See, I told yo short ass!" T hollered.

"Fuck you, T!" Kim yelled back. "Big, tall, brown, Big Bird-ass bitch!"

"Ooh, she said yo mama," instigated Jay in the background.

Amidst the laughter and more shit talking, Ronnie murmured into the phone, "See, baby, this what boredom and drinking do to you. But look, I'ma be over there in fifteen minutes. Call Layla and Sayvonne and see if they wanna meet us up there."

"Okay, Ronnie."

"Aight, see you in fifteen."

"Okay."

"Bye."

Kenni exploded off her bed with a new wave of energy. She opened her closet door, peering inside at its contents, trying to figure out what to wear. Excitement bubbled within her again, prompting her to grab a few pieces of clothing, throwing them onto the bed. Spotting her phone partially covered, she grabbed it, remembering she needed to call her friends.

"Lay, what you doing?" Kenni inquired when the ringing cell phone was answered.

Layla yawned into the phone. "Nothing. Just woke up. Why? What's good?"

Heading into the bathroom, she turned on the shower. "Well, wake up and get dressed. Meet me at Tagged."

"Bitch, I'm going back to sleep." Layla smacked her lips together in annoyance. "I ain't trying to play no damn laser tag."

"Yeah, whatever, bitch. Ronnie's friends gonna be there," she mentioned coyly, sitting on the toilet, naked. "You said you wanted to meet them, and I know two of them definitely yo type."

"Yeah, aight. We'll see. I'm about to get dressed."

"Okay, call Von and see if she wanna meet us there, too. I'm about to hop in the shower. Ronnie gonna be at my house in a minute."

"Aight, K. I'll see you in a lil bit."

"Bye."

"Bye."

*   *   *

"Hey," Shyna called out to Ronnie, who was walking towards her truck in the parking lot. She turned her ignition off.

Ignoring her like a professional, Ronnie unlocked her doors and got in. Something was wrong with Shyna. In two weeks, that night at the club seemed to have completely disappeared from her mental.

"Really, so you not gonna speak at all?" Shyna questioned, getting out of her car. She ripped Ronnie's truck door open. "So, we can't be friends? For real?"

"What the fuck is you doing touching my fuckin' ride? What don't you get, ma? I'm fuckin' over you, shorty. I don't want no fuckin' parts of you. Stop fuckin' talkin' to me." Ronnie yanked her door out of Shyna's hands, blasted her radio, and pulled out, leaving tire tracks in the parking lot.

In record time, Ronnie pulled up to Kenni's house and knocked on the door. It took a minute before Kenni opened the door in nothing but a towel and a smile. Her eyes raked over her body, tongue wetting her lips at the sight.

"Shit, we ain't even gotta go to laser tag no more," Ronnie suggested lustfully.

"Shut up," Kenni giggled, grabbing Ronnie's hand, tugging her into the house.

On the steps, she stopped her with her arms wrapped around her waist, dotting kisses along the back of her neck. "What time yo mama coming home?"

"In a lil while, that's why I'm trying to hurry up," she responded, breaking free of Ronnie's grip and going up the stairs to her room.

"So, I guess it gotta be laser tag then." Sad that they didn't have time for sex, she drifted into her bedroom.

Kenni shot a smile over her shoulder to her girlfriend. She dropped her towel and began to lotion. Pebbled nipples responded to the taut sexual tension emitting from a rooted Ronnie, whose eyes never strayed from her body. Done with the lotion, she spun around, looking for the outfit she had sat out. *Damn, I left them in the bathroom*, she remembered.

Nerves slightly frayed, there was no way to avoid Ronnie, who stood, blocking the doorway, gazing at her in wonderment. Speculating if she was going to allow her to pass, she got her answer. Ronnie drew her into a kiss when she approached. Her hands traversed down her body, grasping her ass, lifting her into the air and laying her down on the bed.

"Baby," breathed Kenni, about to remind her about their plans and her mother, but before she could say anything else, she felt Ronnie's tongue sliding languidly from the back of her pussy, back up to the front, over her growing clit. She bit her lip as her phone started ringing. When she reached out to answer it, Ronnie grabbed her hands and placed them back on her ears.

"We ain't got that much time, remember?"

Nodding, she dropped her head back against her pillows, succumbing to the pleasure of her pussy being tongue kissed. Her cell phone protested with her mother's assigned ringtone. "Shit, baby, that's my mama. Let me… let me… answer the phone."

Ronnie handed her the cell phone, pressing the talk button for her.

"Kenni?" called out Beaunna when the ringing stopped, but all she heard was silence.

"Yes," whimpered Kenni.

"I'll be home in a few minutes, do you want me to pick you up something to eat before I come home?"

Her mouth opened in a silent scream. Ronnie had taken to flicking her tongue across her clit. She shivered, fingers clutching her nipples. "No, no. I'm coming," responded Kenni, stifling a moan, the climax ripping through her. "I mean, I'm about to go somewhere."

"Where are you going?"

Kenni let out a small scream of ecstasy, unable to contain herself. "Laser tag," she gasped out.

"Kenni, are you okay?" Kenni's mother asked with concern.

Pushing her girlfriend's head from between her legs, she stammered, "Yeah, Ma, I'm fine, I just stepped on something. But I gotta go, Ma, my ride outside." She darted to the bathroom, retrieving her clothes and beginning to dress.

"All right, well, you better bring yo ass in at a decent hour."

"Yes, ma'am."

"Aight, go 'head. Be safe."

"Okay, Ma, you too. Bye."

"Bye."

"C'mon, Ronnie, she'll be here any minute," she told Ronnie, grabbing her cell phone and house keys.

Ronnie chuckled to herself. "Yeah, so we can finish that up."

*   *   *

"It's 'bout time y'all got here," commented T, observing Ronnie and Kenni walking up towards the entrance where the family waited for them.

"Fuck you, nigga. That's why you gonna get yo ass beat when we get in here," responded Ronnie. "I'ma make it my mission to find yo ass and shoot you, nigga."

T glanced at the youngest of their crew, Chantel. "Oh, so you want some with Lil Buddy then? Aight, it's on. I got twenty on my team. What you got, Lil Buddy?"

Chantel grinned. "Shit, nigga, I got twenty-five on it. You ain't sayin nothin' but some words. What you got, Ron?"

"Shit, I got thirty on it," proclaimed Ronnie. "Soon as Kenni's friends get here, we gonna make it happen."

T turned to Kenni, grinning widely. "You having some friends meet us up here? Sexy ones on my team."

"Shit, me too," announced Jay. "Kim, Kenni, the time has come," she began seriously. "The team you choose today will be one of the biggest decisions you will ever make. Everything that happens after you choose your team will be based on this decision. So, choose wisely," she said solemnly.

Kenni giggled. "Well, I'm on Ronnie's team. Sorry, T, but yo twenty 'bout to go towards a pair of new shoes for me."

"All right, okay," she said, mock offended, turning to Kim. "Kim, you on the winning squad, or you gonna fuck 'round with these niggas and get got?"

Kim patted T on the arm. "See, look, it's lonely over there with just Jay, ain't it? And it's 'bout to get lonelier 'cause I'ma make it my mission to tag yo ass, too, for talking shit earlier."

"The pain," T joked with a fist over her heart.

Everyone giggled at their antics, and Jay stepped forward again. "Your team has been chosen unwisely, now you four must suffer the consequences. Your time will come."

Everyone laughed.

"There they go right here." Kenni pointed out her friend's car that was sliding into a parking space in front of them. She went to the driver's side as the doors opened. "Damn, Lay. I said laser tag. How you about to play?"

"Girl, I'm dressed for success." She winked at Kenni.

"Whatever. What's up, Von?" she greeted her other best friend, who was on the passenger side of the car. "I'm sorry to let y'all know, but y'all on the losing side of things."

Sayvonne chuckled. "And how you figure that?"

The trio walked up to where the family of lesbians bantered on the sidewalk. "Layla, Sayvonne," she gestured to her friends.

Ronnie nodded at them, then introduced her friends.
"This T, Kim, Jay, and Lil Buddy."

"Lucky ladies, y'all on our team," Jay assured them, standing next to T.

"I think we the lucky ones, bro." T stepped toward Layla, licking her lips like she was LL Cool J's daughter. "What's good, shorty?"

Layla grinned at her from under a hat. "Hey."

"Aight, let's get this shit started, so we can get y'all money," broadcasted Chantel, turning towards the doors.

Collectively, the group began moving towards the entrance. Side conversations and laughter sparked throughout the group while they waited to be assisted. When everyone had paid and was putting on equipment, the shit talking started again.

"Aye, Lil Buddy, don't be tryin to have Mya fight me when you lose yo money, dawg," snickered T, talking to Chantel.

"Shit, baby know what time it is. She gonna thank you for treatin' her, Kim, and Kenni out to eat."

The group chuckled. In turn, Ronnie spoke up. "Baby, where you wanna go with Jay and T money?"

"Aye, before you answer that, think about what you wanna say. We might spare you in there," Jay reminded her.

"Jay, shut the fuck up. I'm shootin' you," responded Ronnie before Kenni could comment.

Giggling, Kenni locked eyes with Sayvonne and jutted her chin over at Layla. The two friends watched T walk over to her, helping her with the gear. Layla grinned at her when T walked away.

"Let's get it crackin'!" hollered T to the associate of Tagged, who walked over to the small group and began to go over the procedures and protocol.

He finished reviewing the instructions and safety practices, then he opened the door for T's group to go in one way, and Ronnie's group to go through the other entrance.

Hands clasped together, the couple entered the darkness, watching their partners, Chantel and Kim, dart off separate ways. Ronnie moved to lead her on the hunt for the other team, but she pulled her a different way. Pushing her against a wall, Kenni attacked the lips on her face.

Gun clattering to the floor, Ronnie broke the kiss, sucking on her neck and unbuttoning her pants. "Ssh," she whispered to Kenni, giving her a kiss and dropping to her knees.

"Oh my God." Her eyes fluttered at the sensations from her nether region. She struggled to keep her breathing composed. The sense of her presently being in laser tag with friends, playing a game, drifted from her mind. Kenni's eyes squeezed shut; hips began to wind in fervor. "Fuck, baby... shit," she moaned.

Abruptly, Ronnie pulled her face from between her legs. She cut off her protests with a kiss, one hand undoing her jeans. Glancing around furtively and seeing no one, Ronnie whipped the two around, so Kenni's back was against the wall. The attachment nestled at her center pierced the inside of the young woman.

"Oh, shit, baby... Fuck... Ronnie... Daddy... Ooh, baby... shit... shit... shit. I'm cummin', boo," screamed Kenni, juices charging out of her.

Attempting to smother any further screams, Ronnie kissed her face while she continued to hammer away. She thrashed her yoni, demanding another orgasm to overcome her. Hands pawing at her shirt, and Kenni making growling noises beneath the attack of her lips was the indication that her mission had been successful. She climaxed hard. Ronnie eased her strap out of her, tucking it back into her pants.

"Y'all some nasty muthafuckas," professed Jay, bursting their sexual haze from her position on the side of the couple, laughing.

They joined in on her laughter with bashful grins. Ronnie tapped Kenni surreptitiously and snatched their guns up. Laughter accompanied the three running and shooting. Ten minutes later, the lights came up, and everyone proceeded to the doors marked exit.

"Yo, can you tell us who got shot the most?" Kim asked an employee.

He smiled at Kim. "It's all on these slips I'm about to hand you guys," he responded as, true to his word, the printer began to print out eight pieces of paper coordinated with the equipment they had picked up.

"Hell yeah, T, yo ass ain't get me, nigga!" Kim exclaimed. "Ain't nobody get me."

T chuckled. "Aight, well, I was shot a hundred and seventy-five times."

"Yeah. I got yo ass," admitted Chantel.

Kim gave her a high five.

"Kenni, how many times you get hit?" Layla questioned Kenni slyly with a glint of mischievousness in her eye.

Kenni looked down at her paper and laughed, "It say six people unloaded they clips in me."

Everyone burst out laughing.

"Ron, what yours say?" T inquired laughing.

Ronnie looked down at her paper and laughed, "Fuck y'all. It say the same shit."

Everybody guffawed again and started to head out of the business. Kenni's friends drifted away from the main group, who had found parking together. Ronnie hung back with her girlfriend so they could say bye to her friends.

"Aye, don't forget my mama barbecuing tomorrow, y'all. Layla, Von, Kenni, y'all all welcome to come," boomed T.

"Nigga, ain't nobody forgetting Ma Dukes cookin'," commented Chantel.

"Thanks, T," Layla yelled back.

"Thanks for the invite, T. Call you later, Kenni," called Sayvonne, giving Kenni a hug and getting into Layla's car.

Her friends pulled off, and the two went over to Ronnie's group, exchanging hugs and hand slaps. Back in the truck, Kenni grinned at herself. Insecurity tugged at her heart, making her bite her lip, realizing T had taken the initiative to invite her to a family function, and not her girlfriend.

"What's wrong with you?" Ronnie questioned.

"Nothing." Kenni flipped the radio on.

"Girl, quit lying."

"I'm good, baby. I promise," she lied.

"Yeah, whatever. So, what's up, you gonna come to our BBQ tomorrow?"

"Do you want me there?"

"Didn't I just ask you?" Ronnie quipped. "If I ain't want you there, T wouldn't have said shit, and I wouldn't have asked you again to be sure."

"Okay, baby, well you know I'm in there. Just let me know when you on the way."

"I got you, baby."

"I know you do, now give me a kiss before you hop up out my ride," she demanded, putting the car in park.

Smiling, Kenni leaned towards her girlfriend and kissed her lips. "I love you, baby. See you tomorrow."

"Love you, too, baby. See you tomorrow."

Chapter 6

"So, I guess I can't get no weed from you either, huh?" Shyna questioned Ronnie, who walked into the foyer of their apartment.

Ronnie huffed to herself. She had almost made it in and out without interacting with that crazy bitch. She walked into her apartment, slamming the door shut behind her. Shyna pushed it open and stepped inside, spying her dropping her keys and phone off on the counter as she made her way to the bathroom. Shyna picked up her phone and scrolled through it. She smiled devilishly at a text message from Kenni that had come through, then she quickly put the phone down.

"Why the fuck is you in my house!" Ronnie demanded to know, coming out of the bathroom and into the kitchen. "Get the fuck out, yo!"

"So, you gonna miss out on fuckin' money? I need some fuckin' weed," Shyna snapped back.

"Find another weed man. I ain't got shit in, and I'm not re-upping." Ronnie opened the door. "Now get out."

"You gonna let a lil bitch stop yo paper?" she muttered, strolling out.

Ronnie slammed the door on her. She went to her kitchen and grabbed her mother's pot, the reason why she had to double back before picking up Kenni for the bbq. Keys and phone secured, she took a deep breath. Hopefully, she wasn't in the hallway waiting for her. Ronnie opened her front door and smiled. Shyna wasn't waiting for her.

*   *   *

"Umm, Kenni, where do you think you going?" Beaunna questioned, watching her daughter slide out of one outfit to put on another and criticize it in the mirror.

Kenni smiled at her mother through the mirror. "Ronnie's peoples havin a bbq."

Smirking, Beaunna took a seat on her bed. "And what does that mean?"

"Ma, stop playin'!" she stomped her foot.

Gray eyes shot to her daughter, staring daggers at her. "That's not how you ask."

"Ma, can I go to Ronnie's people barbecue?" Kenni inquired sweetly with a roll of her own gray eyes.

Beaunna touched a light-skinned finger to her high cheekbones, pretending to think on it. "Well, I guess. Look at you, Mr. Ronnie got you cheesing and a sparkle in yo eye."

She lit up at her mother's words. Peering at her through the mirror, Kenni stated, "I know. I love Ronnie so much, but Ma, what you think about this?"

"Wear that outfit," she told her daughter, standing behind her in the mirror. "And do yo hair like this." She weaved her fingers through her hair to show Kenni the style she was talking about.

"Okay, mama." She criticized the outfit and design mentally. "Will you do my hair, though?"

"Of course I will, baby. Go hop in the shower and start getting ready. Call me when you ready for me to do yo hair."

"Okay, mama."

*   *   *

"Damn, baby." Ronnie hopped out of her truck to go around and open the door for her lady. She whistled, eyes roving all over her. "Look at you. We might have to make a pit stop, baby. I need to eat you now, you look so good."

Tickled with delight, Kenni kissed her and pulled down the mirror. "My hair look okay, baby? My mama did it."

"Yeah, baby. It's cool. I like it. Shit, I told you I wanna eat that ass up right now."

"Nope. Let's go." Kenni grinned and drew Ronnie into a kiss before they took off. "I'm ready to meet yo mama."

"You can see that old lady later. I'm about to stop by my house and suck the soul out you, girl."

"Whatever, Ronnie, you better take me to eat. I'm hungry." Her phone went off, and she immediately pressed the ignore button.

"Who was that?" Ronnie inquired suspiciously.

Kenni shrugged. "I don't know, my phone been ringing off the hook since I got out the shower, but it's all private calls."

"See, look, that's what you get for cheatin' on me. You and Layla—" A hard shove to her shoulders stopped the rest of Ronnie's sentence.

"Don't play like that, I ain't cheatin' on you!" Kenni exclaimed with her arms folded across her chest.

"I was just playing with yo ass, girl. It was a joke."

"Well, I ain't think it was fuckin' funny," she spat back, rolling her eyes and sucking her teeth.

"Whatever," Ronnie muttered.

Twenty minutes of silence passed. Outside of T's mother's house, Ronnie turned the car off and looked at Kenni. When she refused to acknowledge her presence, Ronnie snatched her hand.

"What?" Kenni snapped.

"Give me a kiss," Ronnie demanded.

"No."

A thrill of challenge zinged through Ronnie. She pulled her chin towards hers, and their lips touched sweetly. "Truce." She kissed her forehead.

"Truce," smiled Kenni, chasing her girlfriend's lips with her own. "I love you, baby."

"I know," she said, smiling and getting out the car.

"Forget you then." Kenni attempted to push her out of the car.

"Too slow," Ronnie laughed. She opened her car door, taking her hand. "Girl, you know I loovvee you!"

"Well, look at y'all!" an older female voice called from across the street."Don't you be over there acting like you sensitive!" the woman screamed at Ronnie, who peered across the street with the sunlight beaming in her face. "It's Ma Dukes, nigga!" The couple burst out laughing, catching sight of her on the porch, gripping the middle of her jeans.

"What's up, Ma Dukes?" Smiling, Ronnie greeted her, stepping into a hug from Ma Dukes.

Ma Dukes kissed her cheek. "What's up, baby?" She turned to Kenni. "And who is this, Ronnie?" she said, teasing her with a smile.

Chest puffed out, Ronnie couldn't wipe the grin from her face if she wanted to. "Ma Dukes, this my baby, Kenni. Baby, this Ma Dukes, T's mama."

Kenni's mouth dropped open at the revelation, shock keeping her still in the hug Ma Dukes had pulled her into. Speak of the devil, and who should appear. Kenni laughed to herself as T burst out the front door, screaming, "Mamaaa!"

"What?" Ma Dukes turned around. "I'm right here, big head."

T grinned, ignoring her mother and hopping off the edge of the porch. "What's up, nigga?" She slapped hands with Ronnie. "Kenni, you ain't beat my nigga's ass no more, did you?" she replied, talking shit instantly. "Ma, Kenni blacked her eye, put it on some swoll—" T ducked before she could finish the sentence. She abandoned the lies to play fight with Ronnie.

"And boys will be boys," she muttered, inviting Kenni up onto the porch with her. "Plus,

they at home. Drinks and good weed, they cuttin'
up here like some kids," she commented, staring
down at the two wrestling on the ground.

"True," Kenni laughed.

"So, you and Ronnie got a good thing
going?"

"Yes, ma'am."

"Aye, fool, you love her?" she called out to
Ronnie, who stood, brushing her shirt off.

"You ain't hear me when I got out the car,
Ma?" Ronnie responded, smiling and sending a
wink at Kenni. "Hell nah, I don't love her!" she
exclaimed, running up the stairs with T. A bird
flipped up, aimed in her direction from her
girlfriend. "I looovvvveee you, girl," continued
Ronnie, attempting to drown her face in kisses.

"I told you," Ma Dukes stated to Kenni with
a shake of her head. "And she ain't even drunk or
high yet. They gonna be a mess."

"Where my mama at?" Ronnie questioned,
pulling Kenni near her and planting a kiss on her
cheek.

"She back there somewhere." The tall
woman waved in the direction of the house. Those
two skedaddled away, leaving her on the porch with
her daughter. She recalled T calling her name.
"And, T, what did you want?"

"Nothing," T said, adopting a serene
expression as she gazed out at the scenery in front
of the two. Once her mother's attention was
diverted, she scooped up her glass, drained the rest
of her liquor, and took off running into the house.

"T, I'ma kick yo ass when I catch you! It's on, nigga!" yelled Ma Dukes.

Ronnie and Kenni turned around smiling when they looked back to see T behind them.

"Nigga, where the weed at?" Ronnie fired at T when she caught up with them. "Who got it? Yo ass high as hell and drunk as fuck, bruh."

"Nah, I ain't drunk, bruh." She stood up straighter and cleaned the drunk-ish grin off her face. "Now that you here, we can start takin' rounds. A nigga is high as shit, though. Lil Buddy got some shit in, nigga."

In the kitchen, they found Moryah, Ronnie's mother, bustling around, making a plate and dancing by herself. She sang along to the loud music blaring throughout the house. Taking Kenni's hand in her own, Ronnie walked up to her mother and kissed her on the cheek.

"What's up, mama?"

"Hey, baby," said Moryah, hugging her youngest daughter.

"Mama, this Kenni." She began to introduce the two most important women in her life to one another. "Kenni, this my mama."

"Well, this is new." Moryah smiled at the two. Ronnie had never introduced her to a past girlfriend. "I like it," she approved, nodding at her daughter, then turned to question Kenni. "How you doing, baby? That knucklehead treating you right?"

"Ma, come on now, I know how to treat a lady," argued Ronnie with a smack of her lips.

Pointedly ignoring her and staring at Kenni, she spoke, "If you have any problems with her, you let me know, you hear?" Turning to address her daughter, Moryah dismissed her. "Gone and smoke, T waiting on you. Let us ladies get to know each other."

The acceptance and inclusion her mother extended her girlfriend brought a smile to her face. She kissed Kenni's cheek. "I'm downstairs if my mama start getting on yo nerves, baby."

"Okay, baby." She giggled when Ronnie ducked a swat from her mother. "I'll have a plate ready for you when you come up."

*   *   *

"Hello?" Kenni snapped into her cell phone at the unknown caller. "Hello?" She hung the phone up again, shoving it down into her jean's pocket. In the last two hours, her phone had started to ring continuously from a private number. Whoever was playing on her phone had successfully ruined the great mood she'd had two hours ago. Leg tapping impatiently, she answered the call again when her phone started to ring. "Who the fuck is this?! Stop fuckin' calling my phone, damn!"

"Baby, just stop answering," Ronnie smirked, squeezing her thighs with her hands.

Adjusting herself on her lap, Kenni faced her. "No! Tell them muthafuckas to stop calling my damn phone." She threw her phone in Ronnie's face when it started ringing again.

"Two hotheads," Ma Dukes commented to Moryah, who walked next to her to join the family outside. "I see you cussing now. You ain't shy no more, huh?" she teased.

"Oh, nah, she ain't shy, Ma Dukes," laughed Ronnie.

"Hell nah," concurred Kim, laughing and winking at Kenni. "Tell them what you did at Tagged, Kenni."

Jay and Chantel laughed.

"Yeah, you definitely wasn't shy then," said Jay.

Sucking her teeth and rolling her eyes, she squirmed on Ronnie's lap. "Now yo phone vibrating, baby."

Unlocking her phone to view the message had Ronnie quickly deleting it. Her balloon eyes darted up to Kenni, praying to God she hadn't caught sight of the unwarranted picture message that had been sent to her phone. Another one came through.

"Who was that, bae?" Kenni inquired, feeling the vibration again.

"T dumb ass, talking about hi," she lied smoothly, sending a smile to her stud brother, knowing she would play along with no questions asked.

"Damn, T, y'all talkin' about me?" laughed Kenni when she felt the buzzing of the phone again.

"Aye, bruh, ignore that message," Chantel spoke up. "My bad, wrong person."

Ronnie nodded. "Roll up one, and I'll forget about it."

"Sho nuff. Ma, you smokin'?" She directed her question at Ma Dukes.

"I might if it come my way," Ma Dukes told her.

"Now you know you don't need to be smoking," Moryah interjected, laughing.

"I know, that's why I'ma pass it to you after I hit it."

Amidst the laughs of the family of friends, Ronnie's phone started to hum again. Eyes narrowing, neck whipping, Kenni faced her girlfriend. She stared at her, waiting for her to pull her phone out.

"So, you ain't gonna answer it now? It's everybody here texting you, right?" She reached to pull the phone from her pants pocket. "Answer the phone."

"Chill." Ronnie smacked her hand down.

One of her hands lashed out in retaliation, smacking her girlfriend in the chest. "Whatever." She relaxed back onto Ronnie with alert eyes, waiting for the phone to present itself. "Who number is that?"

"I don't know." She deleted the message without opening it. "I don't know no seven-eight-oh numbers."

"Why you delete it?"

Ronnie sighed. She went to shove her phone back into her pocket, but Kenni snatched the vibrating device from her. "Give me my fuckin' phone."

"Who the fuck is that?" She stood, throwing the phone at Ronnie after opening the picture message to be greeted by a woman's boobs.

"I told you I don't fuckin' know! I just fuckin' said that shit, while you throwing my phone and shit! Yo ass would've broke my shit—"

Kenni pushed her. "Then what? You better have that bitch buy you a new one. Don't forget to call her ass later," she remarked snidely about the text accompanying the picture. "Call her now."

"I'll call," Jay joked, waving a hand in the air.

Head snapping towards her, she snapped, "No. You call." Kenni pointed a finger at a stoic Ronnie, who stood with a clenched jaw, breathing harshly through her nose with anger.

Nostrils flaring, Ronnie stated, "I ain't calling shit." She took a seat and pulled out her phone. It notified her of another message, so she opened it, ignoring her girlfriend.

"What she send you this time? A picture of her pussy?" Kenni spat.

"Yup, sho did, wanna see it?" she retorted, holding out the phone.

Smacking the phone away from her, and the audacity of Ronnie to even ask. "Hell nah—"

Cutting off the rest of whatever Kenni was going to say by grabbing her by her arm and yanking her towards her, she snarled in her face, "Bitch! The fuck I just say, Kenni?"

Unable to watch further without saying anything, Moryah ordered, "Ronnie, let her go."

"Nah, fuck that." Ronnie pushed her towards where her phone had clattered onto the ground. "Pick my shit up."

"You got me fucked up," she laughed.

"Pick my fuckin' shit up!"

"Pick my fuckin' shit up," Kenni mocked her, amassing snickers from the women observing them.

"Ronnie." Moryah advanced closer to the pair. She stroked her daughter's back. "Let her go, Ronnie."

"Listen to yo mama. Let me go, Ronnie."

That condescending tone prickled Ronnie's ears, so she shook her and shoved her away from her. "Fuckin' bitch," she mumbled, heading over to the oversized balcony where everyone was congregated, watching them.

Snagging Kenni's hand in her own, Moryah led them to where Ronnie had retreated to. "All of y'all gone in the house. Bye, Ronnie."

"Well ain't this 'bout a bitch," complained Ma Dukes, standing up with the rest of the group. "We ain't even get to smoke yet. Ma makin us all go in and shit."

Snickers riddled the group. Moryah turned to her, smiling. "Now, Lina, you know I ain't talking to you."

"Oh," she laughed and took a seat. "Lil Buddy, you got the blunt, so you gotta stay out here."

Halfway to the door, Chantel turned around. She looked from mother to mother, unable to choose who to obey. Her eyes went to Moryah.

"Sit down, Lil Buddy," Ronnie's mother instructed. "You, too, Kenni."

Scooting closer to the smaller group, Ma Dukes picked up Ronnie's phone, looking at the picture displayed on the screen, then scrolled up to view the priors. "Well, damn." She passed the phone to Chantel.

Involuntarily, Chantel licked her lips at the seductive pictures on the screen. She handed the phone off to Moryah, who gazed at the phone in confusion. "We gonna call her," declared Moryah.

"Hey, baby," a feminine voice cooed, shattering the silence between the four.

"This ain't yo baby. This is Ronnie's mother. Now, you interrupting our BBQ and my daughter's relationship. Who is this?" interrogated Moryah calmly, staring at Kenni, whose foot beat a rhythm onto the ground.

"Oh, sorry, wrong number." A giggle floated over the phone line before a click indicated that the woman had hung up.

"That was fuckin' Shyna." Disgust spewed from Kenni's voice. "I hate that bitch." Her phone began to ring, and she answered. "Bitch, quit callin' my girl phone!" she yelled and hung up.

"You know you gotta apologize, right?" said Ma Dukes, hitting the blunt Chantel had passed to her. When she nodded yes she understood, Ma Dukes directed Chantel, "Lil Buddy, tell everybody to come on back out."

"How she get my number, though?" Kenni questioned. "And she talkin' about wrong number, like, girl, stop." The two mothers offered her a shrug in response.

"Ask her when she come out here, calmly," Ma Dukes told her.

"Yes, ma'am," Kenni smiled.

"Look, Moryah," Ma Dukes laughed. "She got manners now."

The group of friends trailed out of the house slowly like ornery teenagers with lit blunts and horseplay. Ronnie came to a halt in front of Kenni, staring at her expectantly. No part of Kenni wished to be the bigger person and apologize. Hence, she stood, staring back at her.

"Tell her who it was. Ask yo questions and apologize," Ma Dukes whispered loudly to the young woman, causing everyone to smile or laugh at her antics.

"Sorry I threw yo phone," Kenni finally spoke. "It's Shyna texting you and probably playing on my phone, too. Stupid bitch."

"Baby, I swear to God I ain't fucking with that bitch. I ain't fucked with her since that first time. I ain't kicked it or nothing with her. Its turtles for that bitch. She can't even get no weed from me."

Sighing, Kenni released all of the anger coursing through her body. She refused to let that petty bitch get under her skin and fuck with her feelings. "I trust you, baby. I do wanna know how she got my number, though."

"Shit, you and me both. Let me find out y'all really besties," Ronnie winked. A sudden epiphany made her mouth drop. "Aww, I think I know. When I stopped by the house earlier, she was trying to talk to me in the hallway. I swerved her shit and went to the bathroom. When I came out, her crazy ass was in my kitchen."

"Nigga, you don't believe in locked doors?" Jay had taken the words right out of Kenni's mouth. "Stupid ass."

"Fuck you." Ronnie flipped her off. "I just ran in to grab something."

"Didn't we have this discussion at the club?" chuckled Jay.

Kenni chuckled, recalling the memory. A special ringtone to let her know when her mother was calling made her frown. "Hello?" she answered, walking away towards the back door. "Yes, mama… Ma!"

"How old is she?" Ma Dukes questioned.

"Almost seventeen," Ronnie grinned.

Moryah shook her head, pseudo sad. "My baby robbing the cradle."

"Shit, she then made the cradle rock, Ma," joked T.

"More like broke that muthafucka," added Kim.

"Ask her 'bout Tagged," egged Jay.

"Fuck y'all," Ronnie told them playfully, eyes twinkling, taking in Kenni's pout as she walked up to them. "What's wrong, baby? You gotta go?"

"Yeah," Kenni sighed.

"Aight." Ronnie turned to her family and proceeded to give daps and hugs goodbye.

"It was nice meetin' you, Kenni." Moryah hugged her.

"Thank you. You too," replied Kenni politely.

"Such manners!" Ma Dukes bantered, pulling her into a tight embrace.

Kenni smiled. "Aight, y'all." She waved goodbye to Ronnie's friends.

"Holla."

"Yup."

"Aight."

"Aight, lil sis."

"Y'all be safe!" Moryah called out to their retreating backs.

"They gonna fuck in the car, watch," muttered T.

"Maybe," shouted Ronnie.

"Whatever," said Kenni, playfully running away from her.

Ronnie took off after her.

*   *   *

"Look, baby." Ronnie glanced at her girl sitting in the passenger seat next to her. "I'ma change my number right now, so this shit don't get outta hand."

A grin slowly spread across Kenni's face. "Okay, baby. I'm sorry for how I acted earlier."

"Just quit getting so mad, baby. Chill. I only want you. I love the fuck outta you, baby. Know that."

Leaning across the middle console, Kenni turned Ronnie's face away from the road and kissed her face. "Okay, baby. I trust you."

"Here." Ronnie handed her the cell phone that was on speaker, calling in to customer service. "Speak to a representative," she prompted after going through several dial pad-prompted responses. "Speak to a representative!"

"And you told me to chill," laughed Kenni at her demands.

"Speak to a fuckin representative!" she shouted into the phone.

Gray eyes rolled into their sockets. Kenni to the rescue. She tooted her own horn mentally, vowing to help Ronnie chill in this situation. Oblivious to her girlfriend still arguing to be transferred, she leaned over and kissed her neck.

A shudder rippled through the stud. "You better quit playin'. I ain't got no problem fuckin' you in this truck."

"Whatever," Kenni giggled. "I'm trying to help you calm down."

"You trying to start something."

"Is it working?" She smiled devilishly, pink tongue darting out to glide along her lips.

"Customer care, this is Adam. How can I be of service to you?" The cell phone chirped, interrupting whatever Ronnie's reply was going to be.

You lucky, she mouthed to Kenni. Out loud, she said, "Yeah, I need my number changed. This crazy broad I used to mess with won't stop callin' my phone, texting me hella and shit."

"Your account number, sir?"

"Two…" Her voice faltered. The sensation of Kenni's lips exploring her neck again dumped an overload of endorphins into her body, begging for sexual gratuity. "Four-five-six-nine-one-one-oh-eight. The name on the account is Ronnie Carter."

"All right. Just a minute, sir."

Pulling into Kenni's driveway, she immediately hit the lock button. "Hold up."

"Like I was getting out."

"If you know what's good for you, you most definitely not," she said, breath tickling Kenni's lips, who stared at her with lust-ridden eyes.

"Miss Carter?" the voice questioned.

"Yes, sir?" Ronnie spoke up, winking at Kenni and pinching her nipples.

"All right. Well, we'll have no problem changing your number. I've pulled up your records, and I see the numerous phone calls and text messages. Would you like to block incoming calls from that caller as well on your new number?"

"Yes," answered Kenni, playfully fighting Ronnie from unbuttoning her jeans.

"All right, well, hold on for just a second while I take care of that," he trailed off.

Taking advantage of the muted conversation, Ronnie succeeded in unbuttoning her jeans. She put the phone on the dashboard, the upper half of her body clambering over the middle console so that her lips could mesh against her partner's and her hands caressed her nipples. Pulling, prodding and pinching the nipples until they drew up into taut buds, they poked through her shirt. She reached around, unsnapping her bra and lifting the shirt covering them so she could take the dusty brown mounds into her mouth.

"Mmhmm," Kenni moaned, desire flaring through her. The continued nipple manipulation increased the moisture coating her nether region.

"Yeah, I told yo ass," Ronnie whispered, tugging her pants down. "I know you wanted this, though. Shit, me too." She plunged a finger inside of her.

"Ooh, fuck," gasped Kenni.

"Shut up." She collared her throat, undoing her own pants. "Get over here," Ronnie ordered, strap sitting up, waiting.

Biting her lip, Kenni obliged. She hovered above the strap, breasts pressed into the steering wheel. Hands grasped her waist, slamming her down onto the dick.

"Shit! Ooh, fuck, Ronnie." The moans poured from her.

"All right, Miss Carter, your new number is seven-oh-nine, four-five-nine-six. Is there anything else I can do for you today?" the representative questioned.

Back arched, ass tooted up in the air, and Ronnie digging into her, had her holding onto the steering wheel for dear mercy. Thank God for tinted windows. Screams of pleasure bubbled out of her.

"Ooh shit, baby… Fuck… I'm cummin'… I'm cummin'…" Kenni stuttered, feeling her body alert her to the news of an orgasm coming full speed her way. "Fuck, baby… Damn, I'm cummin'."

Ronnie continued the onslaught until she fragmented on her dick. Kenni caved in on herself, then began thrusting her hips backward, slowly riding out the orgasmic waves.

"Here come yo mama," Ronnie groaned.

"What?" Kenni's eyes snapped open, and she froze. She peered out the window. "Fuck."

Amused, Ronnie watched her ease the strap out of her and fall back into the passenger seat. Hurriedly, Kenni pulled her clothes back on. Opening the door, she almost tumbled, attempting to stand up. She went around to the driver's side, and Ronnie rolled the window down.

"I love you, baby," Kenni murmured, her voice dripping with lust as she pulled away from their kiss.

"I love you, too, girl."

Eyes trained on her lover, a smile plastered on her face, she watched her attempt to sort out her balance issue. When Kenni turned back around to face the truck, she brought her window down to hear.

"What's the new number?" she hollered.

"I'm callin' you now, baby. I love you."

Kenni beamed as her phone began to ring in her back pocket. She answered it. "I love you, too, baby," she responded, hurrying past her shocked mother, into the house.

*   *   *

Beaunna walked into Kenni's room and stood in the doorway, staring at her daughter, who was gathering her clothes for a shower. She cleared her throat.

"Ma!" Kenni exclaimed, clutching her chest when she turned around. "You scared me. What's up?"

"Unt-unh. You tell me what's up."

"What you mean?" She smiled nervously, butterflies taking flight in her stomach when she thought about Ronnie again.

"Either I'm going deaf and hearing things," Beaunna began, "or you said you love that boy and he love you, too."

Kenni giggled and kissed her mother's smooth forehead. "Do we need to take you to the doctor, mama?"

Laughing, she swatted her daughter's leg. "Yeah, all right, smart ass. So, tell me more about the one you love. And when are we gonna do this properly? Like, Ronnie comes over for dinner."

Kenni laughed as her subconscious corrected her mother about the *woman* she loved. "Oh my God, Ma. You met Ronnie, ain't that enough?" she giggled, thinking of how they'd met. "Soon," she added in afterthought as she thought about Ronnie. "What do you want to know?" Kenni questioned, stifling another laugh.

"Cupid then shot you dumb, baby." Beaunna rolled her eyes and shook her head. "How about how old is he? Where does he live? Does he work?"

"Yes, Ronnie works, mother. Ronnie and her friends own a club. Ronnie lives over in Threshold Apartments. Birthday four months ago, nineteen years of age."

"And you love him?"

"Yes, ma'am."

"Why?"

"Ma! I just do, okay!" Kenni whined.

"Yeah, all right. So, the sex good, huh?"

"Ma!"

"What? I saw how shaky yo legs was when you got out of the car. And unless you can't walk in heels, and I know you can, yo legs was shaky from

getting yo rocks off." The two shared a laugh.
"Seriously, Kenni," Beaunna began, "I don't have a
problem with his age. He probably has his own
apartment, and I don't have a problem with that
either, or with you having sex, but," she paused. "If
he hurts my baby again, we will have a problem."

"He won't hurt me, Ma. He love me," Kenni
stated with exasperation. They were good this time
around.

"Just because there's pain doesn't mean it
has to be physical."

"Yes, ma'am. But we love each other. We'll
work through any problems we have," she
pronounced with a hint of defiance.

"Okay, and another thing. You will be
getting on birth control. I ain't having no babies pop
outta you yet. I'm too sexy to be a grandma," she
said, standing with her hands on her hips, admiring
herself in Kenni's mirror. "What you laughing for?
You know yo mama sharp, baby."

Cutting off her laugh, Kenni leaned up off
the bed. "Ma, don't nobody say that no more."

A wink flashed at her from the mirror.
"Well, you know I'm jazzy; that's way past fine."

"Aight, Halle Berry," Kenni laughed.

Beaunna stuck her tongue out at her
daughter as she strutted out the room. "I'm glad you
happy."

Kenni grinned, thinking the same to herself.
*   *   *

"Yo, Shyna!" yelled Ronnie, banging on
Shyna's apartment door before continuing to her
own apartment, leaving the front door open. She

grabbed a beer out of the refrigerator and came back around the corner to see Shyna barely clothed, standing in her doorway. "Come in."

"Oh, I'm allowed in now?" questioned Shyna.

"Did you ask the last time?" Ronnie shot at Shyna, who smiled. Annoyance made her release a tsk sound. "Man, come in and sit down."

Shyna strutted in, smirking, taking a seat on the couch with her legs crossed. "Yes, Ronnie?" she replied, opening her legs and closing them seductively.

Stalking over towards her, Ronnie paused, leaning down in her face. "Look, Shyna, all these games and shit you playin', they stop now. Right now." She closed Shyna's legs with her hands. "I'm tellin' you flat out I love Kenni. I don't wanna be with you. I'm sorry for how things turned out. You a beautiful woman, so I know it's a nigga or a bitch out there for you." Ronnie rose off of her.

"Aww, thank you," Shyna smiled, standing back.

"Did you hear everything else I said?" she asked with confusion.

"Yeah, and you know what, Ronnie, you right. There is somebody out there for me." She stood up. "I'll see you around."

"No the fuck you won't."

"You will. Ron, you live here. I'm sure I'll see you and your lil bitch again. I'm honestly lookin' forward to it," she grinned, heading out of the apartment.

"Fuckin crazy bitch," Ronnie mumbled, locking up behind her.

Chapter 7

It had been a month with no drama, only bonding and building their relationship. Kenni stretched out onto her bed, content with the way things had been going lately. She and Ronnie were solid after withstanding the test of lust.

"Guess what, bra?" Jeremy barged into her room, interrupting her basking in the serenity of her relationship.

"You saved time and money by switching to Geico?" Kenni joked sarcastically.

"No, asshole." He ruffled her hair. "I met somebody."

"Ooh, look at you back dating, brother." She smacked his hand away from her. "Hopefully, she's not a whore."

"Nah, she ain't shit like that." He took a seat on her bed, a dopey grin slapped on his face. "Baby sexy as fuck, though. She know exactly what to do with that mouth, and how to throw that ass back."

"Eww," Kenni squealed, swatting him with a pillow. "Jeremy, I don't wanna hear about that."

Jeremy chuckled. "Yeah, whatever. Act like you ain't doing nothing. Mama told me she walked in on you."

"Oh my God!"

"And y'all ain't stop when she walked in. I ain't never been caught," he boasted while laughing.

"Anyways! Me and Ronnie good. This last month with her has been everything. I love her so much!"

"Sprung ass."

"Fuck you, I'm in love," she stated matter of factly. "You sprung."

"So?" he questioned, grinning big like the Joker.

Little sister bells started ringing in Kenni's head. She stared at him shrewdly, observing his body language. "So you like her, like her then? When you bringing her over? I'll have Ronnie come, too."

"We can do that. Let's do that Friday."

"Okay, bet. And I'm glad you done with yo whole lil dyke-bashing bullshit," she mentioned slyly, wanting to see how he'd react.

"Oh, it's still fuck that gay shit. I love you, though, but fuck them dyke bitches," Jeremy stated, lacking his usual passion when speaking on his homophobia.

"Whatever. Can't wait to meet your lil friend," Kenni told him sincerely, thinking of what kind of woman had brought about this change of heart in her brother. *If she hurt him, I'ma hurt her,* she promised herself.

"You gonna like her."

"I better, or you can't be with her!"

"Shut up all that yapping." He pushed her down on the bed and walked out of the room, whistling.

"This nigga whistling," she chortled to herself and grabbed her phone. She quickly told Ronnie about the new dinner plans for Friday, but also about Jeremy's new behavior because of a woman.

*   *   *

Later on that week, Ronnie sat across from Kenni at a restaurant. It was her seventeenth birthday. Ronnie had already surprised her by standing outside her truck at school with candy, flowers, and jewelry. The restaurant the two were dining in was an upscale joint full of couples, dinner parties, and special candlelit moments.

Sitting across from her girlfriend, she couldn't wipe the grin off her face if you paid her to. Butterflies still soared in her stomach from all of the romantic gestures displayed. She loved the balloons attached to the table, the necklace adorning her neck was a real gold herringbone, and she had earrings to match.

"What you cheesing for, baby?" Ronnie smirked.

"'Cause, baby, this like the best birthday I ever had, and you made it official." She waved her left hand where a ring stood up proudly.

"Hell yeah. I had to. You my baby, and I love you. I had to do it big for yo birthday, and I'ma marry you when you turn eighteen next year." Kenni's eyes ballooned at the statement, but Ronnie killed the sentiment, jutting her chin in the direction of a bald man at a table with a colorful female. "Baby, look at dude right there. Nigga look like he can't stand the bitch he with. Like they only together 'cause she lied and got him believing they got like six kids together."

Words went in one ear and out the other. "I love you, Ronnie," she gushed.

A tug on her heartstrings prompted her to lean across the table and peck Kenni on the lips sweetly. "I love you, too, baby."

"I gotta go to the bathroom, baby," Kenni muttered, extracting her hand.

"Aight. I'ma talk about people till you get back."

"Don't get us kicked out," she warned.

"Man, watch out. Gone to the bathroom, baby." Ronnie shooed her away, smiling and perusing the environment for victims.

Kenni pressed a kiss to her lips once more, then walked off in search of the bathroom. She spied it after walking around, trying to find it, and when she hit the corner, her heel slipped. A pair of chocolate hands grabbed her before her ass could meet the ground.

"You good, lil baby, I got you," her captor murmured, eyes roving over her.

"Thanks," Kenni muttered, sidestepping the stud to make it to her destination.

"Hold on, lil mama." The stud caged her wrist. "Slow down. What's yo name, baby?"

Huffing, Kenni told her calmly with a smile, "Look, I'm not interested in whatever you got to say. I'm happy where I'm at." She fluttered her other hand with the ring on it.

"Fuck all of that. Everybody need a friend, and yo nigga ain't doing too good if that's what she got you to show off. You deserve better," she attempted to kiss her hand.

"The fuck," Kenni snatched her hand away. "You better gone with that bullshit!"

The stud's head cocked back and as the first curse word dropped from her lips a brown skin hand clapped her on the shoulder spinning her around. "Fuck you want with my girl nigga?" Ronnie growled at her.

"Shit, it's what yo girl want with me."

Lips twisted up, jaw twitching, Ronnie's eyes sought Kenni's. She stared into them for a second until she felt the resolve of their relationship coursing through her, pacifying any doubt attempting to spark. "Nah, she don't want yo ass, nigga. But I suggest you back the fuck away from both of us. I ain't above fuckin' you up in this fuckin' restaurant, nigga."

Eyes going between the couple, she scoffed. "I don't fight over no females, bra. That shit lame." She walked away.

Tension ridden, body itching for an altercation, Ronnie tracked her until she couldn't see her anymore. Upon entering the bathroom, the toilet flushed, and Kenni came out of a stall. She threw herself on Ronnie, planting kisses all over her face.

"Girl, you better chill before you get fucked in this bathroom," Ronnie warned, hands roaming up and down her body.

She laid another kiss on her lips. "Nope, not in the bathroom. I'm yo lady, not a whore."

"Damn right you is."

"You ain't wonder if she was lying?" Kenni questioned, washing her hands at the sink.

"Nah." Ronnie shook her head. "I ain't got to. We solid, ain't no lies between us. You all I want and I know I'm all you want. If we ain't got trust, we ain't got nothing, and I trust you with my life, baby."

Pure happiness washed over Kenni. The muscles in her face expanded into a grin. This was one birthday she would never forget, she thought, envisioning their future of what was to come.

"Come on, let's go see if our food ready." Ronnie led her out of the bathroom, holding the door open for her.

*   *   *

Skewing the bar, cleaning and checking bottles while writing down numbers and labels, Ronnie moved methodically, head bouncing to the beat. A ringtone brought Ronnie to a halt. She pulled her phone out of her pocket. "What's good, baby?"

"Hey, baby. Why you ain't been answering the phone? I been calling you all day," Kenni responded.

"I been at work, baby," Ronnie told her, resting her back against the bar. "And I ain't know you was calling. I just took my phone off the charger."

"Well, what time you coming?" she questioned impatiently. Her insides tightened in anticipation of seeing her.

"I'm coming soon as I'm done here, baby. Shit, I'm almost done, for real. This the last lil shit I gotta do. Gimme like five minutes, and I'll be on my way to you."

"Okay, baby, hurry up and finish then."

Ronnie chuckled. "Yup."

"Love you, baby."

"Love you, too, baby. Bye." The two hung up, and Ronnie smiled, then turned around to see all of her family and co-workers staring at her. "Fuck y'all lookin' at?"

T shook her head. "Lovey-dovey ass muthafuckas," she cajoled to the amusement of everyone. The middle finger Ronnie flashed her didn't deter her from the banter. "Shit, between you and Lil Buddy, I might find me a lil baby to settle down with."

"I'ma get you a pocket pussy. You can call it whatever you want, and she ain't got a face. Or do you want the face? I can get you a doll," Kim jested.

Ignoring the wisecracks between her family, Ronnie quickly finished the inventory list. She'd been busy with the club the last few days and hadn't seen Kenni. Anxiety rode her movements.

"Where you going?" Jay called out to her after she had input the list into the computer system.

"Shit, I'm gone. I might fuck with y'all later, though," Ronnie called, heading for the door.

"Well, aye, hold on, muthafucka," T said. "Let's smoke real quick, bra."

Collectively, the group congregated in the lobby and stepped outside to the patio of the business. Blunts were sparked and passed around. Ronnie's leg tapped a rhythm from her seat at a bench-style table.

"Aight, I'm out." She jumped to her feet.

Kim and Jay immediately began chortling. T took the blunt she offered and said, "Man, chill, yo. Yo lil baby ain't going nowhere."

"Man, fuck what you talking about. I'm trying to get to my baby, man," Ronnie told her, striding out the fence to the parking lot.

"You picking somebody up?" T spoke to a woman walking towards them.

The light-skinned female ignored T and stood in Ronnie's way. "What's up, daddy?"

"Married," Ronnie told her tersely, sidestepping and breezing past her without a look back.

"Shit, I ain't!" T called out to the female who meandered back to a car idling in the parking lot. "How you doing, beautiful?"

"Nigga, that's Sean little sister," Jay told her, talking about one of their employees.

"Ron, that's why you ain't holla? Because of Sean?" T instigated over the distance.

The sound of a whip snapping permeated the public noise until Ronnie put her truck window down. She hollered, "Man, I told y'all I love Kenni.

Nigga, fuck them hoes," and sped the fuck off, leaving tire tracks.

*   *   *

"I ain't ticklish," Ronnie denied, smiling and lightly smacking Kenni's hands away from her body.

"Then why you smacking my hands away?" she said, attempting to tickle her again.

"Because it's fuckin weird, yo," Ronnie tapped her hands again.

Kenni stomped her foot, "Just hold your arms up and let me try."

Slowly, Ronnie's arms lifted into the air, but before her fingers could make contact, she tackled her onto the bed. "Why, when I can just tickle you?"

"Okay! Okay!" Kenni wheezed between laughter. "I tap! I tap!"

Ronnie rolled off of her. It took a second, but once Kenni caught her breath, she straddled her. "Now, lift yo arms up." Her hand smacked her chest.

Pinning her arms down on the bed, she grinned. "Nope."

Rolling her eyes in defeat, Kenni leaned down. "Fine. Give me a kiss then."

"Nope," she told her playfully and thrust her pelvis up to smack against Kenni's.

Eyes bucked, and biting down on her lip, she rocked her pelvis down on the stud beneath her.

"Time for dinner," Beaunna called out to the couple, dousing the flames of their sexual appetite.

Irritation bubbled up in Kenni's soul. "Damn, I wish we was at yo house," she pouted, trailing her hand down Ronnie's chest.

"Why?" Ronnie asked, fingering her nipples.

Again, she smacked her chest. "You know why." Kenni rolled off her, standing up and extending her hand to Ronnie. "Come on, I wanna see what this girl look like that got my brother's nose open."

"So? I don't," Ronnie told her blandly, not moving.

"Ronnie!" She stomped her foot. "Come on." When she didn't budge, Kenni rolled her out of bed.

Keeping up the act, Ronnie allowed herself to fall to the floor, lying there like an invalid, staring at her girlfriend. Kenni shook her head and walked away. She waited to see if she was going to come back for her, but when she didn't, Ronnie shot to her feet, following her, prompting Kenni to take off towards the kitchen.

"Is this a fuckin' joke?" Kenni snapped from the entry of the kitchen.

"Girl, move. I thought you was nosey," Ronnie jested, coming up behind her, hands resting on her hips.

Shifting positions so that Ronnie could have a view over her shoulder, Kenni waited for the ball to drop. Beaunna and Jeremy stared at them, mirroring confused expressions. And who was sitting next to Jeremy, smiling? Shyna.

"Nice to meet you," Shyna greeted them both. "Jeremy told me a lot about you," she addressed Kenni.

Unable to process what she was seeing, Kenni gaped at her. Finally, she blurted, "Are you fucking insane? Like, do you suffer from a mental condition?"

"Kenni!" Beaunna rebuked her language and attitude.

"What?" Her eyes darted back to Shyna, then back to Ronnie. "Baby, is this a joke or she real live crazy as fuck?"

"Sis," Jeremy chuckled, standing up. His facial expression threatened her to stop her shenanigans and promised retribution. "Quit fuckin' with her and sit down." His arm draped across her shoulder. He forcibly steered her to a seat next to Shyna, quietly whispering in her ear, "Don't fuck this up for me. I like her."

"Kenni, right?" Shyna smiled encouragingly. "No, I'm not crazy or insane, sweetie, but I really do like your brother.

"You a fuckin' weirdo."

"Kenni, fuckin' quit, bra! Damn!" Jeremy fumed. "She not Monica, bra. She not crazy, and she not on that dyke shit! Fuckin chill and be happy for me."

"Jeremy—"

"No, fuck what you talking about! I chilled with this lil shit." He fanned his hand from Ronnie to Kenni. "I ain't said nothing about it, so shut the fuck up and be happy for me."

"You know what? Fuck it." She crossed her arms over her chest. "You got it, big brother. Congrats."

Puzzled, Beaunna watched the exchange, fully aware that some pieces were missing. "Soo, dinner?" she suggested, letting it go. "Shyna brought green beans."

*   *   *

Later on that night, Kenni lay in bed, curled up on Ronnie's chest. The TV was on, showing a movie, but the movie was watching them instead of the opposite. Her mind was still reeling from discovering Jeremy's mystery woman.

"That shit's fucking weird. She crazy, like really."

"Maaannn," Ronnie chuckled. "Weird as fuck, yo. She real live a lil crazy bitch. I thought she poisoned those green beans, for real. But shit, like you said, fuck it."

"He like it, we love it," she quipped, knowing her next words. "Do you think I should say something to him when he get back?" Kenni pondered out loud after a moment's pause.

Quietly mulling over the question and situation at hand, she didn't answer right away. "Nah. He happy," Ronnie concluded. "And besides, this might not even last that long. At least we ain't gotta deal with her crazy ass. If it do go the distance, fuck it, everybody need love. He happy."

"Okay, well, we ain't doing this dinner shit no more." Shared laughter between the couple was cut off abruptly when they noticed Beaunna in the doorframe. "What's up, mama?"

"Anything you want to tell me?" her mother asked with an eyebrow raised.

"Nah." Kenni glanced at her girlfriend. "Like what?"

A smile toyed on Beaunna's lips. Why her daughter couldn't come right out and tell her the truth, she didn't know, but she continued to play along, just like she would with this new situation. "How do you really know that girl? Shyna."

"I don't! But I don't like her for my brother."

"Why is that?"

"I just don't. Her vibe was off," Kenni sniffed, looking away with her nose in the air.

"Yeah, whatever. You know half of that money he blow on you about to get spent on her is what it really is," she said on a hunch.

"He better not!" Kenni seethed to the amusement of her girlfriend and mother.

"Spoiled ass," Beaunna teased. "Ronnie, what time are you leaving?"

Parent code meant it was time to go when you heard that, so Ronnie rose off the bed reluctantly. "Right now, actually." She pressed a kiss on the side of Kenni's pouting face.

"Goodnight, Ronnie. Kenni." She pointedly looked at her daughter, whose face was twisted up, frowning.

Huffing, puffing, and dragging her feet, she followed Ronnie to the door for more parting kisses. She watched her pull off with her bottom lip poked out.

"Girl, goodnight. I'm done with you and your shenanigans," her mother told her when she entered the living room.

Kenni sucked her teeth and walked off to her room wordlessly.

*   *   *

"Oh my God, he is just everything," Shyna gushed to a perplexed Ronnie.

Ronnie had not too long ago gotten home when Shyna knocked on her door, then invited herself in with a dreamy sigh. She pulled a blunt from the middle of her tits, lit it, took one drag, and sighed to herself, smiling.

"I didn't know he was Kenni's brother at first, but I figured it was a perfect way to fuck with Kenni if I dated her brother, then I really got to know him." She continued to smile, staring off in a dreamlike trance. "I'm sorry about everything that happened between us, but I'm really happy I met Jeremy. He fills that void inside of me that's been left." Her voice faltered, but Ronnie knew what she meant since she'd lost her father figure and fiancé all at one time several months ago. "Like, I really like him. He's so sweet, but rough all at the same time."

"Well, that's what's up," Ronnie told her, hitting the blunt she'd passed. "Congratulations."

"Thank you!" Shyna beamed. "I do need a favor, though. Like, I need your word on it."

Suspicion flooded Ronnie, but she questioned anyway, "What?"

"Promise not to say anything to him about you and me or Kenni. Hell, everything. That's why

I acted like that. I want to start fresh. I'm done being petty to yo lil girlfriend."

"Aight." Ronnie smirked and wanted to call bullshit, but opted to say, "You got my word. Me and Kenni already talked about it after y'all left. We ain't gonna say nothing."

"Thank you so much! Damn, it feels so good. It's like I'm finally healing."

"Well, I'm happy for you, you and him," Ronnie nodded.

"Thank you."

Shyna's phone rang in her pocket, and she lit the fuck up like Fourth of July fireworks in the night sky. "Aight, Ron. I'll holla at you later."

Filled with disbelief and mirth, Ronnie stared at her closed door. "Man, lemme tell Lil Buddy." She grabbed her phone, chuckling.

"What's up, fool?" Chantel's voice floated over the phone.

"Nigga," she exaggerated the word. "Nigga, you won't believe what the fuck happened to me today."

"Yo girl learned to fight and kicked yo ass?"

Ronnie laughed off the sarcastic comment and quickly filled her in on the details.

"Nigga…" Chantel dragged the word out between bursts of laughter. "What the fuck? Aye, fuck it. Good riddance, G. At least you ain't gotta deal with her crazy ass no more."

"Man, I already know it. I dodged a bullet with that one. Na mean? I think she might have started shit out with him on some messy shit, but she genuinely like that cornball-ass dude, too."

"Aye, fuck it, bro. Shit, let her ass be, nigga. You got yo girl, and she got yo girl brother," Chantel cackled.

"I know, right? Shit crazy."

"But for real, Ron, y'all let her ass have that slice of heaven. Stay outta grown people shit."

"Nigga, I'm too good on that bitch. I wish them nothing but the fuckin' best," Ronnie declared.

"All right, nigga. I'ma get at you. It's date night."

"Y'all old asses," Ronnie chuckled.

"Catch up, lil nigga. You got you one now. No excuses."

"I'm older than you!"

"Barely. All right, fool."

"Aight, fool."

*   *   *

"Baby, can you come pick me up, please? I'm about to die," Kenni dished out two weeks later, not bothering to greet her, but getting right to the point. "I'm staying for the weekend."

"What's wrong with my baby?"

"Fuckin' Jeremy and Shyna. They been over here all week, it's disgusting," she complained.

Snickering, Ronnie replied, "You already talked to yo mama about it?"

"Ma, I'm going to Ronnie's for the weekend!" she hollered.

"I'm going, too. I'm tired of them at this point, and they just left," Beaunna joked.

"Ma, kick them out," Kenni begged.

"He's happy," she sighed. "I would never rob either of you of your happiness, whether you were bi, gay, straight or in love with a blow-up doll."

"That's yo inch. You better take it and tell her you a lesbian," Ronnie whispered over the phone line.

"Not yet," Kenni told her, smiling at her mother. "I'ma go get ready."

"Aight, baby. I'll call you when I'm outside. Be dressed, and I need my shit braided."

"Okay."

Phone in pocket, Ronnie grabbed her keys off the counter, heading out. In the hallway, she smiled at Shyna exiting her apartment, dressed to kill with the phone glued to her ear.

"Look at you, all glowing and shit," Ronnie commented about the glow of her skin, due to the happiness that oozed from her.

The only indication that she heard her was a smile. Other than that, Shyna hurried out the front door. Heading out of the door also, Ronnie took no offense at her mannerisms. She nodded at her sitting in Jeremy's car, who sent her mean mugs. She laughed to herself. If he only knew what she knew. *Shit, he can have her!* Ronnie thought, cranking her engine and flying out the parking lot to pick up Kenni.

Forty-five minutes later, her mission was accomplished with the bonus that Kenni had also washed and conditioned her hair and greased her scalp.

"Quit yankin' my shit." Ronnie swatted her leg before positioning her game controller back in both hands.

"Quit moving yo head," Kenni retorted. She reached over her shoulder, pressing a few buttons randomly on the game controller.

"Girl, quit playing. You see all these opps coming at me?"

"Whatever." Kenni kissed the side of her cheek.

Someone rapped on the front door, killing their conversation. Kenni's hands fell away from her head. Ronnie stood, going to the door cautiously, stuffing her gun in the back of her jeans.

"You expecting anybody?" Kenni questioned.

"Nah."

"It's probably my brother."

"Why you say that?"

"Because I ain't tell him you and Shyna was neighbors, and I don't think she did either because of his face when we pulled in."

"What's up?" Ronnie greeted her brother, standing on the opposite side of the door with a scowl. "It's yo brother." She spun on her heels to give the siblings space to talk, but his words made her halt.

"Focus on my sister, but don't talk to my bitch," he bit out, glaring harshly at her. "I don't give a fuck if y'all neighbors."

"Nigga." Face clouded with exasperation, she turned to face him. "Listen, man, first of all, bra—"

"Fuck what you talking about. I said—"

What he was going to say was never finished because Ronnie slammed the door in his face. She went back into the living room and dropped down between Kenni's legs again so she could resume her hair.

"What's wrong, baby?" Kenni posed.

"Yo brother goofy ass trying to check me about Shyna."

Jumping in, Kenni charged across the hall to bang on Shyna's door. Jeremy opened the door.

"What?" he growled.

"Really?" she screeched. "Why the fuck did you come over there on that bullshit? Stay yo ass over here."

"Tell yo dyke not to talk to my fuckin' woman!" Jeremy roared, pulling the front door close.

"She ain't said nothing to her!"

"Yes, she did! I fuckin' heard her. You wasn't even there."

Spinning around to accost Ronnie, who was standing in the doorway of her own apartment, she fired at her, "Why are you talking to her?"

"I'm grown as fuck, shorty," she expressed. "I talk to whoever the fuck I want to."

"Oh, you do?" Kenni shrilled rhetorically. "Fuck you, Ronnie! Take me home!"

"No, my fuckin' hair ain't done! I told her ass she was glowing because she fuckin' happy. It's called being polite. She still my fuckin' neighbor and shit," Ronnie argued.

"I don't care!" Her volume carried down the hallway of the apartment. "I wanna go home!"

"No! You gonna finish my fuckin' hair!"

"No, the fuck I'm not!"

"Kenni, I swear to God—" Ronnie began.

"Swear to God, what?" Jeremy interjected. "Go get yo shit. I'm taking you home, sis."

"No, the fuck you're not. I don't even wanna see yo fuckin' face right now, either."

"Go get yo shit," he demanded.

"I'm not fuckin' going with you."

"You ain't staying here with this dyke," Jeremy countered stubbornly.

"I bet I do," she retorted, filled to the brim with stubbornness, turning her back to him.

Her brother reached out and grabbed her arm. Kenni yanked her arm out of his grip. Shyna opened her front door and surveyed her surroundings. All eyes went to her.

Stepping out into the hallway, she caressed his arm. "Jer."

He huffed and went back into the apartment without a word and Shyna on his heels.

"That was fuckin' weird!" Kenni spat and went back into Ronnie's house. "Sit down so I can finish it," she ordered.

Chapter 8

"Mama, Jeremy don't even live here. Why do he always bring her over here? Kick them out or something. You don't even like her," Kenni pleaded with her mother for the umpteenth time, following her around the kitchen.

"Who said I don't like her?" Beaunna laughed, adding seasonings to a pot of food on the stove.

"Me," she told her. "You like her?"

"There's something about her I don't like," admitted Beaunna, sitting down at the dining room table. "But I don't know what that is yet. Like I told you both, I won't stand in the way of y'all happiness."

"But they're soooo annoying," Kenni complained.

Laughter belted out of Beaunna. "That they are," she finally ceded.

"So, just kick her out then! Ban her from coming, then they won't even be here."

"Kenni," she groaned.

"Mama, he don't even live here! Put yo foot down and make him entertain her at his house!"

"I am not forbidding that girl from being over here. Jeremy's happy with her."

"Fuck her!"

"Fuck who?" Jeremy asked, coming into the house.

"Yo girlfriend! I'm tired of seeing y'all together. Why you don't just go to her house or take her to yo house? Why you always bring her here?"

"I fuckin' like her!" His chest puffed out. "I'm happy! This ain't even yo fuckin' house. Mama ain't said shit."

"Mama think y'all disgusting, too, she just don't wanna say nothing to fuck up yo happiness," Kenni snipped. "I don't care, be happy, but be happy with her at yo house."

Like a lance had pierced his chest, his shoulders drooped slightly. "Mama, for real?"

"Jeremy, I want you and Kenni happy above anything else. I understand why you bring her over here, but you can't force bonds, baby. You just have to let them develop." Soft, honest advice given in a firm, patient, motherly tone appealed to dissuade the tension in the air.

"But they won't because no one likes her," Kenni stabbed him verbally again.

"Kenni!" Beaunna reprimanded.

"I do!" Jeremy boomed, his eyes blazing in a fury.

"And you the only one!" she shouted. "And I bet you wouldn't like her if you knew she fucked with girls."

"She had a fuckin' fiancé before me," he sneered. "Nice try, wrong guy."

"And truth and a lie mixed together is still

bullshit." Kenni turned to face her mother, who was watching the two bicker back and forth.

"Fuck you!"

"Don't be mad at me because I know her truth and her lie," she said simply, unfazed by his anger. "Is the food done yet, mama? I'm hungry."

Jeremy stormed out of the house, slamming the front door on his way out.

"Was you telling the truth?" interrogated Beaunna, staring at her daughter, disapproval seeping from her.

"Maybe," Kenni smirked.

Shaking her head, Beaunna turned the stove off and walked out of the kitchen, murmuring, "God don't like ugly, and He not too fond of pretty, either."

*   *   *

The music blared in Ronnie's apartment mingled with the sounds of the shooting game she was playing. Over all the commotion, you could still hear shouting voices from across the hall. Mostly Jeremy's, but every now and then, Shyna yelled.

Glaring at the front door, she picked up the remote to her stereo system and cranked the music up to its max level. Satisfied, she grabbed her game controller. Not even five minutes later, Jeremy's baritone soared over all of her noise again.

"The fuck, man?" Ronnie hopped up, throwing her controller down. She strode across the hall, banging and kicking the door.

"What?" Jeremy ripped the door open. "The fuck is you here for?"

A deep breath to calm herself, and she started to ask him to keep it down. "Bra—" The door slammed shut in her face. "Muthafucka." She went back to banging on the door. Ronnie wiggled the doorknob, discovered it was unlocked, and stepped into the war zone. "Can y'all bring it the fuck down?!" she yelled over the two. "Damn, the whole fuckin' apartment complex and outside can fuckin hear y'all arguing. Don't nobody wanna hear that shit."

"Sorry, Ronnie. We—" Shyna began.

"Get the fuck out! Nobody asked for yo fuckin' opinion!" Jeremy spewed.

"Nigga, this ain't even yo fuckin' apartment!" she shrieked. "Shut the fuck up! I can't even hear my fuckin' game and music over y'all fuckin ass!"

"Get the fuck out!" Jeremy yelled.

"My nigga, this is not yo spot!" She turned to Shyna. "Can you please get yo nigga to lower his fuckin' voice, yo, so I can leave?"

"My bad, Ronnie—"

"Don't talk to my bitch!" he yelled at Ronnie, then rounded on Shyna. "The fuck is you apologizing for? You fuckin' me or the dyke? Shut the fuck up when fuckin' men talking."

"Nigga, yo dumb ass don't even know how to talk to a woman. That's why she talkin because yo ass obviously don't comprehend shut the fuck up. Damn, I don't wanna hear this shit!"

"So, why is you here? Leave. Get out, muthafucka," he bucked. "Ol' confused-ass bitch, don't know if you wanna be a bitch or a nigga. Sensitive-ass fuckin' dyke—"

"My nigga." She took a menacing step towards him. "I ain't gonna be too many more dykes. Fuckin' chill, that's all the fuck I'm asking."

"Dyke be gone." Jeremy waved her off. "Take that dyke shit across the hall."

A quick step forward and a jab flew Jeremy's way. He leaned out of the way of it, and Shyna jumped between them, pushing the stud back. Ronnie grabbed her wrists to remove them from her chest.

"Ron, please," Shyna begged. "We'll keep it down, just go back to your apartment."

Glancing between the two with his head cocked, Jeremy uttered, "The fuck?" He snatched Shyna up by her arms. "Is you fuckin' this dyke? What the fuck was that?"

"No, I'm not! I'm fuckin' you!" Shyna snapped, pulling herself out of his grip. "Ron, go, please. Thank you."

Ronnie nodded and started to leave the apartment.

"Nah, Ron, stay," Jeremy countered. "You wanna fuck this bitch and my sister?" he taunted as she retreated. "Aye, bitch, you hear me talking to you?" When she didn't bite, he sneered, "Fuckin' hoe-ass dyke."

Control splintered, Ronnie rushed him, shoving him into the wall behind him. "Nigga, I already fucked yo bitch," she lashed out, spewing the truth. "You getting my leftovers, muthafucka!"

she snarled, releasing him and stepping away. "Hoe-ass nigga. Do something, muthafucka."

Shyna punched her in the jaw, making her head snap to the side, screaming, "Fuck you, Ronnie!"

Her mouth moved, gathering the blood from her busted lip. She spat it out and cocked back in retaliation, but Jeremy snatched her up by the throat and threw her over the couch, sending her crashing into the table in front of it. He sneered down at her and surveyed the area, looking for Shyna, who'd pulled a magic trick by disappearing from the living room. Ronnie got up gingerly, watching Jeremy recede to the bedroom. Slowly, he backed out, hands up in the air. Shyna stood in front of him with a gun aimed at him.

Tears fled down her face like a flood as her eyes and barrel sought Ronnie. "I specifically fuckin' asked you," her voice faltered. "I fuckin' told you how happy and complete he made me feel."

"Shyna, my—"

"Shut the fuck up!" Shyna hollered, taking the safety off the gun.

"So, it's true, huh?" Jeremy concluded. "That's what Kenni meant?"

A bark of a laugh came from Shyna. "That little fuckin' bitch." She took a deep breath and gazed at Jeremy. "It was before you, Jeremy. That don't change how I feel about you. Tell him," she insisted to Ronnie, jutting the gun in the air at her.

"Save that shit." He cut Ronnie off. "I'm good, ma." He turned and started to walk out.

"Jeremy!" Shyna screamed. "Jeremy! I swear to God." She panned the gun in his direction.

He glanced over his shoulder at her. "This yo fault, yo mess," Jeremy said. "You love me, though, right? I'm supposed to believe that? And you upping on me? What you gonna do, shoot me in the back? Spare yo dyke and shoot the nigga you said you love, huh? Fuck you, do it then. I don't give a fuck about you or this bullshit no more. Just remember all this shit yo fault." He turned and walked out the front door.

"Dammit," Shyna cried.

Words of declaration that she wouldn't get involved in Shyna's love life spun around in Ronnie's head. She and Kenni had both promised they wouldn't. Regret blossomed inside of her. "Aye… damn, man. Look, I'm sorry, Shyna," she apologized. "My temper got the best of me. I fucked up, yo. My bad."

"Shut up!" Shyna fired a shot. "You and that fuckin' lil bitch!" she screamed and fired another shot into the wall, next to Ronnie.

"Shyna, bra, chill!" Ronnie shouted. "I swear to God, yo, if you hit me. Man, put that shit up, yo! I said my bad, damn!"

"Fuck you and yo fuckin' bad!" Shyna screamed at her. "Get the fuck out before I stop missing on purpose."

Not needing to be told twice, Ronnie dashed across the hall to the safety of her apartment. Shyna crumbled where she stood, sobbing long, body-racking cries. The gun rubbed against her head. Rampant thoughts of her father's funeral, her fiancé's funeral, the feelings Jeremy provoked within her, and Jeremy stating he didn't care about her anymore fucked with her. Her stomach heaved, and chills brought goosebumps on her body. Alone, she cried. Alone, Shyna thought. She fired off one last shot.

*   *   *

"Wake up," Kenni said into her phone, dialing Ronnie's number again. "Wake uuuuppp. Hey, baby," she perked up, grinning.

"What's popping, baby?" Ronnie greeted her. "You ready?"

"You know I'm ready. I was ready last night, but you had to work," Kenni pouted.

Ronnie peeked out her bedroom window, gazing into the parking lot. Shyna's car wasn't outside, and she hoped to hell they didn't run into each other again after the episode last night. "Yeah, well, I'm on the way now, baby."

"Okay, baby. I'll see you in a little bit." She blew kisses into the phone.

"Going to play dyke?" Jeremy scowled from Kenni's open bedroom door, where he leaned against the door frame.

"Really?" Kenni rolled her eyes. "We back on that, huh? Whatever, Jeremy. Where yo hoe at? Go play house with her."

"Fuck that bitch, and fuck you, too," he bit out.

"I tried to tell you, bro."

His eyes crashed to slits, malice sparking. "Yeah, I guess it's no great way to say that the bitch I was fuckin', yo dyke used to fuck. So, that bitch a hoe and yo dyke a hoe because she fucked on her, too. At least I cut the hoe off."

"Fuck you, Jeremy!" she hollered. "You know we was broken up!"

Jeremy chuckled and scoffed at her disdainfully. "Yo stupid ass. She was fuckin' her and trying to get back with you. Shit, they still fuckin' around."

"No the fuck they not!"

"Why you think I broke up with her, dummy?" he shouted in her face, spraying her with spit. "Yo dyke told me she fucked her, still fuckin' her and fuckin' my sister. It wasn't a one and done, stupid ass."

Unable to contain the rage and insecurity, she open-palm slapped her brother across the face. "Fuck you! She fucked her once! ONCE! We was broken up! Just because you sad, don't mean you get to fuck up my happiness!" Snatching her bookbag off the ground, she bulldozed past him.

"Stupid bitch," he snapped back, following her to the front of the house.

"You Mama's only bitch, I'm her daughter," Kenni retorted, barging out through the front door.

Surprisingly, Jeremy let her seethe silently on the porch. She stood, waiting for Ronnie to pull up with her bag thrown over her shoulder, foot tapping a rhythm on the ground beneath her. When she finally pulled up, Kenni didn't even wait for her to park but jumped into the car.

"Just drive."

"I was gonna do that anyway," Ronnie told her. "The fuck wrong with you? I ain't get no love or nothing."

Her leg stopped bouncing, and Kenni exhaled harshly. She pecked her on the lips and sat back in her seat. She didn't even register Ronnie asking her what kind of kiss that was, though it did register in the dim recesses of her mind. Her brain, however, was only attuned to Jeremy's accusations. She heard his words in her ears over and over. A part of her felt slightly bad for slapping him. They'd never crossed that bridge before, but he deserved it, she rationalized. His words painted a picture in her head, and she saw Ronnie fucking Shyna in different places and positions. Kenni's hand flew out, smacking Ronnie in the face.

"What the fuck?" Ronnie snarled, jerking the steering wheel so she could get back in the right lane.

"Fuck you, Ronnie." Her hand connected with Ronnie's face again.

Ronnie's hand flashed from the steering wheel and wrapped itself around Kenni's throat. "Quit fuckin' hittin' me! Don't you see I'm fuckin' drivin'?" she barked, tightening her hand around her neck. "What the fuck is wrong with you? Don't put yo fuckin' hands on me, Kenni!" she roared, throwing her into the passenger window.

Kenni's head snapped and rolled as her words took flight. "You gonna hit me, Ronnie? Hit me then. I ain't scared," she challenged as Ronnie pulled into a gas station parking lot. "Take me home. What the fuck is we doing here?"

"What the fuck is wrong with you?"

"You still fuckin' Shyna? How many times did you fuck that bitch?"

"For real? You back on that?"

"How many times did you fuck her, Ronnie? And is you still fuckin' that bitch?"

"One time!" Ronnie roared. "I fucked her once! And I don't want that bitch! I only want yo fuckin crazy ass!"

"Don't lie to me!" She slapped her again. "You still fuckin' that bitch? You told my brother you fuckin' us both!" She hit her again.

"Listen," Ronnie growled, grabbing her by her throat. "I ain't gonna keep letting you fuckin' hit me." She flexed her fingers. "I ain't told yo brother shit. I fucked that bitch one time, one fuckin' time, and I don't want that bitch. I don't wanna fuck that bitch again. I want to fuck you and be in a fuckin' relationship with yo crazy ass." Her hands clenched around Kenni's throat until she pawed at her hand frantically to let her go.

Finally released, Kenni sucked in air, rubbing her neck and eyeing Ronnie warily. She rasped out, "Then why the fuck Jeremy say that?"

"He in his fuckin' feelings. Him and Shyna broke up last night."

"And how the fuck do you know?" she glared at her accusingly. "I just fuckin' found out."

"I was there." She saw Kenni's mouth open and stated harshly, "Shut the fuck up and just listen. I was playing the game, and they was arguing. I turned the TV up, music, everything, and could still hear they ass, so I went over there and told them to shut the fuck up. Yo brother started acting like yo brother, talkin' mad shit, acting the fuck outta crazy and shit. Finally, I let the cat out the bag and told him I fucked already."

"Oh my God," Kenni groaned. "Why would you do that?"

"Who planted the fuckin' seed?" she fired back. "What the fuck did you say to him before all that?"

"That his bitch a liar and a fuckin' whore."

"Why?" Ronnie looked at her, perplexed. "We said we was gonna stay out of it. They was fuckin' happy."

"So? She wasn't right for my brother."

"He was happy!" she shouted at her.

"I don't like—"

"It wasn't about yo ass!" Ronnie spazzed. "HE was happy. You should've left that shit alone!"

Shaking her head back and forth furiously, she didn't understand Kenni's reasoning at all. She picked up a blunt out her ashtray and turned the music back up. Neither one of them said anything to each other the whole ride back to Ronnie's house.

Cutting the engine off in the parking lot, Ronnie asked, "So, is you done, or do I need to fuck that lil hissy fit up out you?"

"I better be the only one you fuckin', the fuck."

"Shut the fuck up!" Ronnie told her, getting out the car.

Scrambling out on the passenger side, she said, "You shut the fuck up." Raising her hand to hit Ronnie again, Ronnie caught one, then the other hand, and forced her backward, flush against the truck.

"You the only one I'm fuckin' and the only one I want." She kissed her, littering kisses from her lips to her neck.

"Well, take me inside and get me right then."

The two headed inside, lightly kissing and caressing each other. They entered the apartment, falling across the couch with Kenni on top, sucking on her neck. Ronnie's hands slipped up under her shirt, pinching her nipples, provoking moans. Hands unbuckled her jeans, her thong got pushed to the side, and Ronnie rubbed a finger against her clit. Juices started to seep from her.

"Go away!" Ronnie yelled towards the door where somebody knocked. The person banged harshly, and she stopped tending to the writhing woman. "Hold on, baby, shit."

"Fuck whoever that is," she purred, stripping off her clothes, pulling her hand back to her pussy.

Ignoring the incessant knocks, her fingers went back to playing on Kenni's pussy playground. Another finger joined the fun, coaxing her to an orgasm. Ronnie bent down, sucking her pearl into her mouth while her fingers speared inside of her.

"Yes, daddy... Fuck, baby... Ooh... I'm about to cum," Kenni moaned.

The person at the door upped the racket, pounding on the door, making it cringe under the abuse. Ronnie slurped her juices up, tickling her clit with her tongue. She stood up and kissed Kenni's lips.

"Go in the room, I ain't finish with you yet," Ronnie dictated. "Who is it?" she hollered at the door, then ripped it open to find Shyna on the other side in a red, hollowed-out mini dress that hugged the little bit of body it clothed. "Bra, what the fuck do you want?"

"I want some dick. You ran mine off, and I need a nut," Shyna answered, grinning evilly.

"Bitch, I don't wanna fuck you," she spat. "You just fuckin' shot at me."

"If I wanted to hit yo ass, I would have. I missed on purpose. Now, I said I want some dick. I don't give a fuck if you and yo lil bitch good now. I was good enough to fuck on the whole damn time y'all wasn't together, so you can go strap up and give me a fuckin nut or—"

"Crazy bitch." Ronnie slammed the door in her face.

Standing behind Ronnie, fully clothed with tears streaming down her face, Kenni said rhetorically, "Only once?"

Turning around, Ronnie's face fell, and Kenni took that as a yes. She immediately began launching everything in arm's reach at her. In an effort to grab her to avoid the items flying her way, Ronnie lunged for her. Like water slipping through fingers, she broke away, darting into the kitchen. Quickly, Kenni snatched up something off the counter and hurtled to the bathroom, locking the door behind her.

"Baby, she full of shit! It was only one time." Ronnie jingled the doorknob. "Baby!" She knocked.

"Leave me alone!"

"Man, open the door before I break this shit, Kenni! I'm telling you, baby, she lying. You know that bitch a fucking liar."

The toilet flushed, and water turned back on. "Leave me the fuck alone!" Kenni hollered, shaking her head.

She took two steps back and aimed a kick at the door. It didn't open, so Ronnie kicked the door again. The door flew open, and Kenni flew at her, throwing punches.

"You the fucking liar, Ronnie! Fuck you!" She threw wild punches. "I hate you! I fuckin' hate you! Leave me the fuck alone! I'm going home!" Kenni wriggled out of her grasp. She ran to the front door, bolting out of it to find Shyna leaning against the front door of her own apartment, filing her nails.

Shyna blew a kiss at her. "You big mad or little mad, sis? It looks like"—she peered into the apartment over Ronnie's shoulder, who was exiting the apartment—"you fucked up her apartment. No worries, though, we'll fuck at my house again. Oh, and I heard her lie to you. Good for you for sticking up for yourself because, baby, we fucked several times in my house and hers. The last time being at my house. That was my first time sucking a fake dick, but she seemed to enjoy it."

Heartbroken and no time to pick up the pieces, Kenni lifted her chin and uttered, "Fuck you, bitch." She punched her in the mouth like Ronnie had taught her and sprinted down the hallway.

"Try it, bitch. I will fuck you up," Ronnie threatened Shyna, yanking her up by her neck so she couldn't go after Kenni.

Ronnie tossed her to the side and dashed outside. She didn't see Kenni anywhere. Rushing to her truck, she searched her pockets frantically for her keys but didn't find them. "Where the fuck is my keys?" she muttered to herself, going back in the house to check. "Fuck!" Her fist smashed into the wall when she still didn't find them. "Fuck. Fuck. Fuck." Her knuckles crashed into the wall over and over again until her hands were cut up and bleeding. "Damn, I fucked up."

*   *   *

"Kenni, what's wrong?" Sayvonne questioned.

She was passing up Ronnie's apartment building when she spotted Kenni walking. So, like a good friend, she picked her up. Kenni stared out the window. Two silent tears rolled down her face. "Nothing." She bit her bottom lip, trying to stop the tears.

"Girl, what happened?" asked Sayvonne, glancing at her as she stopped at a red light.

"Nothing, aight? Just drop it," choked out Kenni.

Sayvonne glanced at her again but didn't say anything. They drove for ten minutes in silence, then she pulled over into Twinkle's, a twenty-four hour store. She probed gently, "Y'all broke up again?"

Kenni sniffed. "Yeah," she admitted painfully.

"What happened?"

"Jeremy and Shyna been dating for like the past two and a half months."

"What?"

"Yeah," she sniffed, snickering a little. "When I first found out, Ronnie did, too, because you know Jeremy was really feeling her and being cool again. So, we had them both over for dinner. At dinner, she acted like she ain't know us, and I was trying to tell Jeremy she a snake, but he wasn't trying to hear it, so I let it go. Sis, when I tell you they was fuckin' sickening; it was fucking gross. So, I tried to tell him again because I could see he had really started to like her. He blew me off, and I guess he confronted Shyna about it. I don't know what happened, but Ronnie said she told him she hit. And you know Jeremy, he had a whole-ass big fit about it, and they broke up.

"So, I'm at home, kickin' it, waitin for Ronnie to pick me up and he come in, back on that bullshit, trying to say Ronnie been fuckin' Shyna and still fuckin' her. So, me and Ronnie get into it when she picked me up. And she swore, like, she fuckin' swore she only fucked Shyna one time. That was it. I believed her. So, we getting to it now, but somebody keep banging at the door. She go get the door, and I was gonna go to her room, but then I heard it was Shyna. Man, sis." Kenni's eyes filled with tears again. She sniffed and stared Sayvonne in the eyes. "This bitch get to talking like she salty at Ronnie for coming between her and Jeremy. So, she like well, I wanna fuck. Ronnie ain't going, though. Then Shyna say, so I was good enough to fuck the *whole* time you basically wasn't in a relationship, but now I'm not? Man, that shit fuckin' cut me deep as fuck, yo."

"Kenni, why you believe that hoe? You know misery loves company. Her and Jeremy both hurting and want y'all fucked up like them," responded Sayvonne.

"Nah, you had to hear her," Kenni defended her belief. "That might have been the realest shit that bitch ever said. One, she ain't even know I was there, and two, she really sounded hurt. Like, damn, you can fuck me when you not in a relationship, but now you act like you don't know me type shit. C'mon, Von, you know how niggas do."

"And you know Ronnie. She wouldn't—"

"Fuck her! She couldn't even say nothing after she saw I had heard what Shyna said. She ain't say, *bitch, quit lying* or nothing, she just slammed the door in her face. You know when she said she was lying? When she realized I was done. I'm cool on her. Then she wanna holler, oh she lying, she a liar; hell, everything you saying right now. And guess who was right outside the damn door when I left out. Shyna. Talking about she glad I ain't believe Ronnie's lies and yes they did fuck at her house and Ronnie house the *entire* time. And she still ain't say shit. I know she heard her, bra! I know she did! I ain't that damn fast to get out the door before you and hold half a damn conversation."

Lost for words, Sayvonne opened her arms to her friend. "C'mere, girl." She embraced her, rubbing her back while Kenni cried on her shoulder. "Ssh, girl, it's aight. You don't need her then if she can't value you enough to just tell the truth. A relationship built on lies is a relationship that won't stand the test of time. I like Ronnie, she cool peeps, but when it comes to your heart, she hurt you, so fuck her."

Pulling away, Kenni stared at her, dazed. "Von, I love her. Like, I love her so much it fuckin hurts. Even now, I'm pissed, but I want her to be the one consoling me, and she fuckin did it. Like, why lie? We was supposed to start over fresh; no lies, no bullshit."

"I know you do, sis." Sayvonne wiped away the tears crawling down her face. "You know you ain't never cried over nobody before. Honestly, though, sis, communication is the most important part of a relationship. It's vital, sis. If you can't trust her, y'all ain't got shit to stand on. You need to really think about if she the one for you. I know you love her, but following your heart can hurt you sometimes. You need to really think about if you wanna be with her and what all that means to you and to her. Hell, she need to think, too."

"You right." Kenni twisted away from her, placing her face against the window. "Von, will you take me home now?"

"Nope, I'm holding you hostage for a ransom," Sayvonne told her, starting up the car. "I ain't pick you up for nothing, sis. Let's get you home."

*   *   *

"Ron," T called from the front of her apartment.

"Damn. The fuck happened here?" Jay filed in with the rest of their crew. "Hurricane Ronnie or Kenni? Or both?"

"Both," Chantel commented, pointing to the new decoration of holes in the walls.

"Bra, bra!" T called out again, heading towards Ronnie's bedroom. "Aye, y'all wanna start straightening this shit up?" she delegated.

"Don't touch shit," Ronnie raged, barging out of her bedroom, chest heaving and fists clenched. She continued past them, towards the front door.

"Lil bra." Kim blocked her path, reaching for Ronnie's fists that were swollen and bloody from her wall assault.

"Move the fuck out my way, Kim. I'm about to go kill that bitch." Ronnie glared at her.

Kim smirked. "Only if I can help."

"Ain't nobody fuckin playing, yo! Kim, move!" She went to shove past the feminine woman of their group but was grabbed by her two older stud brothers.

Chantel moved in front of Ronnie while Jay and T held onto her struggling ass. "Ron, chill, nigga. You know that bitch ain't even worth it, fam."

"Fuck that bitch! I'ma make it worth it."

"Shit, let her go," Kim grinned. "Fuck that bitch."

"Shut up, Kim," T told her while Jay snickered on the other side.

"What? Fuck her," Kim declared. "Shit, don't even trip, lil bra. I'll beat her ass for you. Where she at?"

"No, I'ma beat her ass!" Ronnie said.

"I just got a text saying to check on you, but, my nigga, what happened? Niggas can't keep holding you like this. You know we smoke. Tell us what happened first, G, then you can go fuck her up," reasoned T.

Ronnie struggled a little more, then sighed heavily when she couldn't get away from her brothers. "Fuck."

The two older studs released her and Ronnie lurched for the door. Kim tackled her, and the two tumbled to the floor with Kim straddling her, laughing maniacally. She kissed Ronnie on both cheeks.

"Bra, you gotta tell me who the fuck we fucking up, and for what." Kim poked her in the chest.

"Yo ole Super Saiyan ass," cracked T. "Bitch, when you turn into a football player? You hit her ass like a linebacker. Aye, Ron, what you gonna do, bra? I know you ain't gonna let her do that to you. Look, you can't even get up," she teased.

Kim was a tough little thing, absorbing blows from her brother and dishing them back out. The other three studs, Chantel, T, and Jay, circled them on the ground. They laughed, continuing to goad Ronnie, but were ready to intervene at any moment.

"Bra, I'm signing you up for the WFA," Jay commented to Kim.

"The fuck is that?" T wondered.

"Women's Football Alliance," Chantel answered. "It's an all-women league of teams, playing full-contact football."

"Oh okay, like that lingerie shit that be on TV?"

"Nah, nigga." Jay grabbed hold of T and Chantel, moving them back from the two on the floor who were swinging at each other and rolling. "These muthafuckas dressed up like the NFL, full gear, and smacking shit."

"Oh okay, okay," T nodded. "Kim gonna be humping bitches after she tackle them."

The three studs snickered and watched as Ronnie finally broke away from Kim and managed to put some distance between the two.

"You play too fuckin' much, yo! Damn!" she hollered at Kim, falling onto her couch and grabbing a blunt out of the ashtray on the table in her living room.

Kim exchanged fist bumps with the rest of the crew, a smirk on her face. "But yo ass calm now. So, spill it. What happened?"

Ronnie exhaled harshly through her nose and began to tell her family the events that had transpired.

Chapter 9

"Hey." Beaunna gently knocked on her daughter's door before walking in. She found her daughter stretched across the bed, TV on in front of her, but she was staring at the floor. Beaunna walked over to the bed and sat down, but Kenni didn't even glance at her. She laid motionless. "Baby, will you please talk to me? What's wrong?" she asked, brushing Kenni's hair back over her face to feel her forehead.

"Nothing," responded Kenni dully.

"I know you and Ronnie broke up again, or I'm guessing y'all did because I haven't seen Ronnie lately and you been moping."

"Fuck her—Ronnie." She covered up her lie lamely, knowing her mother had heard that slip up, then Kenni rolled over. "Ma, I gotta tell you something."

"What's up, baby girl?"

"I'm gay. Ronnie a girl. She was my girlfriend." An intense feeling stabbed her in the gut, twisting with her feelings of missing Ronnie and being hurt by her. "She my ex-girlfriend."

Beaunna laughed. "Girl, you really thought I ain't know? I been waiting on you to tell me this whole time."

"You knew?" Kenni shrilled. "How?"

"Girl, you couldn't lie to save yo life," she chuckled. "All those times you said she instead of he. Me and Ronnie both laughed over those. I don't care, though, baby." Beaunna kissed her forehead. "As long as you're happy, and you are with Ronnie. I actually like you and Ronnie's relationship, besides walking in on y'all having sex. But, I adore Ronnie. She's great for you."

Kenni scoffed. "Fuck her. We broke up again, and she knows this time."

A shadow of a grin flashed across Beaunna's face. "You wanna talk about it?"

"No."

"Okay, well, do you know what happened with Jeremy and Shyna? Why did they break up?"

"Fuck that bitch, too."

"Yes," Beaunna smirked. "We all know you didn't like her."

"Like ain't even a strong enough word," she insisted. "I hope that bitch die so I can pee on her grave."

"Kenni!" Beaunna shouted rebukingly, sending a stinging slap to Kenni's thigh.

"No, fuck her. I hate her, and I hate Ronnie, too." Tears blasted from her eyes, scurrying down her face.

"Is there anything I need to know?"

"Nooo. Can you just leave me alone for a while, Ma? Please," Kenni begged.

"All right." She stood, dropping a kiss onto Kenni's forehead. "I love you, and I'm here when you ready, baby."

"Love you, too," Kenni replied, tears staining her bed sheets.

*   *   *

The day Kenni stormed out of her apartment, Ronnie wore a white t-shirt and baggy black jeans. Today, a week later, Ronnie sat on her couch in the same clothes. Clothes were everywhere from her failed attempts to get dressed, dishes were piled up in the sink from her random eating binges, and the floors needed a good vacuuming. Somebody knocked on her door.

"Damn, Ronnie!" Layla exclaimed, seeing the inside of Ronnie's apartment.

"Yeah. Whatever. What you need?"

"Kenni told me to come over and pick up her stuff," said Layla, looking Ronnie up and down.

"Come on," Ronnie beckoned her inside.

Layla stepped in but didn't stray too far away from the door. Ronnie disappeared into the back, leaving her to look around in disgust. She pulled her phone out to send picture evidence to her best friend.

"Yo, Ronnie, what's up with yo crib and this ass print on the couch?" Layla called out, capturing pictures of the pizza boxes, empty beer bottles, ashes, blunt roaches, cigarillos packs, and a big bag of weed.

"Here." She thrust a box into her arms and answered, "Ain't felt like cleaning."

"I guess," murmured Layla, following her back to the front door.

Ronnie opened her front door. "Yeah."

"Well, uh, bye," stammered Layla, uncomfortable with this subdued version of Ronnie.

"Bye," said Ronnie in a monotone.

As soon as Layla was in her car, she put her cell phone on speaker, called Kenni's house phone, and started backing out.

"Hello?" her mother answered.

"Hey, Ms. B!" Layla greeted her mother from another. "Can I speak to Kenni?"

"Hey, Layla. Hold on, I'll go take it to her."

"Okay."

"Hello?" Kenni picked up the line a few seconds later, and her mother hung up.

"Yo girl look like shit."

"That ain't my girl."

"Bullshit. Trust, it is. Y'all both doing the same damn thing: moping around, not doing shit, sad as hell. And she smelled like she ain't had a shower in some days." Layla's nose wrinkled, offended by the memory of the smell. "Whatever she was wearing when you broke up with her, I think she still wearing it."

Kenni chuckled hollowly. "White tee and black jeans?"

"Yeah."

"How's her hair?"

"Girrl. That shit look like it could do some damage," Layla told her friend, laughing.

Part of Kenni wanted to give in and go to what her heart desired the most, but her brain pushed her to demand better treatment for herself. If they were going to be great together, they had to be great individually, and Ronnie wasn't right now.

She thought of how convincing Ronnie was when she lied. It made her even sadder at the ease of which she'd done so. Nope, they needed some time apart to really be sure this was what each other wanted.

"Why don't y'all just get back together?" Layla rooted for them as a single unit. "It's obvious y'all miss each other and y'all love each other."

"It's deeper than love, Layla."

"Just think about it, Kenni. So what she fucked her more than once. Y'all was broken up anyway, and y'all had already got back together and was over that shit," Layla told her with exasperation. "Do what makes you happy. You only get one life. Live that shit to the fullest."

"Lay, I hear you, but listen to me. She fuckin lied! She's a fuckin liar, Lay! How can I trust her if I can't believe shit she say?"

"So! Fuck that, we all lie sometimes. Think about the eighty-twenty rule. You gonna leave Ronnie, a whole-ass eighty percent, and meet a muthafucka that only got twenty percent to offer you."

"Fuck you and that dumb-ass logic, Layla. You supposed to be on my fuckin side."

"I am on yo side, but you being difficult! Y'all both love and miss each other, and you mad over something from the past that y'all already worked through," Layla countered.

"What-the-fuck-ever." Kenni flopped down onto her bed. "Look, I'll see you when you get here."

"Whatever. All right."

*   *   *

Arianna banged on Ronnie's door, waiting for an exaggerated hour before her little sister opened the front door. "You stank!" she exclaimed when Ronnie opened the door in the same white tee and black jeans that had been fresh days ago.

Ronnie cracked a smile and almost busted her crusty-ass lips doing so.

"No, I'm not playing." She covered her nose. "You really fucking stink. Why ain't yo lil funky ass cleaned up or showered?"

Grabbing a beer out of the fridge she handed one to her sister and sat down, "Man... I... Man..." she choked, sighing heavily.

"Okay, so..." Arianna picked an area and started to clean up. "Where yo girl at? I know she ain't letting you go out like this."

Exhaling harshly, Ronnie threw her head back over the couch. "Man, we broke up. I don't go with her no more."

"Why not?"

"'Cause."

"Well, if you don't wanna tell me, it's all good, but you taking a shower 'cause yo ass is foul. Just foul."

"I will later," Ronnie laughed, attempting to steer Arianna towards her front door.

"No, you will now," her sister dictated, turning Ronnie around and pushing her back towards the bathroom. "We can do this two ways. Either you do it yo-damn-self or I'ma do you like I did when we was kids and wash you up. Yo choice."

Her answer was to close the door. In the shower, Ronnie scrubbed her body thoroughly, reminiscing on better days when Kenni was by her side. She wondered if she had been honest, admitting she had fucked her more than once, if they would still be in this predicament. They still would've been, she concluded. Kenni already didn't like her.

Almost an hour later, she emerged so fresh and so clean, clean, noticing Arianna had cleaned her apartment for her.

"You owe me seventy-five dollars."

"For what?" Ronnie said.

"Do I look like a damn maid? It's been an hour and a half, and I cleaned yo shithole. You lucky we family."

"Yeah, yeah. It ain't been that long, yo over exaggerating ass."

"Go sit down and take them funky-ass braids out yo hair. I'ma tame it—"

"You gonna do what?"

"Tame. It," spoke Arianna clearly and loud. "Yo shit look wild as hell. Then I'ma braid it over for you."

"Ari, I'm cool. I ain't going nowhere," Ronnie told her with a smile.

"See, this is where I come in," T said, coming from out of her walk-in closet with an outfit for Ronnie to wear.

"T, what you doing here, bruh?" Ronnie grinned.

"We having a studs' night out, bra." She turned to Arianna. "But, Ari, you know you more than welcome to come."

"Nah, I'm straight," Arianna declined.

"Yeah, I know that. But do you wanna go?" T said, joking.

The three laughed.

"You is a fool."

T smiled at her. "Ron, let's bounce. We gotta pick up Jay dumb ass, too."

"Damn, can I put my clothes on?" Ronnie asked, pulling a pair of blue jeans over her boxers.

"Yeah. Hurry up."

The two studs and Arianna left the apartment, joking with one another. They went down one flight of steps, and both studs froze with eyes locked onto Shyna pulling mail from her mailbox. T slid closer to her stud brother with her hands loosely at her side, versus Ronnie, who stood stiffly with fists balled up.

"The fuck y'all stop for?" Arianna shoved between the two. "How you doing?" she said to Shyna and waited for the studs at the front door.

"Hey, Ronnie," Shyna smirked.

T grinned, dropping one arm over Ronnie's shoulder, a hand clasping her arm. "Shorty, you messy as fuck, but I'd still fuck the shit outta yo ass," her eyes appraised her body while she maneuvered Ronnie to the front door.

"You fuckin stupid," Arianna laughed, pushing T. "Who was she, Ronnie?"

Ronnie swallowed and exhaled, releasing her fists. "The reason me and Kenni broke up."

*   *   *

"Bra, I know you all heartbroken and shit, but nigga, get a dance. Smack a bitch on the ass or something," T jested, grinning at Ronnie.

"Bra, I appreciate what y'all doing, man, but real shit, the only thing that would put a smile on my face, or better yet, put me in a better mood, is my lil baby. I love that girl, man."

"Well, she ain't fuckin' with yo goofy ass right now," T stated matter of factly. "And you ain't cheating by being in a strip club unless you fuck somebody other than her at the strip club."

"It's just not the same, bra." She looked around the strip club full of gorgeous women of all shapes and sizes but wasn't impressed by any of them. " I ain't happy if I ain't got shorty love. I'm telling you, I love her, man."

To herself, T pondered her words. She honestly didn't understand what she meant. Being that she was the oldest, however, she knew the responsibility that fell on her shoulders. "Nigga, what's her number? I'm about to call her. Big brother T to the rescue."

Woefully, Ronnie shook her head. "Man, she don't wanna see me. You should've seen the way she looked at me."

"Bra, what's her number? I'ma handle it."

Filled with bitterness, Ronnie shook her head. She couldn't even allow T to try. It wasn't going to change anything, she resolved to herself. A small light of hope stood out in her mind. T did have a way with words, she mused to herself. Just maybe.

"Ronnie."

"Five-two-one, oh-seven-seven-four." The number tumbled out of her mouth before she could process everything.

T whipped out her cell phone and dialed the number. "What's her name again?" She glanced at Ronnie with a joker's grin.

"Fuck you." Ronnie rolled her eyes. Her stomach clenched in anticipation, that small beacon of hope blossoming. T was going to fix it. She had a way with words and had never been turned down by a female. *T was going to fix it*, she told herself.

"How you doin', ma'am?" T spoke into the phone. "May I speak to Kenni? She ain't there? Well, can you tell her T called? Ronnie's brother… Yeah… Okay… Thank you… Bye." She hung up and looked at Ronnie. "She ain't there."

"No shit."

"Aight, nigga, we tried yo way, now you try mine, man. C'mon, let's get up on these hoes."

"Nah, man, I'm cool," declined Ronnie, not even looking around at the naked ladies surrounding her.

Deflated with concern, and unsure about what her brother was feeling, T sat down. She hated for Ronnie to suffer and thought some more on what she could do to get the two back together.

*   *   *

Kenni walked through the door, fresh off a shopping excursion with Layla and Sayvonne. She dropped her bags by the door and went into the kitchen. Her mother stood by the stove, sipping tea.

"Where you been?" Beaunna yawned.

"Layla and Sayvonne took me shopping," responded Kenni, fixing herself a sandwich and popping open a can of pop. "It was cool," she answered the next unspoken but known question.

"Some boy called you."

"Who?" Kenni took a bite of her turkey sandwich.

"I don't know. It may have been a girl, though, I don't know. I saw Ronnie, and she fooled me. I think he or she said they name was T."

Her eyes went flat. T could call to try to mend the relationship, but Ronnie couldn't call? "I don't know a T," she lied and started to move upstairs.

"Whoever the person is, supposedly, they're Ronnie's brother," Beaunna told her, dogging her footsteps to her room. "So, I guess you know who T is?" she asked when Kenni refused to respond but began hanging up her clothes, tears making their way down her face. "Sit down, Kenni." She prompted her onto the bed, next to her.

"Ma." Kenni started to protest, but the motherly look she received made her shut her mouth, wipe her face, and sit down.

"Listen, while y'all was together, that was the happiest I've ever seen you. You walked around like you were glowing and walking on clouds all the time. Now, I don't know what happened since you won't tell me, but I don't think it's serious enough to stop yourself from being happy, so when are y'all going to get back together and quit playing this game?" Stubbornly, her daughter remained quiet.

"Kenni?" Beaunna said her name in a tone that said she had better answer her.

"I don't know," Kenni shrugged. "She lied to me. Like, we had moved past it, but damn."

"Love is a battlefield, Kenni. You will get hurt, no matter how small. There will be fighting, whether it's with each other because y'all arguing about something, or to stay together because something is trying to come between y'all. Just think about it, baby. Hell, make a pros and cons list. Do you want Ronnie and the relationship? Yes or no? Why or why not? Pros? Cons? If the good outweighs the bad or vice versa, you know what to do."

Kenni batted her eyes quickly and looked away from her mirror where she still had a picture of Ronnie and herself, which she had been staring at. "Ma." She glanced back at the picture and turned towards her mother. "Look, Ma, I, um." A lump rose in her throat, which she swallowed with difficulty. "I'm… I-I'm tired and want to go to sleep."

Beaunna stood. "Okay, baby." She kissed her forehead and left the room without another word, understanding her daughter's pain, which shone brightly through her eyes.

Alone in her room, Kenni gazed at the picture on her mirror. The lack of having Ronnie in her life and the intense feeling of missing her bubbled over. She threw herself onto her bed, burying her face in a pillow, crying uncontrollably.

*   *   *

"Ooh, look at you, lookin all daddy-ish," Shyna flirted, catching sight of Ronnie coming into the apartment building. "Don't tell me you still mad?" At her scowl twisting further and no reply, Shyna slid in front of her door, barring entry. "So, we really back to this now? You
need to open yo fuckin' mind and think." She jutted her in the temple with a finger. "Yo lil bitch barely fuckin' legal and throw tantrums like a damn child. Why the fuck would you even want the spoiled lil bitch? I did you a fuckin' favor."

Rant over, Ronnie's hand flew to her neck. She sneered, "Call her a bitch again."

Shyna narrowed her eyes at her. "You only put yo hands on me because you know deep down, I'm fuckin' right. Y'all toxic as fuck together. She act a fuckin' fool,
and you run right after her like a lil puppy dog with its tail tucked. So, that makes who the bitch?"

"Fuck you," Ronnie snarled in her face, banging her back against the door.

She wet her lips and smiled. "Well, fuck me then and leave yo hand right there, too." Wrapping a leg around her, Shyna pulled her in closer and undid the top button of her jeans. "Yeah, yo lil bitch—"

Clutching her throat tight, Ronnie took her up top like she was about to chokeslam her and threw her into the wall on the opposite side of the hall. "That lil bitch is mine. Fuck you and what you talking about, miserable, crazy bitch." Ronnie turned to leave out the apartment building.

*   *   *

Nerves jumbled around Ronnie's stomach, coated in anxiety. She knew she shouldn't be here. It wasn't going to solve anything, but she had to try. Slowly, she approached Kenni's front door, swallowing the apprehension boiling inside. At the door, Ronnie took a deep breath and adjusted her hat. She knocked.

"Ronnie?" Beaunna opened the door, smiling approvingly.

"Hey, mama. Is Kenni here?"

"You know she is." She opened the door wider, inviting her into the house. "She's upstairs," Beaunna mentioned. "Now, you know since y'all been broken up, Kenni been moping around here, sad as can be, not doing nothing."

In shame, her head dropped. "Man, it's all my fault, mama."

"Yeah, well, maybe," Beaunna retorted. "But I'm sure Kenni played a role in everything, too. You want something to drink? How about a bottle of water?"

Ronnie nodded.

"So, what did you do? And don't say nothing. I wanna know how it relates to Jeremy and Shyna as well," she stated, handing her the water bottle.

"Damn, well, shit." She shook the bottle up. "You got something stronger?"

"You gonna be good to drive home?"

Mock offended, Ronnie replied with a grin, "I'm a professional, Ma."

Taking her word for it, Beaunna pulled down two glasses and a bottle of vodka that was hidden in the pantry. She filled their glasses and set one in front of Ronnie. "Talk."

Immediately, she chugged the contents of her glass, then refilled it to take a sip before beginning her sordid tale. "Aight, so the first time we had broken up, I fucked Shyna. We was friends, but we had got super fucked up when it happened. Kenni say we wasn't broken up then, but she came over that night, and Shyna was still in my house."

"Okay. So, to sum this story up, y'all got past that and got back together. Shyna ended up talking to Jeremy and Kenni spilled the beans to Jeremy about you and Shyna's dealings. So, what happened now?"

"I told Kenni I had only fucked her once when we was broken up. Shyna told her differently."

"Well, did you?" Beaunna arched an eyebrow at her.

"Yeah, I hit her twice while we was broken up."

"So, Kenni's mad that you lied. Jeremy's mad that Shyna lied. Why did you lie?"

"I ain't think it was that important," Ronnie shrugged.

"Ma, who you talking to?" Kenni bellowed from her room. "Who was at the door?"

"Come and see!" she called back. Silence was her response. "Kenni!"

Kenni grudgingly got off her bed. She came to the top of the stairs and her eyes slanted once she caught sight of Ronnie. "Yes, mother."

"Don't you see her standing here?" Beaunna gestured.

"I don't have anything to say," she hollered petulantly, retreating back to her room.

The fake confident swagger Ronnie had fizzled out like an extinguished flame. She shook her head sadly.

"None of that. Go talk to her. You said it's your fault, so you gotta go through the heat." She killed her pity party. "Go make it right."

"She ain't even trying to hear me."

"So? Make her. Gone now, she waiting. You know where the room at. No funny business unless you put a sock on the door."

A smile couldn't help but surface on Ronnie's face at her words. She walked to Kenni's room with determination. *I'm not leaving here single!* Ronnie declared in her head. Walking into her room, she took a seat on the bed. Kenni was on her computer, ignoring her and the pitter patter in her chest.

"I wanna get back together," announced Ronnie.

On the inside, Kenni's heart swelled. Verbally, however, she uttered, "That sounds like a personal problem to me."

"Why you being so damn difficult?" Ronnie exploded. "Damn! I said I ain't want no other bitch! I want you. I fucked up, baby. Shit, I'm sorry! Why you won't let me make it fuckin' right? Fuck! I'm here, ain't I? I'm trying, too, ain't I?"

"Wasn't you just at Silk's the other night?" she shot at her, talking about the strip club.

"Yeah, T took me. It was a studs' night out, but I ain't touch no-damn-body or get no lap dances. The—"

"So, why the fuck was you there?"

"Shut the fuck up and listen! The only reason I was there was because my niggas got tired of me looking all crazy because I'm stuck on yo ass! Why the fuck you think T called yo ass? Middle of a fuckin' strip club, full of naked bitches, and I'm salty as fuck I ain't with yo ass."

"Yeah, whatever, you can save that shit," stated Kenni, turning back to the computer.

Jaw working overtime, she took a deep breath, calming herself. "Kenni?"

"What?"

"I love you, baby. I apologize, and I'm willing to do whatever to work through this as long as we back rocking together. I want you, baby. I only want you."

Kenni chuckled lightly. "Ronnie, you can miss me with all that. You was just cussing me the fuck out. You don't want me."

"Yes, I do," said Ronnie firmly. She turned her chair around to face her, holding onto her armrest so their faces were only a few inches away.

"Answer me this then. How many times did you fuck Shyna?"

"Man, really? We back on that shit? Fuck that bitch, I want you!"

"How many fuckin' times did you fuck her?!" Kenni spazzed and slapped her.

Recoiling back, Ronnie glared at her. She bit out softly, "I then told you. I then asked you fuckin' how many times to keep yo fuckin' hands to yoself. So, you know what? Fuck her and fuck you, too. Yes, I fucked that bitch more than once. There, you happy. It shouldn't have changed shit. We already moved past it. You really let that bitch come in between us. I don't fuckin' like that bitch. I don't fuckin' want that hoe. I don't want no other bitch but yo dumb ass. But if you can't understand that I love you, I'm in love with you, well, fuck it then. Either you gonna learn or I'ma learn to be without yo ass." She stalked out the house with fire in her eyes.

*   *   *

Kenni sobbed into her pillow uncontrollably. She curled up into a ball and hugged the pillow tight to her body. Tears raced rapidly down her face, her nose started to run, and a headache started to creep up.

Hearing her daughter's cries, Beaunna came into the room. She sat down on the bed, cradling Kenni's head and stroking her hair. "What happened, baby?"

"I-I blew it, mama," Kenni cried out. "Sh-she told me she loved me and wanted to be… to be with me, but I just couldn't get past Shyna and her. I-I hit her again. Mama, I don't think she wants me no more."

"Aww, baby," she crooned. "It's gonna be okay. She stay in Threshold Apartments, don't she? What's her address?"

"Two-five-six-nine Woodlane. Why?"

Beaunna shushed her. "Don't worry about it. What's the number?"

"Apartment four," Kenni yawned.

Beaunna hummed Kenni to sleep, still stroking her hair and singing to her softly. Beaunna murmured a quick prayer of healing for her daughter's pain, then left her daughter's room to go handle the business of her daughter's heart. Beaunna drove to Ronnie's house.

"She's not home," Shyna spoke in a singsong to Beaunna, opening her apartment door.

Turning away from Ronnie's door, she faced her. "You sure got your nerve."

"I do. How's Jeremy?" Shyna agreed.

"Unt-unh." Beaunna shook her head no. "Save it. See, I know all about yo ass now. I had a feeling, but now I know for sure. And you got both me and my kids fucked up."

A devilish grin descended on her face. "So, that's where that lil bitch, I mean, yo daughter, got that lil mouth from, huh?"

"Look, heifer." Beaunna's finger flew in the air, and she took steps towards her. "You keep the hell away from my damn kids."

"Or what?" Shyna taunted her invitingly, grinning maniacally.

"Ma?" Ronnie questioned in confusion, coming up the stairs, flanked by Arianna and T.

"Hey," Beaunna greeted her curtly, side-eyeing her, focus still on Shyna. "I was just coming to see you when *it* popped out."

"Aww, look at you, mama. You mad?" Shyna jeered again.

"Bitch, beat it," Ronnie snapped, opening her front door. She beckoned everyone into her apartment and began making introductions. "Kenni mama, this my sister, Arianna." Arianna smiled and waved when she was introduced. "My brother from another mother, T." T smiled in greeting.

Beaunna smiled at the two, then turned to T. "So, you called my house?"

"Yeah. I was calling for this fool." T stood and mushed Ronnie in the head. "Her and yo daughter need to quit bullshittin' and get back together."

"Hell yeah," Arianna murmured, turning on the television.

Beaunna smiled.

Ronnie started to peel an orange, ignoring the general consensus. She was literally just at Kenni's house. She tried, it didn't work, it's over. No need to keep harping on and on about it.

"That's why I'm here," Beaunna commented, moving from the doorway and standing in front of Ronnie. "You know she cried after you left?"

Curiosity piqued, Arianna stared at her then turned to her sister, who continued to peel her orange. She jostled her in the shoulder. When Ronnie looked at her in question, she bucked her eyes and looked at Beaunna.

"Ronnie, she talking to you," Arianna scolded her younger sister.

"I know," she scowled. "Kenni don't want me. She playing fucking games. Bet her ass show up here in a couple days sayin what I just said. I'm through with her. She can kiss my ass—"

"Ronnie!" Arianna interjected before Ronnie could work up a good steam.

"Don't take no offense to what she saying. We keep it gutta all the time," T grinned.

Not at all understanding the slang T had just spoken, but able to deduce it was something along the lines of being honest, she nodded slowly. "So, Ronnie, you don't care?"

Disregarding her question, Ronnie's scowl tightened.

"Ronnie?"

"No, fuck her," she spat, retreating to her room.

"Don't mind her, she just mad, that's all," Arianna told her, then picked up the cordless phone. "I'ma get yo daughter over here to work this shit out. What's the number?"

"Five-two-one, oh-seven-seven-four."

"Aight."

*   *   *

Bring! Bring! Bring! Kenni's phone rang, but she ignored it, seeing Ronnie's name on the caller ID. Layla and Sayvonne, who had stopped by, rousing Kenni out of her sleep, glanced at each other.

"You want me to get that?" Layla asked when the phone rang for the fifth time.

"No," Kenni responded, turning on the TV to BET.

Sayvonne sighed, rolled her eyes, and picked up the ringing phone. "Hello?"

"Is this Kenni?" a woman's voice asked.

"No, but she right here. Who is this?"

She raised an eyebrow, wondering who was calling her from Ronnie's house if it wasn't Ronnie.

"Arianna, Ronnie's sister."

"Aight. Here go Kenni." She handed the phone to Kenni, repeating, "It's Arianna, Ronnie's sister."

"Hello?" Kenni spoke into the phone.

"What's your address?"

"Why?"

"I'm about to come scoop you up. You and Ron 'bout to settle this," Arianna said loudly enough for Sayvonne to overhear her.

"Ronnie don't want me," Kenni told her somberly.

"Yeah, right, and pigs can fly," she said sarcastically. "Y'all not 'bout to stay on this stupid shit. Y'all can move past this shit. So, y'all can make up by y'all selves or… nah, it's too late for that. We about to have an intervention. Now, look, either way, whether you give me your address or not, I'm on my way. I just thought I would tell you. Be ready." She hung up the phone.

"What she say?" Sayvonne asked, even though the conversation was heard loud and clear. She put the phone back on the charger.

"Nothing," Kenni lied. She turned to Layla. "Run me to the store right quick."

Layla raised an eyebrow. "Yeah. Sure." She threw a quick look at Sayvonne when Kenni reached across the bed for her purse.

"Wait for me," Sayvonne said, jumping up.

Layla shrugged as if she didn't care, and the three trooped out the house. Fifteen minutes later, they pulled up into Threshold Apartments.

"Aww, you a bastard," Kenni told Layla softly, but not meaning it.

"I love you, too, girl," Layla smiled. "C'mon."

They got out the car, walked into the building, and up to Ronnie's floor. Kenni stopped her crew in front of the door. She turned to say something to them, but Shyna's door opened first.

Before Shyna could say anything, Ronnie's door swung open, and Arianna growled, "Don't say shit," then pulled the three girls into the apartment.

Kenni's mouth dropped open seeing her mother sitting on the couch. "Ma, what you doing here?"

Beaunna smiled. "Trying to fix a fucked-up situation."

Kenni smiled gratefully at her mother.

"Have a seat," Arianna ordered Kenni and her two friends. "I'ma go get Ronnie." She passed T, who was staring at Layla, and tossed the remote in her lap. "Watch TV instead of her."

"What?" Ronnie barked at her when she barged into her room.

"Kenni here," she announced.

"So?" Ronnie said and stretched out on her bed, her hands behind her head.

Arianna rolled her eyes. "Go in there and talk it out with her."

"No," Ronnie responded stubbornly.

"Fine." Arianna's jaw flexed. "Fuck it." She left out of the room and went back to the living room where T had everyone watching a female-only porno.

"T!" she cried, snatching the remote out her hand and changing the channel.

"What?"

The girls laughed, and Beaunna grinned at her antics.

"Kenni, you gonna have to go back there and talk it out with her." The words came out of her mouth, but her eyes sought out her mother, wondering if she would have a problem.

"Okay," Kenni said, noticing her mother was unperturbed by anything being said. She went to Ronnie's door and tried to open it, only to discover it was locked.

"She so damn difficult," Arianna muttered, standing on her tiptoes to get the key, which was at the top of the door. She opened it and pushed Kenni in.

Sauntering back into the living room, she didn't know Ronnie had also trailed behind her until she took a seat at the counter. T burst out laughing as Kenni came moseying into the living room behind the two, drifting to Ronnie's side.

"Ronnie, I want you back," she whispered.

"So, I don't want you back," Ronnie responded, not bothering to lower her voice.

Her head whipped, gauging the reactions of the others peppered throughout the living room. All of their eyes were glued to the TV, seemingly lost in fascination at a commercial advertising

Neutrogena. Sayvonne and Layla peeped their friend. They stood together.

"We gonna roll out," Layla stated.

"Hell, I might as well, too." Beaunna stood. "It ain't like she can get pregnant."

"Yeah, me too." Arianna stood. "C'mon, T."

T flipped back to her porno. "Nah, I'm cool," she said, earning a slap from Arianna.

Once everyone cleared out, and the door was locked, Ronnie exploded, jumping to her feet, facing Kenni. "What, you think this shit a fuckin' joke? My heart and my feelings ain't nothing to fuckin' play with. And that's what the fuck you doing right now, right? I just said let's be together, and you wasn't with that shit. Now, hours fuckin' later, you with it. Man, fuck you. You was just cool, remember! Quit fuckin' playin' with me, yo!"

"I'm not playing with you! I fuckin' love you!" she shouted back.

Ronnie's lips smacked together in disbelief. "You love what the fuck I can do for you. You don't love me for real; otherwise, this shit would've been dead."

"Really?! Really?!"

"Really, really?" Ronnie mocked her. "Yeah, really, muthafucka. Bra, just leave. Leave me the fuck alone. You cool on me, remember? I ain't 'bout to keep playin' this dumb-ass game with you."

"Fuck you, Ronnie!" Kenni threw the chair down she had previously occupied. "All this shit is yo fuckin' fault! YOU fucked Shyna. YOU lied about that shit."

"And! You can't keep yo fuckin' hands to yoself. You like to fuck up my shit when you mad."

"Well, if you wouldn't have fucked her, then I wouldn't—"

"What the fuck do you mean?" She squared off in Kenni's face. "I been warning you to keep yo fuckin' hands to yoself since you damn near met me. I be trying to spare yo lil dumb ass. My sister ain't always gonna be here, and you putting yo hands on me will make me fuck you up."

Internally, she wanted to scoff. Ronnie wasn't going to do anything to her, even if she did put her hands on her. That little prickly feeling of awareness thought about what she was saying. She recalled when she hit Jeremy. It didn't change anything, but it changed something between them. At the moment, she'd felt it. That was a line they had never crossed. Thinking about their relationship, Ronnie had asked multiple times for her to control herself. Kenni took a deep breath. She could do this.

"I'm sorry," she admitted. "I'll keep my hands to myself from now on, and I won't mess up yo house no more. I promise."

"Man, get the fuck outta here." Ronnie ridiculed her with a laugh. "No, you won't. And even if you did, then what? You gonna let this Shyna shit go now?" She watched her facial expression contort. "Yeah, I thought so. Man, quit wasting my time playing with me, yo. There's the door." Her chin jutted in the direction of the door, and she started to head back to her room.

Flashes of being alone without Ronnie in her life permanently spurred her into action. She loved her and wanted to be with only her. "Fuck Shyna."

"Oh, now it's fuck Shyna," Ronnie said sarcastically. "So, what? You gonna keep yo hands to yoself, finally let go of that Shyna shit, and we gonna live happily fuckin' ever after?"

"We can!" Kenni fired back. "I just wanted to know how many times you really fucked that bitch."

"Oh my God! And we back here," Ronnie cried out incredulously. "I thought you wanted to dead this shit. What the fuck, man? What the fuck do you want from me? You either wanna fuckin' be with me, or you don't. Earlier, you didn't, now you do. What the fuck, man?"

"Because I need to fuckin' know! I heard you tell my mama earlier that it was twice, but you told me only once. So, how many fuckin' times was it?"

"It don't even fuckin' matter! It's fuckin' old news! You letting that bitch come in between us still. We had moved past that shit. How the fuck you wanna get back together and stuck on that same dumb shit?"

"And rebuild on top of lies again?" Kenni screamed. "*You* fucked her, Ronnie. I hated that bitch and wished she would drop fuckin' dead before you even fucked her. To be honest, it was never even just about you fuckin' her. I had got over that shit! The point was, after apologizing, you fuckin' lied about how many times you fucked her! Hell, you probably fucked her more than twice.

First, you said it was once, then it turned into twice. What the fuck, Ronnie? Damn. I'm trying to move past this shit, I just need you to be fuckin' honest. How the fuck can we move forward without you being honest? Your dishonesty is what caused all of this!"

Ronnie balked, "My dishonesty? My dishonesty? Get the fuck outta here, bra. Nah, it was yo childish ass—"

"You know what, Ronnie?" Kenni huffed and took off her promise ring. Pushing aside the pangs in her heart, she tossed it at her. "You right. So, whatever, you ain't gotta be with my childish ass. I ain't about to keep arguing with you about this shit."

Cradling the ring in her hand, she looked at Kenni in bewilderment. Ronnie followed her back to the living room. "So, you just gonna leave? Straight like that?"

"What else is there to talk about, Ronnie?" Kenni stared at her. "It's all my fault, remember? I'm childish. I can't keep my fuckin' hands to myself. So, congratulations, you ain't gotta deal with me no more."

Like a broken record, she repeated, "So, you really just gonna fuckin' leave me?"

"Yes, Ronnie!" Kenni shouted at the door. "I'm not about to keep sitting here, doing this with you. Just like you said earlier, I'm tired of the same shit. So, if I'm childish and can't keep my hands to myself, leave me the fuck alone. Yo ass can't fuckin' tell the truth. You a liar. So, yes, we done. Call it a break, whatever, but until you ready to be fuckin' honest with me, I'm cool on you. Leave me the fuck alone like you told me earlier." She walked out the door, slamming it shut.

Chapter 10

"Thanks, y'all, for coming to my track meet," Layla told her besties, parking outside of Kenni's house.

"Girl, like we would've missed it," Kenni laughed. It was coming up on the end of senior year, and for the last three months, they had been back to hanging thick as thieves with no significant others. Even prom hadn't changed that. Missing Layla's last track meet of the season was a no go. "You been talking about it all week."

"We caught all the hints," Sayvonne told her with a laugh.

"Whatever!" Layla exclaimed. "Let it—"

"Are y'all coming in?" Kenni interjected, getting out of the car. "Why y'all still in the car?"

Sayvonne rolled her eyes. "All right, Princess. Damn, what's the rush?" She opened her car door.

"Like I was saying, before I was rudely interrupted," Layla jested at Kenni, walking up to the porch.

"What's up, sis? What's up, Lay, Von?" Jeremy stepped out onto the porch.

Layla growled, staring daggers at him. "I forgot rudeness runs in y'all family," she half-joked, walking into the house.

Releasing Kenni from a side hug, he questioned, "The fuck is her problem?"

"Rough track meet. She finished third."

"Aight, well, Sunday dinner at my house this weekend. Von, you coming?" Jeremy asked politely.

"Look at you," Sayvonne smiled in a teasing manner. "All polite, like you know how to talk to a woman. I almost wish I had a sister for you."

His face instantly turned up into a scowl. "You coming or not? Ain't nobody got time for that bullshit."

"You know I'm coming," she grinned.

"And I am, too," Layla announced, coming back onto the porch, sucking on a peach.

He turned his glower onto her. "Nobody invited you."

"Whatever. I'll still be there," she dismissed him, turning her attention to Kenni. "You talked to Ronnie yet?"

"No, and she don't need to talk to that dyke," Jeremy spat.

Kenni rolled her eyes. "C'mon, y'all." She led them inside. "No, I haven't talked to Ronnie since I changed my number," she finally answered Layla in her room.

"Bitch, you lying," Layla blurted.

"No, I'm not." Kenni gave her the finger. "I told y'all what happened. She still ain't called, so I guess she ain't done being a liar."

Sayvonne rolled her eyes. "Girl, is you done messing up her house?"

"My attitude changed. I grew up," she pointed out.

"Girl, it's only been three months," muttered Sayvonne.

"So?"

"She probably waiting on you to hit her up," Layla divulged.

Both of them shot their heads in her direction. Kenni voiced the question, "Why would she be waiting on me? I told her to hit me up when she done lying."

Layla rolled her hazel eyes. "Because you walked away. Niggas is stupid. She not gonna hit you up first."

"If she really love her and want her back, she will," countered Sayvonne.

Laughing, Layla sniped, "What kind of damn fairytale you think this is, Von? In real life, niggas don't be on that sappy shit."

"Dudes you fuck with don't be on that," she checked her.

"Anyways." Layla rolled her eyes. "Soo, you gonna hit her up and catch you a nut at least? I know you miss her."

Feel-good endorphins overwhelmed her body just thinking about the time spent with Ronnie. She smiled to herself. "I do miss her." Nervously, Kenni flipped her phone over and over in her hands. "I hit her up earlier at the track meet," she revealed quietly.

"Biiitt-chh," Layla dragged the word out.

Kenni threw a teddy bear at her. "Shut up."

"So, what happened?" Sayvonne demanded to know. "What y'all talk about?"

"Nothing. She ain't hit me back," she told them with a strong voice, but a sad heart.

"What you say?" Sayvonne asked.

Attempting to come across as nonchalant, she shrugged. "Hey. Told her it was me and asked her how she been."

"Hmm," Sayvonne pursed her lips.

"Girl, that don't mean shit," Layla advised her, chuckling. "You know how niggas is. Now she trying not to be thirsty as fuck for you. Niggas play hard to get, too."

"It's fine," Kenni replied. "I don't even care, for real."

"Then why you hit her up?" Sayvonne interjected.

Her heart clenched and throbbed with a painful ache. "Because I miss her."

*   *   *

"What's wrong with you?" Shyna asked Ronnie, who sat across from her, pushing food around her plate. "You been different since we left the bowling alley earlier."

"I just ain't hungry," Ronnie exhaled her lie, throwing her fork on the plate. What was bothering her was a simple text message. Kenni had finally hit her up, and no matter how far down she'd pushed her heart, and how numb she tried to convince herself she felt, her heart had soared from just a few lines from Kenni. And now, hours later, her name and utter essence thrummed through Ronnie.

"You not hungry?" Shyna questioned with glass in her tone.

Ronnie pushed off and away from her table. "No, I'm not fucking hungry. Did I st-st- stutter?" She grabbed her truck keys.

"Where you going?"

"I need some 'rillos," Ronnie told her, walking out the front door, reminding herself to keep her gait steady.

Once she got in the car, she peeled out, and after a series of turns and watching the rearview mirror, she was sure Shyna hadn't followed her, so she pulled to a stop at the river. Ronnie rolled her blunt and perched on the hood of her truck. Inhaling slowly, she recalled every past memory and emotion associated with Kenni. A smile crept across her face as the memories flitted across her brain. Mentally, she dug her heart up and allowed the air to caress it to feeling again, and before she knew it, tears seeped down her face. She missed her so fucking much. The text message Kenni had sent her brought a smile to her face. Picturing her smiling face, her finger stroked the phone lovingly.

That lasted all of about two seconds due to Shyna's face popping up on her screen, notifying her of a call. Ronnie sent her to voicemail. She quickly sent a message to Kenni saying hey. Shyna's face popped up again, and again, she declined the call and repeated it the third and fourth time.

"The fuck am I gonna do?" Ronnie whispered, staring at her vibrating phone that screamed Shyna was calling but nudged her heart with the text notification from Kenni that read: *I miss you.* "Fuck," she growled, dropping her head in her hands. "Fuck, fuck, fuck."

The phone lit up again, this time, with no face on the screen. Ronnie sighed and glanced down.

"Yo," she said into the phone.

"Nigga, nigga, what's good?" T greeted her.

"Shit, chilling."

"The fuck wrong with you, sounding all dry and shit like you in yo feelings?"

Ronnie heaved a big sigh. "Shit, I am. Kenni just hit me up."

"So?"

"So? Nigga, Kenni just hit me up. Kenni, nigga."

"You still love shorty, huh?" T concluded.

"Man, yeah, nigga. I ain't never stopped loving her."

"But you with Shyna now. Like, with her, with her," T quipped. "In a whole-ass damn relationship."

"Nigga, I know!"

"So, what the fuck you gonna do?"

"Nigga! Man, I don't fuckin' know," Ronnie stated with defeat.

"Check dig, nephew. You gonna have to ease yoself up outta this shit with Shyna. Like, back all the way the fuck up as slow-fast as you can," she instructed.

"Nigga, what?"

"Finesse, yo," T snapped. "Just listen to what I'm saying, yo. You can't just step to Shyna right now and be like, fuck you, I wanna break up, then pop back up with Kenni."

Another text message from Kenni brought a smile to her face, and she quickly texted back, telling T, "Yeah, I know that. Shit, I ain't even bringing Kenni to the house. Shit, won't trick me again." She pressed more buttons on the phone to open and read a new message.

"Ron, who you talkin' to? Why you pressing buttons?"

"My bad, I'm texting Kenni. She had hit me up when I was with Shyna earlier, but I dipped on that bitch and slid to the river."

"Aww, nigga," groaned T. "Bra, you gonna have to go home and fuck Shyna tonight."

"Fuck—"

Immediately, T cut her off. "Ronnie, shut the fuck up and listen to me, bro. Shyna damn cuckoo for cocoa puffs and yo ass probably cussed her out before you left, so she at home, pissed and insecure. You gonna have to go home and fuck her good to get rid of those feelings so she don't suspect shit. Then you gotta start backpedaling like a muthafucka. Attention, affection, all of that. Even arguments. But this the kicker, though. Nigga, you gonna have to fuck her randomly to throw her off yo trail, you feel me? Get high, drunk, whatever, but you gonna have to lay that wood on her."

"And what about Kenni?" Ronnie pretended to humor her, but she was really curious to see if their strategies aligned.

"Nigga, by no means can she come to the spot. Stall it out with her for as long as you can on the talking side. I'm telling you, bra, follow my lead, and I'll take you to the championship like Jordan in the nineties."

Ronnie rolled her eyes. "Yeah, whatever. Aight, I got you. I'm about to go back to the house and deal with this shit. I ain't fucking her, though."

"Nigga, you got to."

"I can't."

"Nigga, *Love & Basketball* ain't teach you shit? Can't should never be in a man's vocabulary because when you say can't, you ain't a man," T quoted the movie.

"I hear you."

"Bra, come to the crib," T told her. "I got you, bra."

"Nigga, I ain't trying to fuck her crazy ass no more. Shit, she already blowing me up now. I'ma just chill."

"Get off that hoe shit, nigga, and come get a drink. I'ma smooth this shit over for you. So, bring yo ass and watch a nigga work. It's all about finesse."

"Fuck you, nigga," Ronnie laughed.

"Yeah, whatever. I'm putting shots out, bring yo ass," T directed her, knowing her stud brother would come over.

     *   *   *

"So, you leave for fuckin' hours and come back home fuckin' drunk," Shyna stated angrily, watching Ronnie stumble around her apartment with a huge smile on her face.

"Yeah," Ronnie agreed, opening the fridge, microwave, and cabinets. "Where that food go?"

Arms crossed over her chest, she snapped, "Oh, now you fuckin' hungry?"

"Yeah, now I'm fuckin' hungry," Ronnie smirked, then slapped Shyna on the ass. "Feed me."

"Nigga, you been fuckin' gone for hours, not answering or returning my calls, and you stroll in here, fuckin' drunk, wanting something to eat!" Shyna exploded.

She slammed a cabinet. "I'm looking in fuckin' cabinets and shit, ain't I? I told you I'm fuckin' hungry!"

"So, why you ain't answer the phone?"

"Why you keep calling if I ain't answer? Goofy muthafuckas! Hell yeah," Ronnie gloated, opening the oven and finding her food. She picked at it, eating it cold, and ambled towards the kitchen table.

"What you mean, why I keep calling? Because my fuckin' girlfriend wouldn't answer the phone! Because my fuckin' girlfriend ran the fuck outta here!" She slapped the plate onto the ground, away from Ronnie's hungry ass. "What the fuck is wrong with you?"

Ronnie fired up out of her seat. "What the fuck is wrong with you? I was fuckin' eating! And you wonder why I got up through on yo shit," she gestured to the mess on the floor. "Yo fuckin' clingy ass, blowing up my phone and shit. Obviously, I was fuckin' pissed, stupid. All I wanted was some fuckin' me time. Damn, I can't never have no space. Shit!" She grabbed her keys off the counter.

Struck speechless, watching her put her shoes on, Shyna hurried to her. "Baby, wait. I'm sorry."

"Whatever." Ronnie shrugged her hand off of her.

"Baby, I'm sorry. Where you going?" She ran to block the front door.

"To get the fuck away from you! Shit, I ain't even hungry no more."

"Baby, I'm sorry." Shyna wrapped her arms around her. "I'm sorry, let me make it up to you." She started kissing her neck.

"Move," Ronnie told her, attempting to angle her neck away from Shyna.

Shyna grinded against her and moaned in her ear. "Take yo anger out on me, baby. I'm sorry." She twisted her nipples.

Ronnie narrowed her eyes at her and threw her back towards the living room. Shyna stripped, watching Ronnie stalk towards her. When Ronnie stood in front of her, she slipped a finger in her mouth, then trailed it down to her pussy, moaning and biting her lip. She rocked her hips to the rhythm of her stroking fingers, her other hand beckoning Ronnie closer.

Lust mixed with the effects of the alcohol she'd consumed brought her to Shyna. She smacked her hand down, spinning her around and bending her over the couch. Her strap-on sprang to attention when she dropped her pants. Shyna leaned up, but she shoved her back down, thrusting inside of her.

"I. Fucking. Hate. You," she snarled with earnest.

"Ooh, shit," Shyna moaned. "I love the way you hate me, baby. Fuck… yess… This pussy yours… This pussy yours, daddy."

Hammering into her from behind, Ronnie's fingers went from digging into her hips to one filleting her ass cheeks. Shyna's screams of pleasure reverberated throughout the apartment, conjoined with the sound of her wetness being penetrated. Ronnie yanked her head back and continued her onslaught until she attempted to run away, climbing over the couch before buckling down on the floor.

"Damn, baby," Shyna panted. "Give me a second. Give me a second, and I'll get you something to eat."

Disgust at herself filtered throughout Ronnie. She glowered down at the woman. "I'm going to bed."

*   *   *

Kenni sat outside the store around the corner from her house with her insides tingling, a slow grin stretching across her face, watching Ronnie walk up to her. Her eyes roved over Ronnie hungrily. After a few months of no contact, and a week and a half of fleeting conversation, they were finally linking up.

"What's good?" Ronnie grinned down at her, standing in front of her.

Unable to contain herself, Kenni broke the nervousness of the situation and shot into Ronnie's arms. She squeezed her tightly and nuzzled into her shirt, inhaling Ronnie's scent. "I missed you," Kenni admitted.

Ronnie squeezed her tighter and kissed the top of her head. "I missed the fuck outta you."

No more words were spoken. The two stayed wrapped tightly in each other's arms, basking in the feelings flooding through their bodies.

"Come on." Ronnie gently took her hand and led her to the counter so they could get ice cream.

"I think this time apart was good for us," Kenni said, facing her on the bench with her ice cream. "You look different. You been working hella. I refocused on school, all my grades is A's, and I'm going to college in the fall."

"Aye, that's what's up. I hope you gonna be here for school." Ronnie kissed her cheek. "Congrats, though. I'm proud of you."

"Thank you, and yeah, I am," Kenni grinned. "What about you? You got a new job keeping you busy or the club?"

"A new job," Ronnie blurted with a pounding heart.

"Aww, shit. Congrats, what kind of job?"

"Security. Mostly nights, but I get some day shifts, too."

"Oh okay." Kenni's mood dampened a little bit at the realization that Ronnie wouldn't have a lot of time for her. "Are you still at the club, too, with T and everybody?"

"Yeah."

"Well, I'm proud of you, too," Kenni told her.

Ronnie grinned. "Thanks." Her phone buzzed in her pocket. She checked the text message.

"Well, look, I just got called in for a shift, so let's link up again another day."

"Can I spend the weekend with you?"

"I gotta work," she grimaced.

"All weekend?"

"Yeah, two doubles back to back."

"Damn, okay, baby. Get that money then."

"Shit, you know it." Ronnie winked at her, then kissed Kenni's cheek. "I'll see you later."

"Okay, see you later, baby."

*   *   *

"How the fuck you lose yo key?" Ronnie thundered, striding into her apartment building.

Shyna eyed her evilly, watching her advance. "I don't know, Ronnie. My house key was right next to yours, along with my car key."

"So, you lost all of them?"

"No, I just don't have yours," Shyna snapped.

Ronnie unlocked her door and walked into her apartment, slipping her keys in her pocket. "Well, I ain't making yo simple ass another one."

"What the fuck do you mean?" Shyna shouted after her, walking into Ronnie's bedroom.

"I mean what I said. I ain't making you another one. You lost my shit. So, if you leave tonight, lock the bottom lock," she said, putting on another pair of clothes.

"Where you going?"

"I gotta work tonight."

"Well, don't go," Shyna stated matter of factly. "I wanna spend some time with you."

Peering at her with disdain, Ronnie stated, "Man, I'm going to get that money. You tripping."

"You own the fuckin' club! You getting paid regardless!"

"So? That's less money we gotta pay out, and more in our pockets if we work. I ain't fuckin' off no more. Excuse me," she said to Shyna, who stood in the doorway of her bedroom.

"Fuck you, Ronnie," Shyna retorted when she was pushed roughly to the side, out of Ronnie's path.

"Fuck you, too," Ronnie called back over her shoulder. "See you later, maybe."

"Swear I hate you sometimes."

Rounding on her, Ronnie stormed into her face, barking, "Well, I hate yo ass, too, then."

"Whatever. So, can I go with you?"

"You just said you hate me." Ronnie gaped at her like she was fourteen karat crazy. "Now you wanna go? Nah, stay yo ass here and think before you talk."

"I wanna go," Shyna stomped her foot. "Please. I'm sorry."

"Nah." Ronnie smiled evilly at her. "We just talked about space. Respect my shit." She walked out the door.

*   *   *

"You just been floating around here, smiling all goofy these last two weeks," Beaunna remarked to Kenni, who'd wandered into the living room with her phone in her hand. "Care to share?"

Kenni beamed. "Me and Ronnie back talking," she admitted.

Immediately, Beaunna raised her hand to hit the mute button on the TV. "That's new. So, y'all back together?"

"Not yet. We just been talking, like, getting to know each other all over again."

"That's cute," she said, forcing her motherly instinct down that screamed to protect her from getting hurt. "So, what you think? You think she's changed? Have you changed?"

A warm flush engulfed Kenni. She reclined back in the loveseat with a sigh. "We both definitely did. She working two jobs right now. We gonna be good when we get back together."

"Good. Then I'm happy for you," Beaunna told her honestly.

"Thanks," Kenni grinned. "Me too, mama."

"You better tell her she better not hurt my baby again, though," Beaunna warned her. "She can catch these hands now."

"She won't," she laughed. "We passed all that."

*   *   *

Parked behind a grocery store, with all of her tinted windows up, Ronnie dialed Kenni's number. "Yo, what's good, ma?"

"Hey," Kenni chirped happily. "I was just thinkin' of you. How work going?"

"It's cool," she lied smoothly, a grin plastered on her face. "It's my lil fifteen-minute break, so I wanted to make sure I called you. I miss yo voice. Shit, I miss you."

"Aww, you so sweet, babe. I miss you, too. When is your next off day?"

"Shit, between these two jobs, I don't have one." Ronnie reclined her seat. "I'ma just have to call off from this security shit to kick it with you."

"No, you ain't," Kenni fired back. "You better get that money!"

"But I miss you, though."

"And when you get some time, I'll be right there waiting. In the meantime, you get that money."

Ronnie chuckled. "Aight, I got you, baby. Yo, I been thinking, though. My lease almost up, and I'm definitely moving. You wanna get a spot together? I'll take care of everything," she told her quickly.

She squealed in glee. "You know I do!"

"Bet. You know where you would wanna move to?"

"Somewhere close to my mama. She would be here all by herself. Jeremy ain't really been coming around like he used to, and I don't wanna be too far from her."

"Girl, leave yo mama alone. She probably can't wait till you leave so she can have some act all throughout the house."

"Eww," Kenni laughed. "She better not."

"Yeah, whatever. Mama got needs just like you do. You like busting nuts, don't you?"

The thought made her pussy jump. Kenni clamped down on her bottom lip softly, murmuring, "I don't know. It's been a while. You gonna have to show me how that feel again."

"Shit, I got you," Ronnie replied, licking her lips. "Let me know when you ready."

"Hey, you the one that gotta find time," she pointed out.

"For you, I got all the time. I got you."

"Yeah, aight. We'll see."

"We most definitely will, but yo, I'ma get at you tomorrow. It's time for me to get back in here."

"Okay. I'll talk to you later, baby."

"Aight, baby." Ronnie hung the phone up and sped off towards her house.

        *   *   *

"Ronnie." Shyna grinded against the sleeping stud. When Ronnie turned away from her, she frowned, climbing on top of her, pulling her ear into her mouth. "Wake up, baby."

"Move," Ronnie grumbled sleepily.

"I need some head. Wake up," she pouted.

Shyna flopped back on the bed in exasperation. She shoved her, but Ronnie continued to snore, making Shyna huff in annoyance. Nipples pebbled, she pinched them herself, squeezing her legs together. Slowly, her hand drifted between her pussy lips, fondling her pearl. Moans crept out of her. Wetness secreted but her orgasm was elusive.

"Fuck," she growled, chasing it. Shyna took a finger and smeared it across Ronnie's lips. "Fuck me, baby, please." Again, a finger darted across the lips on her face.

"Bra, what the fuck!" Ronnie jumped up, tossing her onto the floor. "I'm fucking sleep, yo!"

"So! I'm fuckin' horny!" Shyna hollered back, getting up off the floor.

"Well, grab a fuckin' toy and go ham," she declared. "Leave me alone, damn! I'm fuckin' sleep! Shit, I told yo ass—"

"I know what the fuck you said! You came back from the fucking store, smoked, and went to sleep because of a bitch-ass headache."

"So, what the fuck is you doing putting yo pussy on me?"

"Nigga, I put this juice on yo shit!" Shyna threw a pillow at her. "I'm fuckin' horny!"

Ronnie threw the pillow back at her and went over to the dresser. She popped open a drawer and launched a vibrator at her. "Have fun." She scooped up her clothes and walked out of the room.

"Where you think you going?" Shyna demanded to know, following her.

"To my fuckin' house to get some sleep!" she snapped. "And don't fuckin' follow me! You need to catch a nut, remember?" She slammed the front door shut and went across the hall to her apartment, slamming the door.

Chapter 11

"Okay, I'll talk to you later, baby," Kenni cooed into the phone with a grin. She hung the phone up and spun her chair around to face Layla, who was lounging in her bed. "What you doing?"

Layla raised an eyebrow at her, looking up from her phone. "You don't find it weird that Ronnie all of a sudden got two jobs, always working, always busy?"

"Noo," Kenni rolled her eyes. "She getting that money."

Imitating her eye roll, she questioned, "Where she even do security at?"

"I don't know. I ain't ask."

"Stupid ass. Text her and ask her."

"No," Kenni refused. "I trust her."

"Really? After all this time? She could have a whole-ass girlfriend that you don't know about. What's up with Shyna?"

Pausing before speaking, Kenni took a deep breath. "Layla, I appreciate what I think you trying to do, but we good. We don't even talk about that bitch, she a nonfactor. We starting off again right."

"Yeah, whatever. You need to find out. Closed mouths don't get fed, and if she hurt you again, I'm putting sugar in her tank," she threatened.

  Kenni laughed. "Well, thanks, but we good," she said, pushing away the slight flare up of insecurity.

  "Yeah, whatever. Well, I'ma find out what's up." Layla stood up. "What she doing tonight?"

  "I don't know."

  "Well, get dressed." She opened her closet. "C'mon, let's see if she home and what she doing that y'all can't be kicking it."

  "Lay," Kenni chuckled, not moving from her chair. "It's not that serious, boo."

  "I will go by myself," Layla threatened.

  "Whatever. I trust her," she laughed. "Bye."

  Layla narrowed her eyes at her. "Y'all so fuckin' weird now." She sunk back into the bed.

  Laughing, Kenni replied, "Whatever."

  "I guess y'all did need a lil space to grow up and shit."

  "I know. I'm telling you, we good," Kenni grinned.

  "You like disgustingly happy," Layla told her, standing back up. "I think I am gonna leave."

  "Whatever," Kenni giggled and gave her the finger. "Bye."

     *   *   *

  Boom! Boom! Ronnie turned her vacuum off. "Who is it?" she hollered. *Boom! Boom!* Ronnie exhaled and set the vacuum down. She went to her front door and peeked out. "What's up?" she asked Layla and poked her head into the hallway, looking both ways for Kenni, and to make sure Shyna had truly gone to the grocery store like she'd said.

Layla barged right in, eyes roving around all that she could see. "Why you ain't at work? Kenni said you got two jobs now."

"I do. It's not time for me to go in yet. What's up, though? Where Kenni?"

"At home, missing you," Layla shot at her. "You need to spend more time with her."

"I know, I just be busy with two jobs."

"Yeah, whatever. Where Shyna?"

Ronnie's insides went cold, but she delivered smoothly. "How the fuck should I know? I ain't her keeper. She stay across the hall, go knock on the door. Y'all friends now?"

"Whatever. You better not hurt Kenni again. Go see her. Now," Layla demanded and walked out."

"The fuck?" Ronnie chuckled. She looked around her living room and checked the time. The wheels spun around in her head as she plotted. *Fuck it*, she muttered.

Thirty minutes and a shower later, Ronnie pulled up to Kenni's house. Quickly, she sent Shyna a message, stating she had gone to T's house for a minute. Diversion completed, she put her phone on silent and bounded up to the door and knocked.

"Hey, baby!" Kenni exclaimed, opening the front door and jumping into her arms. "What you doing here?"

Ronnie grinned. "A lil birdie reminded me I needed to spend time with you between my jobs."

"Was that lil birdie named LAYLA?" she shouted the name back into the house.

"She not here," Layla's voice called back. "Try again later." She pushed the front door shut.

Chuckling, Kenni replied, "I'm sorry about her."

"It's cool. Shit, she right. I do need to be spending more time with you. Shit, I told you, what, last week, I was. But check dig, I'ma make it up to you. Well, if yo mama cool with it. I wanna come over and spend the night with you when I'm off work."

Kenni's eyebrows furrowed together. "Why can't I spend the night with you?"

Her chest rose and fell with a heavy sigh. "I ain't talked to you about Shyna, but she still on that bullshit, and honestly, I don't even want that to touch what we starting now. My apartment got a lot of ugly memories, too. I wanna start all the way new with you. I want you to be my girl again, but I know I need to spend more time with you before we can make that happen. I ain't about to ask you to be my girlfriend again and not be spending no time with you."

"Well, I'll talk to my mama about it." Kenni squeezed her tightly. "Baby, I know you gotta work, though. I understand that, and I wouldn't stand in the way of that. I would still be yo girlfriend if you asked."

"You would?" When she nodded, Ronnie grinned and said, "Will you take me back and be my girlfriend again then?"

"Yes." Kenni pressed her lips to Ronnie's. "Took you long enough to ask."

"So, this what the fuck we go back to?" Jeremy spat, walking up to the house, interrupting their moment.

"What, Jeremy?" Kenni looked at her brother with chagrin.

"You back dyking?" he thundered. "After all that bullshit she put you through?"

"Jeremy, I fucking love her. Ain't shit changed! We took a break, and now we back. I love her, damn—"

Jeremy cut her off, screaming, "Ain't no such thing as love!"

"Yo, you sounding real bitter right now," commented Ronnie.

"Fuck you," he glowered.

Ronnie rolled her eyes and kissed Kenni's cheek. "I'ma check you later, baby. Go 'head and deal with yo brother."

"Okay." Kenni kissed her again. "Thank you, baby. I love you."

"I love you, too, baby."

"You just stupid as fuck," Jeremy grumbled, staring at her watching Ronnie drive off with a dopey smile on her face.

"No, you just fuckin' bitter!" she spazzed. "You and Shyna or you and whoever can work some shit out and be happy."

"I'm not—"

"Don't wanna hear it!" Kenni cut him off. Storming inside, she pulled Layla to her room, locking the door and turning her music up.

*   *   *

"Where my bottle at?" Ronnie questioned Shyna, entering her apartment.

"Where it's always at?" Shyna answered dryly. She followed Ronnie to the kitchen. "So, you went to T's house?"

Ronnie glared at her and rolled her eyes. "That's what I said, ain't it?"

"So, why wasn't yo car at T's house?"

"You stalking me now?" She set her bottle down.

"I'm not stalking you! I happened to roll past when I left the store."

"Shut the fuck up lying to me, yo. You only been to T's house one time. And if yo insecure ass would've called, you woulda known we rode together over to Ma Dukes' house." She took a swig from her bottle. "You been acting the fuck outta crazy lately, and I ain't got time for that shit." Ronnie walked back to her apartment and locked the door, leaving Shyna staring daggers at her front door.

*   *   *

"Mommy." Kenni entered her mother's room with baby steps to match her baby tone.

"Oh, Lord," Beaunna chortled. "What do you want?"

"I'm your favorite, right?" Kenni crawled into bed with her, smiling sweetly.

Narrowed eyes flashed to her daughter. "Child, what do you want?"

Batting her eyelashes, Kenni leaned in and kissed her mother's forehead. "You love me, right, Ma?"

"Oh my God. No, I hate you, child of mine," Beaunna joked, feigning exasperation. "What do you want? You're ruining my beauty sleep." She placed a hand over her head dramatically.

"Can Ronnie spend the night this weekend?" Kenni rushed the words out. Say yes. Thank you, Ma." She jumped up to retreat.

"Unt-unh, heifer, bring yo fast tail back in here," Beaunna called her back.

Kenni paused, turning around to face her mother with big, round eyes. "Ma, please. We not gonna do nothing! I promise."

"Yeah, whatever. Says the child who didn't stop when I walked in last time."

She laughed. "You can't just stop yourself from cumming. It feel too good."

"Oh my God!" Beaunna chastised her. "TMI, child. TMI!"

"Whatever, Ma. You wouldn't have stopped, either."

"That is neither here nor there."

"And what happened to, I'm on the best birth control, I can't get pregnant?"

Beaunna rolled her eyes. "Oh my God, you're insufferable. You are a spoiled rotten child."

"So, is that a yes?" Kenni questioned with a grin.

"I guess. That freaky shit better be down to a zero. I don't wanna see or hear nothing."

"Thank you," she squealed. She darted down and gave her mother some affection, then dashed for the door.

"Hey, hey, wait," Beaunna commanded, making her stop in her tracks. "What is going on with y'all?"

Another smile transformed her face. "We back together now, and when her lease is up next month, we getting a place together, close to you."

"Aww, look at my baby growing up. I'm happy for you, baby."

"Thanks, Ma." She grinned again and ran out of the room.

*   *   *

"So, you been MIA all week, and now you not even coming home tonight?" Shyna questioned dubiously.

"Yeah, my sister moving," Ronnie told her in a bored tone. "So, I'm crashing over there when I get off so we can get right to it. The faster we get that shit done, the faster I'll be back."

"Whatever." She cut her eyes at her. "That better be what you doing."

"Or what?" Ronnie threatened. "It ain't like you give me space to breathe or any-fucking-thing else. You always wanna fucking tag along, blow my phone up, or be on that goofy, pop-up shit."

"Because I like spending time with you!" Shyna shouted.

"Yeah, well, I used to like it, too, but now you on that clingy, crazy shit and I don't wanna be around that."

"Crazy? Crazy? I'm fuckin' crazy because I want to spend time with you? You can spend the night here, and we can go to yo sister's in the morning."

Ronnie gave her a look of disbelief. "Did you not even hear shit I said? One, my sister don't even like yo fuckin' ass, and two, I just don't fuckin' want to!" she roared.

"Listen, Ronnie, I will fuck you up if you—" Shyna began.

"Who the fuck you talking to?" She shoved her across the room. "Watch yo fuckin' mouth! You'll fuck me up? Nah, I'll fuck you up. Do something then." She stared at her angrily, waiting for Shyna to retaliate. "You know what, fuck you, yo. I'm good on you. We done. It's over." Ronnie turned her back on her.

"No, the fuck it's not!" Shyna jumped on her back, punching her in the head.

She flipped her over her shoulder and caught her in a chokehold. "Yes, the fuck it is. If I gotta put my fuckin' hands on you and beg for fuckin' space, I don't need to be with you! I don't wanna be with you. Leave me the fuck alone." Ronnie threw her away from her.

Shyna stood, chest heaving, and tears running down her face. "So, just like that, you say it's over, huh? You done?"

"Go get yo lil punk-ass gun," she taunted, smiling. "You ain't the only one packing heat." Ronnie lifted her shirt to flash the gun tucked in her waistband. "We can both die in this muthafucka tonight. What's up?"

"Fuck you, Ronnie," Shyna bit out.

"Yeah, I thought so. Fuck you, too." Ronnie stalked out.

*   *   *

Sitting in T's car, Ronnie slapped hands with her stud brother. "Good looking, bro."

"Fa sho. You still shouldn't have broken it off with her yet. It's only been a few weeks," T commented about Ronnie breaking it off with Shyna.

"Three weeks is almost a month, nigga," Ronnie told her. "A month too long. Fuck that bitch. I couldn't pretend no more. I saw my out and took it. And Kenni my girlfriend now. I couldn't risk fuckin' that up again."

"Yeah, I hear you, but you shoulda waited on that, too. You should've dicked Shyna down a few more times, then maybe we wouldn't be doing this goofy shit we doing now," she said, referring to Ronnie dropping her truck off at her sister's house, only to have T pick her up to take her to Kenni's house.

Ronnie laughed. "But you see, I covered my trail. And she would be stupid to pop up at Ari's house even if she knew where she lived."

"Damn right about that," T chuckled. "But you gotta go home sometimes. What you gonna do about that?"

"Shit, I got some cash stacked up. Fuck all that shit, I ain't going back. All I needed was my scale and weed. I got both, and enough money to crash at a hotel in the meantime."

"Nigga, you can stay with me and Kim," she told her, lightweight offended that Ronnie hadn't thought to include her family in on her plans to lay low.

Declining and shaking her head, Ronnie explained, "Nah, I'ma do the hotel. I got my own shit, you feel me, so when Kenni come through."

"I can dig it, but what about yo truck, though? That muthafucka stands out."

"Well, shit, what's up, can I whip yo 'lac?" Ronnie grinned.

"Nigga, you wanna drive my Cadillac!" she yelled.

"C'mon, nigga," Ronnie chuckled. "She don't even know you got that bitch, only we do."

"Aww, nigga," T began morosely. "I'm just fuckin' with you. You know I got you, lil bra."

"That's what's up."

The two shook hands again, and T expressed, "I'm glad you got it all figured out, bra. I see you then learned something from ya big brother."

"Yeah, good looking, fool." She grabbed her bookbag out the backseat. "I'm about to get in here, though, nigga."

"Aight, get yo sprung ass out then," T chastised with a smile.

"Aight, nigga, be safe."

"Nigga, you be safe," T called out. "You got a lil crazy one out, running around without a leash."

Closing the door, Ronnie laughed. She took a deep breath, glad to be rid of Shyna for good, and excited for her new beginning with Kenni. Walking up the walkway, a punch of nerves smashed into her. She felt giddy at the prospect of finally being done with Shyna. At the door, waiting for Kenni, she thought about all their plans. Kenni was due to graduate soon. They would be together in a new place. Ronnie had proposed a while back, and she still meant it. She was ready to start planning their wedding. There was only one woman in the world for her, and she was standing outside of her house.

"What you doing with that bookbag?" Beaunna cracked, standing in the front door. "You moving in or staying the night?"

"I would def move in for a few weeks if you would let me," Ronnie told her seriously.

Beaunna cocked her head to the side, hearing the seriousness of Ronnie's statement. "And you're entirely through with Crazy this time? No more back and forth?"

"Yes, ma'am. And I don't know if Kenni told you, but my lease is up soon, and I'ma get us a spot together. And I want to marry her, if that's okay with you."

"So, that time apart really made a difference, huh? Yes, that's fine with me as long as my baby doesn't get hurt. You keep her and yourself away from that little shit in your apartment building."

Grinning, Ronnie replied, "Honestly, Ma, like I said, my lease almost up and me and Kenni back together, so I'm not even going back there. My family already know what's up, too. I just don't want nothing or nobody to taint our relationship again."

"All right," she smiled. "We'll see. You know you're welcome here anytime while you're figuring it all out."

Relieved to have this conversation off her chest, she followed her inside. Beaunna veered off

to the living room, stating, "Keep the door open,"
making Ronnie grin. She made her way to Kenni's
room and walked in.

"What's up, baby?"

Kenni squealed and hopped off her bed,
jumping into Ronnie's arms. She smothered her
face with kisses. "Why you ain't tell me you was
here?"

"Surprise," Ronnie grinned, sitting her on
the bed.

"Close the door," she whispered, lying back
on the bed, biting her lip.

"Nah," Ronnie laughed. "Yo mama already
said keep the door open."

She pouted, then grinned mischievously.
"Fine. We'll keep the door open then."

A groan slipped out of Ronnie. She didn't
want to wait either, but she kissed her forehead and
murmured, "Wait till she go to sleep."

"Fine."

Ronnie flicked her on the nose. "What y'all
got to eat? I'm hungry."

"C'mon." Kenni bounded up from the bed,
heading to the kitchen.

*   *   *

Ronnie slid her strap in and out of Kenni
slowly. One hand covered her mouth to muffle the
moans coming from her. When her sounds of
ecstasy continued, she dropped down to her
forearms, placing them on the side of her head,
using her mouth to drown the whimpers of sexual
pleasure.

"Fuck, baby," Kenni groaned, dragging her nails down the stud's back.

Thrusting slow, pounding hard, Ronnie's arms deftly moved, wrapping her up in a headlock. She dipped her head down, attacking Kenni's lips, licking and sucking on them. Frantic scratches on her back ensued, and she could feel the state of orgasmic frenzy she'd worked her into.

Shuddering, Kenni stammered, "Ooh, shit… Fuck, I'm cumming, baby… Ooh, baby, I'm cumming."

A mother of an orgasm slammed into Kenni, making her body convulse. She clawed at Ronnie's back with shooting sparks behind her clutched eyes. Did Ronnie care? No. She pulled out with a plop of her strap and sucked on her clit until spurts of cum shot into her mouth.

"Damn, baby," Kenni panted when Ronnie finally released her from their sexual stronghold. "I missed that." She snuggled into Ronnie.

That warm feeling of contentment mingled with happiness rippled throughout Ronnie. She wrapped her arms around her, pulling her closer, and kissed her forehead. "I love you, baby."

"I love you, too, baby." Kenni angled her head up for a kiss.

"You still got that ring I gave you?"

"Yeah. It's on my nightstand."

Leaping up like they hadn't just engaged in a marathon of sex, Ronnie retrieved the ring. She kneeled down on Kenni's side of the bed, facing her. "Baby, will you marry me?"

Sleep tugged at her, but a grin still surfaced. "You know I will." Ronnie slid the ring on her finger, and the two shared a kiss. "Now, come on, let's go to sleep. I'm sleepy," Kenni yawned.

Elation roared throughout Ronnie. She made her way back to the spooning position they were in and kissed her again. "I love you, baby."

"I love you, too, baby," Kenni murmured, drifting off already.

*   *   *

Loud noises pulled Ronnie from out of her deep sleep. In a light sleep, eyes still closed, she could definitely make out Kenni's screeching and another woman's raised voice. She dragged a hand over her face and opened her eyes.

"Fuck you!" Kenni yelled.

Ronnie jumped up immediately with a one track mind. That damn Shyna had sniffed her way over here! She grabbed her gun out her bag. Playtime was over for that bitch. She headed to the front of the house with a ball of trepidation and anxiety churning, all while praying to God Shyna didn't mention they'd been together during Kenni's absence.

"Speak of the dyke," Jeremy said, glaring at Ronnie, who entered the kitchen. "And who should appear?"

"Who I love is none of your business!" Kenni shrieked with exasperation.

"And who I did was yo business?" Jeremy fired back.

"Bra, get yo bitter ass outta here. If you want that bitch, go get her!"

"Kenni!" Beaunna shouted at her disapprovingly. "Both of y'all, calm the fuck down. Jeremy, can we talk without the extra shit?" Her pleas went unnoticed.

"Fuck you!" Jeremy roared at Kenni. "I ain't bitter!"

"Fuck you!" She spewed venom back at him. "You is bitter. You mad that I'm happy. You really fuckin' loved that crazy bitch, huh? If you want her that bad, man up and go get her, dummy! Ronnie did."

Staring at Ronnie coolly, he questioned, "And what else did Ronnie do?"

Instantly, her insides froze. "Proposed," Ronnie recovered, holding up Kenni's hand. She dropped her fiancée's hand and stepped up to Jeremy. "Listen, man, if you want Shyna, go get her. Have her, yo. Please. Shit, if that's what makes you happy, go get her, but I'ma be around, nigga. Yo sister and me getting married, and yo mama already gave her blessing."

Jeremy rounded on his mother. "You condone this unnatural-ass shit?"

"Jeremy—"

"You know she fucked off on yo daughter? That the whole reason they broke up was because of Shyna?"

"Yes, Jeremy. I—"

"What the fuck, Ma?" he cried out. "So, everybody can fuck up my happiness because shorty ain't right for me, according to y'all, but you gonna condone a nigga cheating and beating on yo daughter and not give a fuck? Well, I'ma not give a fuck what y'all think, either," Jeremy spat, storming out the door and slamming it behind him.

Beaunna exhaled shakily. "That is not how I thought I would be woken up today," she grumbled.

"Yeah. You and me both," Kenni agreed.

Tightening her robe, Beaunna told the couple, "I'm going back to bed. If y'all leave, coffee me, please."

Chuckling, Kenni grabbed Ronnie's hand. "We'll go in a lil bit, Mama. C'mon, baby."

"Like mother, like daughter. You wanna go back to bed, too, huh?" Ronnie joked.

"Hell yeah. His ass came banging on the door all early and shit because he lost his keys last night and started shit. And his bitch ass about to come right back because he ain't even grab his spare house key from Mama."

"Well, hopefully, he'll be cool by the time he come back."

"He won't be. He throws fits and holds grudges like a girl," she yawned.

"C'mere." Ronnie put her gun away, undressed, and pulled Kenni onto the bed. She massaged Kenni's back and temples until sleep knocked them both off kilter.

Two hours later, banging on the door ruptured their sleep. Neither one of them moved to get up. Kenni pushed against Ronnie's chest.

"Answer the door," she groaned.

"This yo house," Ronnie complained.

"Ain't nobody home. You house sitting. Please, baby," Kenni begged. "If it's Jeremy, Mama keep his key in the kitchen junk drawer."

Ronnie groaned and opened her eyes. She heaved a big sigh and rolled out of bed. In the hallway, she waved off Beaunna, who, without a word, headed back to her room. Continuing to the door, she whipped it open, only for her eyes to balloon.

"Wow, so this is your sister's house, huh?" Shyna glared at her.

Stepping out onto the porch, Ronnie closed the door behind her quietly. "What the fuck is you doing here, yo? Leave," she demanded.

"Nah, I don't think I will," Shyna laughed. "So, was this the reason you all of a sudden started needing space and shit?"

Calm, calm, Ronnie reminded herself. *Keep your voice low. Don't spazz, Ronnie*, she chanted to herself. "Listen, you not my bitch, so I don't owe you no fuckin explanations."

Shyna stepped into her personal space. "Ronnie, I will fuck you and that lil bitch up. Quit playing with me," she hissed threateningly.

"You. Not. My. Bitch," Ronnie spat in her face, slow and precise.

The front door opened, and Kenni stepped out, commanding immediately, "Get the fuck off my porch," and standing at Ronnie's side.

Lips curving into a grin, Shyna told her, "Fuck you and yo porch, little girl."

"Well, get the fuck off it then."

"Shut—"

"No, you shut the fuck up!" Kenni hollered. "I don't care what you got to say. Get the fuck off my property! Stay the fuck away from me. I'm done entertaining yo lil bullshit. I'm glad my brother left yo crazy ass."

"First of all, your brother loves me." She winked at Kenni. "He vented to me about what's going on over here, and I put him to bed. Second, lil bitch—"

"Nooobody cares," Kenni interrupted. "Fuckin' leave! Damn! Stay the fuck away from me, my house, and my damn fiancée!"

"Fiancée?" Shyna flinched.

"You know, I wouldn't piss on you if you was on fire." Beaunna stepped onto the porch. "You heard my daughter. Get the hell off my porch before I call the police."

The words didn't quite register with Shyna. She swallowed in confusion, brain spritzing over the intimate memories she'd shared with Ronnie from losing her fiancé and father figure to her past suffrage of trauma and abuse. They did it just like folks had said you were supposed to start a relationship. Friends first, then lovers and partners.

Tears brimming in her eyes tripped down her face. "Fiancée? Fiancée?" Her mind blanked out.

"Shyna, listen, I do not want you."

"After everything we shared? After everything I fuckin' told you?" her words rang out, tinged in anger. These last three months, Ronnie had done everything to solidify their relationship, even badmouthing the young woman who currently wore a ring on her hand. But now, just like that, she was stripped of everything and was alone again.

"Leave me and my family alone," Ronnie said, clasping Kenni's hand with the ring on it.

Multiple epiphanies burst in her mind like fireworks on July fourth. She nodded, wiping the tears off her face. "Oh, I get it. I understand now." Shyna smiled at the cognizance. "This was a fuckin' game, huh?"

Apprehension snaked through Ronnie, the dread prompting her to shove Kenni away from her urgently, stating, "Go in the house." Her eyes were perched on Shyna's hand that had drifted out of sight, behind her back.

"Nah, stay right here!" Shyna shouted, pulling out a nine millimeter pistol, aiming it at Kenni. "Y'all bad, remember?" she gestured at Beaunna, who stood, horrified, hand over her mouth. "This shit funny, huh?" The gun went back to pointing at Kenni, but her words were directed at Ronnie. "So, this was all a fuckin' game, right, Ronnie? Play with me until yo lil bitch took you back. Never mind that I was happy with Jeremy. Never mind my damn fiancé is gone. This was all a fuckin' game, right, Ronnie?! You never gave a fuck about me, right, Ronnie? Only her. I was just good enough to fuck on."

"Shyna, I swear to God," began Ronnie.

"Swear to God, what?" Shyna taunted. "I swear to God we'll never play this game again." She aimed, and a shot was fired, hitting its mark, blood splattering everywhere.

*   *   *

"NOOOO!" Ronnie roared. She dropped to the ground amidst Beaunna's screams, scrambling towards Kenni. Blood poured from the open wound in her chest. "Kenni, baby." Ronnie pulled her into her lap, rocking her. "I'm sorry, baby. I'm so fuckin' sorry. Please hold on, baby. Hold on, baby. Call the police! Somebody get an ambulance here!" she shouted, crying.

"Baby," Kenni gurgled. "I… love… love… y-y-you," Kenni gasped as blood began spilling from her mouth.

"I love you, too, baby. I swear I fuckin' love you," Ronnie told her.

Shyna squatted down in front of them, placing the gun to her temple. "This is why you shouldn't play games with people's hearts, Ronnie," she hissed with fire in her eyes.

Beaunna screeched in anguish, slamming a plastic chair across Shyna's back. A shot popped out from the impact, but she didn't lose the gun. Smiling wickedly, Shyna faced her and fired.

"Fuck you," Ronnie blasted when Beaunna imploded. Hot tears streaked down her face and constricted her voice. "Fuck you. Fuck you. Fuck you." She pressed harder onto Kenni's chest wound to stop the flow, readily accepting that she would be next.

"No, next time, just don't fuck with me," Shyna threatened. Sirens in the distance made her glance around. Neighbors were out, watching the scene from afar. People were in the windows. She kissed Ronnie's cheek and ran to her car, fishtailing out the lot.

Beneath her hands, Ronnie felt the struggle of Kenni's chest to rise once more. She stuck a finger under her nose. The body in her arms went lax. "Fuck, baby! Nooo!" she cried out. "Somebody help! Help me!" Ronnie rocked her in her arms, gazing at Beaunna, watching her chest move up and down.

Epilogue

"Answer the fuckin' phone," Ronnie growled into the phone. "Answer the fuckin' phone. Fuckin' bitch," she spat when the voicemail picked up. "I'm at yo neck, nigga. You and that bitch."

"Ron." T clamped a hand down on her shoulder.

Ronnie shrugged her hand off her shoulder and followed the rest of their family, plus Kenni's friends, into Beaunna's home. Everyone piled into the living room, centering around Beaunna and Ronnie. Ma Dukes, Moryah, and Chantel's girlfriend, Mya, bustled around the crew, passing out drinks, pushing plates of food into unwilling hands. Ma Dukes nudged a plate back into Beaunna's hands.

"Bee, you have to eat, honey," Ma Dukes attempted to persuade her gingerly.

Beaunna set the plate down. "Thank you. I'm not hungry."

Ma Dukes sighed, and Moryah took over. "C'mon, Bee. A few bites at least. You've barely eaten these last two weeks. You need to eat to maintain your strength so your shoulder can heal," she told her, referring to the wound she'd suffered from the encounter with Shyna.

"I need to find my son." Tears gushed from her eyes. "He didn't even show up today. On her—" Her voice broke. "My baby's funeral," she cried, "and he didn't even show up."

"Yeah, I wanna find him, too," Ronnie said, pushing her plate to the side. "And don't let me catch up with that bitch."

"Why did you fuck that girl, Ronnie?" Beaunna's gray eyes locked onto her brown ones. "If you loved my daughter, why did you fuck that girl?" Shame riddled her, and she was unable to respond vocally. Physically, she hung her head. Beaunna continued vehemently. "You the reason my baby gone. If you hadn't fucked that girl and came back—hell, if you never even pursued Kenni—my baby would still be here."

"I wish I would've never fucked that bitch, but I love Kenni." Ronnie glared at her with wet eyes. "Kenni would still be alive if yo son bitch ass—"

"Ronnie," Arianna warned her.

She jumped to her feet, spurring the oldest ones of her group of friends into moving in front of her. "No, she need to know! It's Jeremy's fault! That's why he ain't come to the funeral. He told Shyna to come to the house that day!"

"He would never!" Beaunna shot up to her feet. "Jeremy loved his sister!" Ma Dukes and Moryah held her arms on either side with Chantel and Mya in between the two grief-ridden women. "You get out of my house! All of y'all! GET OUT!"

Ma Dukes and Moryah rubbed her arms. "Bee, we been over this, and just like we told you last time, baby, we not leaving you here alone. Say whatever you want, but we are not leaving you alone."

"I said get out! Let me go!" Beaunna attempted to pull away from the two mothers holding her. "Get out now! Get out!" She fought the women off, but couldn't get away from the four women surrounding her, and crumbled to the floor. "I just want my kids. Where is my son? My baby girl," she blubbered.

The crew parted, allowing Ronnie passage to Beaunna. She pulled her mother-in-law into a bear hug. Layla and Sayvonne approached from where they were weeping together on the couch and wrapped themselves around the two. Ronnie's family followed suit, the sobs rippling throughout the group. Together, as a unit, they stayed until the cries hitched and ebbed away. As everyone peeled off one another, Beaunna's phone began to ring a specialized tone that indicated Jeremy was calling.

"Jeremy?" Beaunna gasped, running to her cell phone on the couch. "Jeremy? Hello? Hello?" She fumbled with the phone and ended up putting it on speaker. "Jeremy?"

"Mama, I love you," Jeremy's voice belted out into the room.

"I love you, too, baby. Where are you? Why wasn't you at your sister's funeral?" Beaunna whined.

"I found her, mama. I found that bitch," Jeremy growled. "She took my sister." A gunshot rang out, and everyone flinched. "So, I took her life, too." He made a spitting sound.

"Okay, baby. Now, where are you? Come home, baby. Please, Jer."

"Mama, I love you." His weeping voice thickened, making him pause to swallow. "But I can't come home. I can't. My sister gone because of me."

"No, no, it's not your fault."

"It is, mama! Y'all pissed me off, and I went to Shyna's house," he scoffed. "I was pissed at y'all and wanted to drive a wedge between Ronnie and Kenni. I was hoping Shyna would be pissed and break them up again, and she did fuckin' permanently. Now, everywhere I fuckin' go, I see my sister's face. I hear my last words to my sister, my voice saying fuck you."

"Jeremy, where are you?" Beaunna screamed frantically.

Ma Dukes pawed at Moryah's arm. Cell phones whipped out throughout the group. Moryah reported to police the situation at hand.

"My last words to you ain't gonna be fuck you, mama! I love you, mama. I'm so fuckin' sorry, mama!" Jeremy cried. "Mama, I love you!"

"Jeremy, WHERE ARE YOU?!" Beaunna shouted with tears streaming down her face. She grabbed her keys, and Ma Dukes took them from her, hurrying outside with everyone else in tow.

"Mama, just say it back," Jeremy begged her. "I can't tell Kenni, and she can't say it back to me no more. So, mama, please. I love you."

"I am on my way wherever you are, baby, just please don't do nothing crazy."

"I love you, mama."

"Where are you?!"

"Last chance, mama. I love you."

"Jeremy, I love you, too! Where—" A gunshot permeated through the phone, followed by silence. "Jeremy! Jeremy!" Beaunna screamed. "Where are you going? My son needs me!" she yelled at Ma Dukes, driving back towards her home. She reached out, trying to grab the steering wheel and maneuver it from the passenger seat.

Ma Dukes threw the car into park and jumped out, taking the keys. Everyone surged around the car, leaning against Beaunna's door so she couldn't open it.

"NO! NOO! NO! NO! MY KIDS! MY BABIES!" Beaunna wailed, lashing out at everything in arm's reach.

Once Beaunna calmed slightly from her frantic state of mind, Ma Dukes opened her car door. "C'mon, Bee, let's go in the house."

Beaunna got out of the car sullenly, and the group surrounded her. She took a few steps in the same general direction as everyone, then broke away, dashing towards the street where traffic sped up and down the block. Layla tackled her, rolling her away from the street. Sayvonne charged over and helped hold her down while she wailed.

"I want to be with my kids!" she cried out in anguish.

Ronnie's crew trickled out of the house. Everyone converged around Beaunna, who was fighting the two girls.

"Get a damn bus here or something!" Ma Dukes barked into her phone.

Police, an ambulance, and a unit from the psychiatric hospital appeared on scene minutes later. Beaunna still struggled, fighting against everyone in uniform and not in uniform. Eventually, a tranquilizer brought her down so the staff could strap her down and transport her to the local facility. The uniformed officers spoke with Ma Dukes, and then Layla and Sayvonne.

Ronnie stood, staring blankly, watching Beaunna get driven away against her will. When she was approached, she turned away. "I'm fine. I don't wanna talk," Ronnie replied curtly, going back in the house.

*   *   *

On bended knees, body wracked with sobs, full of liquor and THC, Ronnie cried out with clasped hands, "God, You know I ain't no praying type nigga, but why? WHY?! Why You take my baby, man? What the fuck? What I'm supposed to do without her? Fuckin' bullshit, man! Why, God?" She jumped up and rammed her fist into the wall. She did it again, barely registering the pain of her knuckles being split open.

Her bedroom door opened. Ma Dukes and Mya swarmed on her, wrapping their arms around her. Tears flowed freely between the three women. Ronnie struggled against their hold.

"Baby, calm down." Mya attempted to placate her.

"Fuck you!" Ronnie shrilled, ripping out of their hold. She assaulted the wall again and crumbled to the floor, burying her head in her hands. "Why He have to take my baby, man? Why Kenni couldn't live?"

Moryah sidled down next to her, pulling Ronnie into her arms. "I love you, baby. I'm so sorry you gotta deal with this."

"Ronnie," Ma Dukes began, kneeling in front of her, wiping her tears away. "I know it hurts, baby. I know it hurts, but we can't question God. Everything happens for a reason. I know it's cliché to say, and it don't do nothing for your pain. When I lost T's brother, Tyrone, it ain't help me none, either, but I promise you, time heals all wounds, Ronnie. You will never forget her; the pain just becomes more bearable with each passing day. But we will get through this together, Ronnie, like always."

The cries hitched with the automatic rebuttal to Ma Dukes words. *Nothing will help,* Ronnie thought somberly. *Not all of them together. Fuck time. If God really didn't want her to suffer, He wouldn't have taken Kenni.*

*   *   *

"Ronnie, you need to eat something." Arianna entered her sister's room and folded her arms, staring disapprovingly at the full plate of food she'd brought to Ronnie an hour ago.

Ronnie looked over her shoulder from where she was perched on the edge of the bed, facing the wall. "For what?" she questioned coldly. "Kenni can't eat. Why should I? You know"—she stood up, facing Arianna—"I really wish y'all would get off this babysit Ronnie shit. I'm fine," she said tersely, punctuating her lie with a swift jab to her punching bag.

"You're not!" Arianna told her with narrowed eyes.

"I fuckin' am!" Ronnie exploded. "Shit, y'all ain't making it no better! What the fuck, I'm supposed to feel better, be happy because y'all fuckin' here all the time?!"

"No, you're not! We know you mourning. So is all of us. We here because we love you and don't want you to do nothing crazy."

"There it is!" Ronnie slow capped. "The real fuckin' reason. I ain't gonna do nothing to myself," she glowered at her big sister.

Arianna took a deep breath. "Ronnie, I love you. I just want you to be okay. I wanna help you any way I can."

Liquor splashed into Ronnie's cup. She finished the cup off and swirled the bottle, sloshing the remnants around. "Another bottle would help. And y'all leaving me the fuck alone."

In a flash, Arianna was there, grabbing the bottle and slamming it onto the bedroom floor. "This ain't fuckin' helping! Being fucked up all the time ain't how you deal with it!"

"Who the fuck is you to tell me?!" Ronnie hollered, stepping into her face. "Who the fuck did you lose? I lost my fuckin' baby, my fuckin' heart." Traitorous tears scrambled down her face. She turned away from her sister, plucking a picture of Kenni off her dresser. Arianna's arms came around her, and she shrugged off her touch. "Can you leave me alone, please? Damn," she bit out.

The bedroom door opened, but Ronnie didn't turn to see if someone else was coming in, or Arianna was leaving.

"I just don't wanna lose you, too, Ronnie," Arianna murmured, then the door closed.

"I just want you," Ronnie said to the picture of Kenni after a few moments of silence. "I swear I would do anything to bring you back. I wouldn't fuck it up again." She lost herself in memories of the past. Liquid continued to seep rapidly from her eyes. She sniffed. "It's all my fault you gone anyway. It shoulda been me." She echoed the sentiments Beaunna had expressed the day of the funeral.

*　　　*　　　*

A knock on Ronnie's bedroom door stirred her from her sleep. Over the past few weeks, or however long it had been, she might have lost a sense of time and couldn't pinpoint her family's babysitting schedule, but only two people knocked on her door before coming in first. Too bad she didn't want to see either of them.

"Ron, I'm coming in, bro," Chantel's voice said from the other side.

And I bet you bringing Mya with you, Ronnie snarled in her head, envious of the couple who was still alive, building and thriving together.

"What's up?" Ronnie sat up in her bed.

"We brought you some food." Mya held up a bag of fast food.

Ronnie sneered at her. "I ain't hungry."

Unconsciously, Chantel's hands sought Mya's for a squeeze and release. *They probably didn't even realize they did it*, Ronnie observed sourly.

"I got some weed," Chantel broadcasted.

She scoffed, "Where my Hennessey?"

"Come on now." Chantel held up her hand. "You know I got you, bra."

Mya stepped in between the two before the exchange could take place. "But you gotta eat and shower first."

Ronnie's lips twisted up. This was another mystery she hadn't solved. Randomly, it seemed someone withheld her liquor until she caved and did something stupid they wanted her to do like eat and shower. "I'm not hungry, and I just woke up. I ain't taking no shower," Ronnie told her defiantly.

Lips pursed in her direction, Mya snatched the bottle from her girlfriend and started to walk out. "No liquor for you until you do then."

Hate unfurled in her stomach. She hated Mya for holding her liquor hostage. She hated Chantel for allowing her girlfriend to pull this stunt. She hated their stupid relationship. It wasn't fair they got to love one another, and she was alone.

"Fine," she growled, throwing the covers off of her.

Ten minutes later, Ronnie was back in her room after a half-ass shower and wolfing down her food. Surprisingly, she was a little hungry. She didn't know the last time she had eaten.

Chantel passed her a blunt while Mya poured Hennessey into cups for the two studs. *Perfect synchronization*, Ronnie scoffed. They complemented and balanced each other well. Kenni had done the same for her, too, she thought. *She was my other half.*

"Why are y'all still in here?" Ronnie questioned, ignoring her cup and swiping the bottle.

"Because we love you," Mya told her simply.

"My nigga, it don't matter what you say. We in here. We ain't going nowhere," Chantel told her.

"Fuck you," Ronnie bit out, still sullen about them having a relationship and holding her bottle.

"Love you too," Chantel smiled, raising a cup at her.

Huffing, Ronnie strode out of her room, into the living room, flinging herself down onto the couch. She ignored the looks from Moryah and Arianna; anything to be away from the happy couple. Two hours later, she felt differently. Arianna had cooked her favorite meal, trying to get her to eat, and Moryah had turned on her favorite movie. Despite it all, she didn't give in and engage with either of them. The Hennessey had her zoned out. She felt alone with jagged knives ripping into her skin whenever she thought about Kenni. When the happy couple finally emerged, Ronnie dashed to her room, craving the solace.

*   *   *

"Why you don't never say nothing when I come in yo room?" T inquired, sitting on a stool she had dragged in. "We just sit in here and stare at each other, but everybody else, you make leave."

"You know why," Ronnie told her with a curled lip. She reached for her bottle, taking a long swig.

T extended a blunt to her that she didn't take. "Nah, nigga. Because you love me the most and I'm yo favorite," she cracked with a smile.

"No," Ronnie denied. "This yo fault, too. You supposed to be the oldest, making sure yo lil brothers straight. And following yo lead, my bitch gone! Kenni dead because I listened to yo ass! 'Cause of you!" she spat.

T licked her lips, attempting to shelve the mental burden that had just been thrown on her shoulders. It was true, though. She had advised Ronnie on how to play the game. "I'm sorry, lil bra," she finally told her. "If I woulda known—"

"Man, save that shit," Ronnie lashed out. "You know what she meant to me when we broke up, and you took me to a strip club. My baby gone, but you got yo hoes, so you good. Nigga, I ain't you. Fuck them hoes, nigga. I want my baby back. Can my so-called big brother fix that?" she asked rhetorically. "Nah, I ain't think so, but you knew how to help make it so my baby gone fuckin' permanently. Fuck you, man." Ronnie finally looked away.

Tongue in cheek, T left the room. Ronnie heard Jay and Kim call out to her without receiving a response. The front door slammed shut, and Ronnie settled back onto her messy bed.

*   *   *

Ronnie's eyelids fluttered as she regained consciousness from a deep sleep she didn't realize she was in. A genuine smile stretched across her face when she recalled her dream. Kenni had visited her. Happiness zipped through her, making her lips tingle as if Kenni had kissed them and left, saying I love you.

Her smile faltered. Kenni was admonishing her in the dream for the treatment she'd been dishing out to her family. She heaved a sigh and pushed herself up off the bed. Looking around, Ronnie smiled; it was like she was still in the room with her, just like in her dream.

Crossing to her bedroom door, she paused. Ronnie heard Kenni berating her in her head at the hesitation. She grabbed her bottle of Hennessey and opened the door. Kim and Jay's faces gazed back at her.

"Shot up?" she questioned with a smile, holding the liquor.

"Aye, let's get it, lil bro," Jay smiled.

Kim turned the stereo up to the max. She gathered the shot glasses for the trio and brought the weed over to the table. Once settled at the table with shots in hand, they held them up, toasting one another.

"Salute to you, lil bro. You gonna be aight. We got you," Kim stated.

Their glasses clinked together, but the liquor ran sour down Ronnie's throat. The remnant feelings from her dream started to ebb away. She pushed away the impending despair. No matter what, she still needed to apologize for her actions. Her family didn't deserve that.

*   *   *

Shot after shot, the three of them slammed them back. Somewhere during that time, Ronnie had gotten drunk. She'd sent out drunk texts, full of apologies and I love you's. They had made videos, laughed, and kicked it down memory lane about Kenni and their high school years.

"All right," Ronnie stood. "I'm fucked up," she admitted, swaying with a smile plastered on her face. "I'm going to lay down."

"Punk ass," Kim slurred.

Ronnie gave her the finger and turned to stumble to her room.

"I'ma have somebody bring us some food!" Jay bellowed.

"Jay, shut up!" Kim demanded, cringing away from her. "Why so loud?"

"Put something in my mouth, and I'll be quiet."

Ronnie closed her door to the rest of their antics. Alone in her room, she made her way over to the bed. Her favorite picture of Kenni lay waiting for her. She picked it up and fell backward against the wall.

"I miss you," Ronnie uttered to the picture, kissing it. Tears sprang forth and ran down her face. She pulled a knife from her pants pocket. Unbeknownst to the two in the other room, she had swiped it after cutting the limes to match the tequila Jay had brought out.

Her brain cleared from the cool metal laying flat on her skin. The only thing pressing her mind was seeing Kenni again. Arianna's words filtered through her brain, her statement of not wanting to lose her. Her heart throbbed, and she pushed all thoughts of her family out her brain. If it was meant to be, then it would be. If not, then it wouldn't. She just wanted to be with Kenni.

*   *   *

T and Arianna walked through the door of Ronnie's apartment, carrying pizza. Arianna plopped down into a chair next to Kim, who was rolling a blunt. T dropped down onto the couch next to Jay and Chantel, who were playing a video game.

"Ms. Bee still getting sedated on the regular," T reported to them. "Ma Dukes and Moryah up there visiting her now."

Kim lit the blunt. "She gonna bounce back. Her and Ron gonna be straight."

"Damn right," Arianna agreed, smiling. "What made her send out those texts?"

"Shit, we had some drinks and shit. Bra bra was in her feelings for a minute," Jay delved.

Arianna smiled and passed a joint. "She getting better."

"How long she been in her room, though?" T questioned.

"About an hour or two. She wanted to sleep that shit off in her bed. She was fucked up," Kim answered.

An uneasy feeling T couldn't pinpoint made her hold onto the blunt. Something wasn't right. She felt it. "I'ma go check on her." She got up and knocked on Ronnie's door. No answer. She turned the doorknob. "Y'all know her door was open?" T questioned, not opening the door.

"Nah," answered Chantel, abandoning the game and going to the closed door with the rest of their family of friends joining them as the energy of uneasiness spread.

She took a deep breath to calm her frazzled nerves and pushed the door open. All five of their mouths fell open when T opened the door. Their stud brother Ronnie lay in a pool of her own blood, her wrists slit, and a picture of Kenni clutched in her hand.

Playing Games Discussion Questions

1. What is the difference between the heterosexual lifestule and the lesbian lifestyle portrayed by the characters?
2. What are the similarities between the two lifestyles based on the lesbian lifestyle portrayed in this novel?
3. Does the statutory rape law apply to lesbians?
4. The character Ronnie had just turned nineteen and Kenni turned seventeen in the book. Does this qualify as statutory rape?
5. On occasions the characters physically struck one another. Even though they are all women does this constitute domestic abuse?
6. Which community has more domestic violence? LGBT or straight? Does it matter? Shouldn't we aim to prevent it?
7. Do you know any preventative methods so you will not have to use violence on your mate?
8. Which community has more suicides, LGBT or straight? Does it matter? Shouldn't we aim to prevent it?
9. The suicide hotline number is 1-800-273-8255 available 24 hours every day. Please talk to someone. Suicide is not the answer.

10. How would you describe the character Shyna?
11. Why did Ronnie continue to go back to her and Shyna continually allow her?
12. Who do you think was at fault for the way things turned out? Why?
13. Do you think Ronnie's friends played a role in Ronnie's actions and decisions regarding Shyna and Kenni? Are your friends influential in your relationship?
14. Beaunna, Kenni's mother was very laidback in raising her kids. What do you think of her motherly ways? Do you think if she was harsher things may have turned out differently?
15. Do you think it is proper for parents to intervene in her kids relationships whether it be in a negative or positive manner?
16. Should parents build and maintain relationships with their kids choice of partner?
17. What could the main characters individually have done for a happier outcome?
18. Do you think all lesbian families are like Ronnie's family of friends?
19. As you were reading did you read and picture as normally like any other novel or was it hard to read and picture because of the characters sexuality?

20. Did the book entertain and/or educate you? How?
21. Would you recommend the book to others?
22. Did the book live up to your expectations for a 'REBOOT'?
23. What do you think about T's interest in Layla?
24. Do you think T may have a shot?
25. Read on for an excerpt from Players Ball, Playing Games II.

Playing Games II

Players Ball

Kendra Spencer

T cut her car off and reclined back into her seat. Gazing off in to the distance at the sea of headstones assembled in the grass made T's mouth tighten as her lips twisted. She pinched the bone between her closed eyes. Being in the cemetery brought back another memory of a death, her older brother's. T shook her head to dispel the memories and reached for a blunt in her ashtray. Pulling on the blunt several times, T filled her lungs with the THC, exhaling before replacing it back in her car ashtray. Once out of the car T straightened her clothes out then started to walk towards Ronnie's grave plot.

With each step T took towards Ronnie's grave, her feet seemed to be getting heavier and heavier. Finally, she came to a stop in front of Ronnie's final resting place. A tear rolled down her face into the dirt as T looked at the up turned ground waiting for Ronnie's casket. Turning away, T went to sit next to Kenni's grave a few feet away from Ronnie's grave plot.

Letting out a sniffle, T began to speak to Kenni's headstone as if she were there next to her, "What's up Kenni. How y'all living up there?" she looked around. "Tell Ronnie's punk ass that was a bitch move she pulled but I still love her doe. What y'all had, had to have been love 'cause I know my nigga wouldn't leave me down here. That shit at da club doe that was fun. I wish we would have had more times like that. Our crew crazy as hell but I'll let Ron tell you our stories. Tell her to tell you some stories about when we was in high school before we hit dat eighteen bar."

Peering off into space again, she revealed a flask that contained alcohol from inside her suit jacket. She took a swig, "My nigga always had my back. Mafuckas in school already knew; you fuck with T, you fuckin' wit' Ronnie. You fuck with Ronnie, you fuckin' wit' T." A lump developed in her throat causing T to pause reflectively before swallowing to continue, "I can't believe y'all gone. All this mainly over Shyna. We should'a let Kim kick her ass when she volunteered. She took you away from her, made my nigga hurt core deep. Then took my nigga away from me. That's about a bitch if I ever heard one."

"Ronnie was my nigga. More than blood. Shit, she gone. Shit ain't gon' be the same no mo'. I feel like a part of me died. I love everybody else in our crew but Ronnie was my *nigga*. I don't know how heaven work, but I know y'all gon' see each other. So, when you see her tell her I miss her and shit ain't gon' be the same down here no mo," stopping T took a big gulp of the liquor before beginning solemnly, "I ain't know you that well but you was cool. You had spunk or fire, whatever da hell you wanna call it. That's probably one of the main reasons Ronnie loved you so much," T drunk some more. "Damn I'ma miss y'all. Y'all kept a nigga laughing."

Ma Dukes, T's mother and Moryah, Ronnie's mother walked up to T. "C'mon T they carrying her up now," Ma Dukes spoke to her daughter with Moryah hunkered under her arm.

Kim who was walking behind the mothers stopped at T's feet as the older women continued on. She stuck her chestnut hand out to T and pulled T to her feet, "You a'ight?"

"Yeah," T said brushing off her clothes. "I was just talkin' to Kenni about Ronnie."

"Oh," Kim said softly glancing at the headstone awkwardly as they started walking away from her permanent home. "You sure you a'ight?" Kim questioned looking at T sideways.

"I'm cool," T said exhaling in Kim's face.

Kim jerked back, "What you been drinkin' on?"

"Hennessy. Ronnie's favorite."

The two smiled and quieted down as more people flooded the cemetery to pay their last respects. They stood next to each other, T drinking silently with tears cascading down her face. A feeling of numbness overcame T as she shook the hands and gave hugs to the people trying to console her. An aching feeling deep within T exposed itself when T looked around the gravesite noticing people walking away smoking and laughing. Her gaze led her around her family of friends to watch Ronnie's mother Moryah being supported by her own mother. To see Chantel being held by her girlfriend Mya, Jay had a female with her as well who had wrapped her arms around Jay's back. Kim stood next to T, but she was on the phone declaring in a quivering voice that she was fine. T's somber gaze connected with Kenni's friend Layla whose watery eyes matched hers. Layla flashed T a smile. Before T could return it Arianna, Ronnie's sister, popped up in front of T. Arianna smiled mournfully and pulled T into a hug. She clenched Arianna tight closing her eyes as the tears seeped out wetting Arianna's t-shirt. When T felt Arianna take a slight step back she opened her eyes to discover, only their family of friends was still present along with Layla and Sayvonne.

T stepped back from Arianna and pulled out her flask again, tipping its contents onto the soil of Ronnie's gravesite.

"T!" Arianna exclaimed grabbing her arm.

"What?" T questioned back incredulously. "My nigga loved her some Hen, so you know I gotta marinate her grave in it."

Moryah chuckled sadly, "T, you is something else. No matter what we doing or where we at, you always make us laugh."

T smiled at her.

"Thank you," Moryah told her, her eyes watering as she held out her hands for a hug. The two embraced and Moryah said in a loud whisper, "Now I know you hurting, we all are. But don't go doing nothing off the wall. All of y'all," she looked around at her youngest daughter's "family" and Kenni's best friends. "I can't take no more funerals y'all," Moryah broke down but still managed to hug everyone before Ma Dukes ushered her to the car.

Arianna watched Ma Dukes sit Moryah, her mother as well, in the car before following her mother's example, hugging everyone. "Make sure you take care of T," Arianna whispered in Kim's ear then hugged T.

"Ooh do it again," T cajoled with a smile when Arianna kissed her cheek but sadness strained her voice.

The family of friends watched them leave then turned their attention back to Ronnie's gravesite. There was a long pregnant pause, as everyone except Layla consumed with their own thoughts running through their heads seemed to zone out while staring at the casket. Layla snuck glances at T who caught her more than a few times.

"T, you a'ight?" Chantel asked breaking the silence.

She looked around to see the family watching her. She plastered on a smile to mask the pain she felt soul deep, "Yeah man. I'm good."

"You sure?" Chantel's girl Mya asked.

"I'm cool y'all. Fa real I'm good."

The family gave way to another silent pause, which caused everyone to slowly drift back to their cars. One by one or two by two everyone rubbed the casket and went on to their car until only T and Kim were left. Kim's phone began to buzz feverishly in her purse vibrating against something. T glanced down at her but neither one of them uttered a word.

Plunking down on the ground, T laughed as a memory began to surface, "I remember the first time I met Ronnie in seventh grade. I was new to her school and had pulled her gurl. We met up at a football game to fight and shit and one of her niggas was like y'all dumb fighting over a bitch. And we just got cool. Started talking and shit."

Kim smiled and laughed not really seeing the humor in the story, "I remember when I first met y'all."

Busting out with laughter T finished Kim's story, "We both tried to get on wit' yo' lil' sexy ass!"

"Hell yeah. Had you first bell, her second bell, and both y'all niggas fa lunch. Y'all was crazy!" Kim exclaimed laughing as a ton of memories hit her.

T's laughter slowly died away as she studied the white casket in front of her. "Them was the days man." She blinked back to focus when Kim asked her if she was ready to go, "Nah you go 'head. I'ma be there in a minute."

Kim stood over her and declared, "T, you been drinkin. You don't need to be driving like this."

Looking up at her T grinned, "Man I'm cool. I told you I was a'ight."

Folding her arms, Kim looked her over skeptically instead of responding.

"Kim. Go 'head. Invite ya gurl over. What's her name Cream?"

Smiling at the idea, she started to walk away, "A'ight. Turn yo' phone on." T took the phone out of her pocket and turned it on showing Kim. "I'ma call you if one of yo' gurls call and you call me when you leave here."

"A'ight."

"Holla."

Watching and waiting until Kim was out of hearing and sight distance, T sprawled out on the ground next to Ronnie's grave.

      *   *   *

A vibration from T's pants awoke her; she didn't realize she had fallen asleep. T pulled her cell phone out of her pocket. She answered groggily, "Hello?"

"Where da fuck you at?" Kim shouted.

T took the phone off her ear and looked around, "I'm at the cemetery."

"What are you still doing there T? The funeral ended at three and it's going on seven."

Standing up, wiping her suit off, T picked up her flask and responded, "I fell asleep."

"We coming to pick you up," Kim said into the phone over the fumbling in the background.

Chuckling T declined, "Yo, I'm good," her phone beeped. "Hold on," T read a text message one of her female friends sent her. "Yo Tricia call me?"

"Yeah. 'Bout an hour or two ago."

"A'ight. I'm going over there."

"You sure you don't need us to take you?" Kim questioned with worry.

She let out a laugh hearing Kim's girlfriend do the same, "My car here."

"A'ight."

"Holla."

T walked over to Ronnie's casket and put her hand on it, "You know Ron, I was just bullshitting when I said I was gon' settle down a few months ago. Now though," she shook her dreads as a tear escaped from her eye. T looked towards Kenni's grave, "Maybe I need too. Life's short. I can't keep playing games with these hoes. Shit I should'a brought a bitch here with me too," T sighed heavily and patted the coffin. "I love you lil' bruh. And I'ma miss you like a muthafucka fam. I'ma come by again soon though. I'm about to go kick it with Tricia. I love you," she dropped a kiss on the coffin and started to walk off to her Monte Carlo while loosening her tie.

Popping open the trunk of her car T placed her suit jacket in it along with her tie. Rummaging around in her trunk for something she could place her flask in, she grabbed her book bag with a smile. "Ha. I'ma put this in here," said T putting her flask in the book bag. She patted her crotch where she had tucked her strap-on in her boxer briefs over her brief harness, "Love my new harness," mumbled T pulling out her cologne and spraying some on her wrists, neck, and midsection. T slammed the trunk shut, went to the driver's side of the car, and opened the door. She paused staring out at Ronnie's coffin then looked towards the sky, "I love you lil' bruh. And I miss the fuck out you already."

Before driving off T sent a text message to her female friend relaying that she was enroute to her house. Driving with one hand the other hand searched the compartments of her car. Her hands ran across a bag of weed, and she put it in her lap. Finally coming to a red light, she fished around for a pack of cigarillos. She sped off once the light turned green only to make a sharp left turn into a convenient store parking lot.

"Yo let me get a pack of White Owls," T spoke to the man behind the counter, still walking through the door.

"Two dollars."

T handed him a five-dollar bill and began to walk away. She turned around when the man called out to her. "Keep the change," she told him already splitting one of the cigarillos.

"Thank you."

Leaving the car door open, T plopped down in her car emptying the guts of the cigarillo onto the ground. T proceeded to break the weed back down in the open cigarillo and roll it up. Just as she held the blunt up for inspection, she noticed Layla coming towards her dressed in a pair of low-rise capri denim jeans with a red v-cut halter-top, a silver chain, and a black and red Cincinnati fitted hat.

She put the blunt in her ashtray only to get out of the car and perch on the hood to watch Layla approach her. Remembering the glances Layla kept casting her way at the funeral, T took in the view from head to pretty manicured toes adorned in black flip flops, "Damn you stay wit' a hat ma," T commented as Layla drew closer. "Who you trying to impress?"

Layla didn't respond at first, she just hugged T tightly. Feeling T stiffen slightly, Layla ran a hand down T's chest and pulled away, "You alright T? I'm sorry about Ronnie."

Staring into Layla's eyes T responded, "I'm sorry about Kenni. I've been better though, but you still skipped over my question."

Smirking Layla released T. She turned around and went into the store switching her ass. T followed behind Layla into the store, eyes glued to Layla's ass while Layla replied, "If I know you gon' be around, you," she glanced back at T catching her eyes glued to her ass. Layla moved towards the chips at the front counter waiting for T to come up behind her, "You stay around here?"

Grinning T replied with, "Hold on now doe," her eyes roamed over the back frame of Layla who had smiled, as she turned around to the man working the register, "You dressing to impress me?"

Biting down on her lip, Layla nodded hesitantly.

T sidled up next to her then spoke in her ear, "Well you doing a damn good job ma."

The man behind the counter watched the interaction between the two. Layla extended a dollar to him but he waved the pair on out the store.

"You on foot today?" T questioned not seeing her car in the parking lot of the one stop shop.

"Yeah. My car in the shop,"

"Well get in," T said, while opening the door of her black Monte Carlo for Layla. "It ain't no way in hell I'm letting yo' lil' sexy ass walk home."

Layla smirked and got in the car.

"So, where you stay?" T inquired hopping in and starting the car up.

"Off Beckenroff," Layla said checking out the interior of T's car.

They pulled out of the convenient store and T stopped at a red light.

"T?" Layla said.

T glanced over at Layla casually and before she could react, Layla was sucking on her tongue.

Kendra Spencer is a 2017 graduate of the Ohio Media School. Upon graduation Kendra Spencer started her company Blaque Diamond Ink, a book publishing company that will operate and run on a full media scale. In addition to the book industry she is a ten year veteran of semi professional womens football with the Cincinnati Sizzle (#33) and team voted defensive captain. Kendra Spencer also has a plethora of years working with individuals with developmental disabilities and at risk youth/teens that have been impacted by trauma. She is also the proud paw parent of a father and son bully breed.